Semi-De

By

Liam McKenna

Copyright © 2025 Liam McKenna

Dedication

For my mother who taught me to read and write

My siblings who taught me to laugh and fight

My children who make the world seem right

My friends, too many to mention by name,
who keep my feet planted tight.

To Teresa M you know how this happened and your part in it,
thank you so much.

Table of Contents

Chapter 1
Ole

"**O**le, ole, ole, ole!"

"Ole, ole, ole, oleeeee!"

The noise was deafening.

I motioned to Ally;

"What you want mate?"

I signalled to the barmaid as I tugged at my wallet, which was a bit tight in my new jeans..

He narrowed his eyes and replied;

"What did you say?"

I hated when he did that, and what's more he knew I hated it!

"What the fuck do you think I said? Here's a clue – I'm standing at a bar in the departure lounge of Belfast city airport – we're going on my stag weekend with the fucking male voice ole, ole choir over there and I'm ordering a pint – so three guesses what I said..."

He shuffled uneasily, scratched his chin, surveyed the draught beer options, took a sharp breath, scrunched his nose, tutted, and said:

"Gis a pint of Coors Light."

I just shook my head – he did that every time, annoyingly – then always ordered Coors Light. I made the victory sign towards the barmaid and pointed at the Coors Light (beer for slimmers – did you ever?), but there was no point in trying to be heard over the racket.

I'm Colin, by the way, and my nuisance mate is Ally. I love him, but this isn't really about him.

You see, I had to tell you this story, and while I couldn't be sure where to start, I thought my stag weekend would suffice. I sipped the froth from my pint as I turned from the dark oak bar and checked for empty seats.

"L...I...V...E...R..P DOUBLE O...L to get blocked you see..."

They all laughed as they downed pints and passed around the hip flask. We chuckled as we squeezed past wee Sean and sat on the edge at a rickety table – we stabilised it with a folded cardboard beer mat.

"Looks like it's going to be nuts."

I suggested as I tossed my thumb towards the choir. Ally grimaced and said; "What is?"

I was about to blow my fuse when I caught sight of his cheeky grin creeping from the corner of his lip;

"Got ya."

He just slouched back, sipping his pint in his own little contented world.

My phone made what I referred to as "the Siobhan noise." I flicked it open to read her text:

"Hi, love of my life, hope you're enjoying the departures lounge! Love you, stay safe xxxxxxxxx"

I was about to close my phone without replying. I hate it when people chat on their phone while they're actually in someone's company. I replied briefly;

"Just arrived, later xxx"

I studied the walls, which were adorned with iconic local images, and offered Ally my opinion;

"Titanic – sank, Harland and Wolff cranes – bankrupt, Geordie Best, (In who's name the airport is eponymous.) Geordie, a genius but nonetheless an alcoholic, Alex Higgins – Geordie's bar companion and so it goes on. Giant's Causeway – what a complete disappointment! Area of natural beauty, my arse!"

We laughed!

The pints were flying!

"Who has the tickets?"

Shouted Jimmy just before downing a pint in three seconds, accompanied by stamping feet, banging tables, and loud cheers. He slammed the glass on the table and rubbed his lips with the back of his hand in a very self-satisfied way.

Sean then started the ball rolling.

You always know when he's about to tell a joke because he ALWAYS prefixed it with;

"Did you ever hear the one about Jack and Jill (Or whoever the main character the joke was) now I didn't make this up I'm only telling it."

Sean is a handsome man, about five foot seven, with sharp blue eyes and a carefully sculpted beard. He was good at telling stories and jokes, usually delivering them in batches of three.

"Well Jack and Jill were in the garden playing and Jill says to Jack."

Ally looks at me and says;

"I've heard this one, it's good."

Frustrating!

Sean continues;

"Fancy playing hide and seek – I'll hide if you find me you can kiss me here"

He pointed between his legs;

"And you can fondle my breasts."

"Jack asks what happens if I don't find you?"

She looked over her shoulder and said;

"I'LL be hiding in the shed."

We laughed as Sean supped his pint and ran his hand through his hair before continuing;

"Did you hear the one about the blonde girl getting her first flying lesson? Now

I didn't write it I'm only telling it."

We all laughed at his prefix.

"She was 20 minutes into her first lesson in a two seater plane when the instructor died from a heart attack. In a panic she lifted the radio and pressed the button."

He replicated the action;

"May day, May day."

He whispered in his best Marilyn Monroe voice;

"May day, May Day"

He said again we were all rolling about;

"Air traffic control comes on the radio."

"This is air traffic control, what seems to be the problem?"

Sean went into full Monroe impression, even standing up for emphasis;

"My lord I'm on my first ever flying lesson and it appears the instructor has died. What should I do? The voice came back, first of all stay calm and I will talk you through how to land the plane safely."

Sean rolled his eyes for effect;

"Ok are you sure?"

He murmured.

"Don't worry came the voice – now first tell me your height and position!"

He paused!

"I'm five foot seven and I'm sitting at the front seat."

We were in hysterics;

"The voice came back, okay say after me.... OUR FATHER"

We lost it in loud guffaws. After things settled, Ally stood up and said, "That reminds me of a joke." He even stole Sean's prefix;

"Did you hear the one about the blind guy getting his first flying lesson? I didn't write it I'm just telling it."

That got a laugh, but unlike Sean – Ally was not adept at the telling jokes;

"So, this blind guy is in a plane on his first flying lesson and surprise, surprise his instructor died. He lifted the radio and said may day may day my instructor has died and I'm blind!"

His voice was monotonous, so not a single word got the proper emphasis. He lifted his pint and took a large gulp;

"The voice came back."

He continued;

"OK sir this is air traffic control we are very sorry to hear this but if you stay calm we will talk you through how to land the plane."

He lifted his glass again but didn't drink.

"The blind guy says will you hurry up the plane is upside down. The air traffic guy comes back and says if you are blind how do you know the plane is flying upside down?"

For dramatic effect, he took three sips of his beer, and as he went to set his pint down to deliver the punchline, Sean shouted;

"Because the shit is running UP my back!"

We all burst out laughing. Ally shrugged in a resigned way and sat down. Jimmy then spoke again;

"Fuck me who has the tickets?"

I shrugged;

"Stephen I think."

Jimmy sighed and with such a look of disappointment simply muttered;

"Who in God's name gave him the tickets? Sure he'll be late for his own funeral."

"Aye, right enough!"

Ally smiled.

"We might be having the stag weekend in the airport!"

Jimmy was always glass half empty.

Speaking of which, I nodded at Ally and waved my nearly empty glass in his face. He shifted uneasily in his seat, stood up, and made his way to the bar. After almost five minutes, Ally left his spot and returned to ask what I wanted to drink.

Really frustrating!

I pointed at the Coors Light insignia on the glass as I downed the last of it, wiped my mouth with the back of my right hand, and said...

"And get me £200 from the till and the blonde bar maid's number";

and winked.

As it was my stag weekend everyone laughed.

We sat around laughing and winding each other up until it started to get ridiculously unfunny how late Stephen was with the tickets. Just as it was getting as close to the wire as possible, Stephen strolled in with the tickets. We grabbed them and made our way to airport security.

Our flight's "final call" was announced as all twenty-four of us joined the back of a queue of about 400 people. I made my way to the front, excusing myself profusely as I pushed past the others in the queue, explaining the situation to the jobsworth security man. He curled his lips downwards, like a Frenchman chewing an onion, and motioned with his upturned palm... "All these people in front of you – there will be a riot."

I held my hands up and shouted;

"Excuse me folks – the guy who had our tickets was in a car accident and our final call has been called – would you mind if my stag party, not too many, made their way to the front, otherwise we will miss our flight."

The whole queue shuffled and grumbled, but no one offered an audible rebuke. I hastily waved to the boys, and all twenty-three of them pushed through the increasingly irate queue. We were almost all through when one of the lunatics shouted back;

"We're only kidding our flight is later we just wanted to get through to the bar!" I think we were the only ones in that building who thought he was funny. One bloke in the queue shouted, "Wanker!" and chucked a plastic water bottle in our direction. We made it through, and apart from John relieving himself in the stairwell, the "uneventful" departure was complete.

Chapter 2
So He Did

During the plane journey— all thirty-five minutes of it— there was singing, laughing, and far too many people buzzing for the irritable flight attendant. I sat in a state of dread. The attendant was as camp as Christmas, mincing up and down past us more times than seemed necessary. I sat patiently, waiting for "it' to start.

Joey asked the flight attendant his name. The attendant curled his hair with his right hand and pointed to a very worn-out badge with his left.

"Stephen Mulcahy"

And continued;

"And I'll have none of your lip so I won't big boy."

We all guffawed. Joey asked for two cans of queer, and Stephen glanced at him before retorting;

"I think you mean beer so you do, and I'll have no more of your guff so I won't or you'll be handcuffed to me on the other side so you will!"

We were roaring with laughter. Stephen scratched the back of his head, made a dramatic left turn, and tiptoed to the back of the plane. Without warning, we hit an air pocket and dropped quite violently. The laughter stopped instantly. One of the guys I barely knew shouted;

"We're all going to fucking die!"

Then burst into laughter.

The pilot reminded us to remain seated with our seat belts fastened. Once we'd settled, Stephen returned with two miniature cans of Heineken, handed them to Joey, and held his hand out;

"That's seven pound twenty so it is!"

Joey coughed in protest at the extortionate price but reluctantly paid after an interminable rummage in the front pocket of his jeans. Bing bong;

"Hello, ladies and gentlemen"

Screeched over the tannoi:

"This is your captain speaking we are just passing the Isle of Man and will soon be beginning our descent into John Lennon, Liverpool airport."

Stephen was checking that we had our seatbelts fastened.

"I would like to thank you,"

Continued the pilot;

"For flying Easyjet today we do hope you are enjoying your flight and we wish you a safe onward journey. We look forward to seeing you again soon."

I thought, I bet you Stephen fucking Mulcahy isn't. I turned round to Ally, who was in the row behind me;

"See John Lennon, that's someone a city can be proud to call its airport after!"

He nodded in agreement but also countered;

"George Best was some player."

He missed my point.

I was just settling back for landing when the bing bong went again;

"Sorry to disturb you but I have been asked to announce that Colin, who is on board,"

It was unmistakably Stephen's voice;

"is heading to Liverpool for his stag weekend so he is, along with all his mates and some hangers on!"

We were laughing loudly, Stephen concluded;

"I hope you boys take it easy so I do."

The ole oles started again, Kieran I think. The plane safely touched down, and all the eejits began applauding. The other passengers saw the funny side of it, but I was certain they were also glad the flight was over. We alighted from the plane, and Stephen shook hands with everyone, chatting merrily. As he shook my hand, he glared over the top of his glasses, pushed them up the bridge of his nose, and said;

"I wish you all the best, so I do."

I winked.

It had begun.

Chapter 3
Ask Your Ma

Taxis had been pre-booked to take us to the aparthotel we had booked for the weekend — nothing too fancy, let's face it, there wasn't going to be much sleeping this weekend! We arrived at reception, which doubled as a bar that sold only bottles of Corona beer and dry white wine. Better than nothing, I thought. Patrick, Siobhan's brother, was sitting there waiting for us. He had come up from London, where he lived, for the stag. Patrick is a good lad but looks for all the world like the skinniest, archetypal Irishman you've ever seen: ginger hair and beard, and he's never shy about wearing one of his mother's hand-knitted Aran jumpers. He was rooming with me as he didn't really know anyone else. He began introducing himself to all the lads; he was always known as a nice guy.

When John, of the empty bladder, shook his hand he said;

"Ya rocket ye."

Patrick smiled as this indicated acceptance and replied;

"Aye you would know."

Jimmy shouted over;

"Takes one to know one!"

And, in John, we all knew at least one.

Patrick and I were in room twenty-nine. It was basic, with a double bed, a single bed, an en-suite toilet, and a walk-in shower, which was a bit on the small side.

On the walls were two mass-produced prints of Parisian street scenes, each fixed to the wall with four large screws, as if any self-respecting thief would bother nicking them. The bedding and walls were magnolia and bland, pretty typical for this sort of accommodation. We had arrived at 7:39 and agreed to meet in reception at 8:15 sharp — and we were, sharp I mean. Patrick threw his bag on the single bed, so I automatically opened my tiny suitcase on the double. He went straight to the bathroom for a pee, leaving the door open so I could hear everything. Disgusting.

I turned my phone on, and it beeped furiously, all the lads sending selfies of them getting dressed — mental! It also made the Siobhan noise, so I read her message;

"Hi, hon, hope you arrived safe and well and Patrick hooked up with you all okay! Miss you, won't be too long until I'm no longer MISS anything, lots of laughs. Let me know all is okay and I won't bother you again until tomorrow! Have a good time, but not TOO good, Lots of love, Siobhan xxxx"

She refused to use text abbreviations — it was her thing. I didn't care! I rolled my eyes and was about to shove the phone in my pocket. She can be so annoying! But I thought better of it and replied;

"All good, Patrick here and in the bathroom, heading shortly!"

Once changed, with hair products and aftershave applied, I took a good look at myself in the mirror. I sucked in my tummy, turned sideways, and convinced myself I wasn't getting flabby. How could I be? I'm only thirty-five. The clothes were standard "pulling clothes," as my mates called them. I'd had my hair cut on Wednesday, and not a single strand was out of place. My new barber was spot on with the skin fade I liked. My two-day beard was perfectly sculpted I took one last look at myself and, in that self-talk way, acknowledged the emergence of a tiny bit of flab. But I had two weeks. "Get it sorted in two weeks," the voice in my head said.

Patrick and I headed for reception, the aftershave stench strong enough to knock you out. As I took the last couple of steps down, I said;

"We look and smell like a million dollars!"

John countered;

"Aye old and wrinkly and smell of pee!"

We exited and jostled our way to Concert Square, all twenty-four of us laughing, ripping into each other, and generally being funny — or so we thought. I was intrigued that not one person was wearing jeans. In fact, all twenty-four of us, including Patrick, were dressed like some sort of army. Various shades, but the uniform was strikingly similar: light blue shirts, tan brogues, navy trousers, all fastened with tan belts. Leo wore cream-coloured linen trousers paired with the most garish Hawaiian shirt. He also wore navy suede desert boots — he did it to be different — and, to be fair, it worked. The rest of us looked like showroom dummies, and trust me, some of us weren't exactly the sharpest tools in the box.

"Your MA likes concert square,"

Suggested Jimmy. We all laughed, this started a chorus line;

"Your ma likes the brown brogues"

We were flying now;

"Your MA likes the tan belts,"

Said Frank, as he held his crotch, and so it continued until we had exhausted every possible thing that could be given salaciously as something our mothers would like... the emphasis on the word MA was given in a sexual tone by the way it was said. It was like "I spy" for grown-up, immature men. It was, however, also very funny!

Almost by accident, we stumbled upon Concert Square. Music was cascading from every bar, the square festooned with chairs — there were women everywhere, and some of them were even wearing things that could pass as clothes. Ally said;

"That's when you know you're getting old you see a girl wearing a skirt like that"

He pointed at a girl wearing a micro-mini skirt, not much wider than some of our belts;

"And your first thought is, fuck she must be freezing!"

We all laughed at that, and Ally had a self-congratulatory grin plastered all over his face. We gleefully rubbed our hands together;

"Let's get this party started!"

Roared a handful of the team ...and we did.

Chapter 4
Tikky Tacky

We naturally broke into groups of three or four. Most bars refused to allow larger groups in at the same time, and, to be honest, it was just easier that way. We did the rounds—Baa Bar, Black Rabbit, Krazyhorse, Tikki Joe's, and the Walkabout, to name a few. Each of them received visits from some of us at different stages. We'd agreed to meet at the Walkabout at midnight to regroup. Knowing that arriving together would likely get us turned away, smaller groups arriving separately worked better.

The craic was ninety!

My small group consisted of five—me, Ally, Patrick, and my two brothers, Joe and Paul. We started our rounds at Baa Bar, a modern, dimly lit "poser's bar" where we fit right in. The bar occupied an old converted warehouse, with bare brick walls interspersed with dark grey ones adorned with various paintings of animals and what looked like chemistry apparatus.

At the bar, we were making bleating noises when I asked, "What's the shout?" "What do you mean?" Ally replied.

I raised my left eyebrow and said flatly, "Enough, you bloody nuisance. You're getting a Coors Light."

He shrugged as if he might fancy something different, but when he was met with *that* look, Coors Light it was.

The night progressed with plenty of laughter, chatting, and a parade of beautiful women. I was thoroughly enjoying myself.

We moved on to Tikki Joe's—more shots, more rounds of beer. It was brilliant craic. We wandered around the bar looking for a poser table to set our drinks on, giving us a chance to properly look around. Tikki Joe's, like many bars in Concert Square, seemed to be another converted Victorian space. Its bare walls contrasted with its bright and modern vibe, perfect for dancing and pulsing with great music. This was the place to be for any stag or hen do.

As I surveyed the bar, lost in thought, I noticed a girl sitting alone in a corner. She looked strikingly like the new secretary from work. She had her head down at first, but when she glanced up and caught me staring, she smiled and waved.

She was stunning in a red dress that stood out beautifully against the black leather bench she sat on. She'd only been in the office for three weeks, but every man there had already developed a mild crush on her She was all woman.

A single glass of prosecco sat on the table in front of her, and an upturned dark green bottle protruded from an ice bucket. There was only one glass—she must have been alone.

She motioned for me to come over. I excused myself and walked towards her. Her fire-red dress hugged her voluptuous curves. She *was* all woman.

"Joan?" I asked.

She nodded. "Good to see you!"

I continued, "What brings you to Liverpool?"

She smiled, her long black hair falling in shiny curls. Her deep red lipstick matched her dress, and her perfectly applied makeup accentuated her impossibly high cheekbones. Even her shoes, like her cheekbones, seemed impossibly high.

My phone buzzed with the Siobhan noise, but I ignored it as I sat beside her. That short red dress somehow made her look even sexier than she did at work, its fiery hue enhancing her mocha-toned skin.

"My friend and I booked a weekend away to celebrate me getting the new job," she explained, gesturing behind her with her thumb.

She nodded at me knowingly, and I nodded back.

"But when we arrived, she got violently ill and went straight to bed in our hotel room!"

"That's awful," I said sympathetically. "Will she be okay alone?"

Joan waved her diamanté-encrusted phone in my direction. Her nails, long and painted the same deep red as her dress, glinted in the light.

"She has my number," she said. "And, at the risk of sounding selfish, I didn't want to sit staring at hotel room walls. So…" She upturned her palms. "Hey presto!"

She playfully jabbed my shoulder with a smile and asked why I was in Liverpool.

"Stag weekend," I offered without elaborating. I was shamelessly flirting. She didn't ask for more details, and I didn't offer any.

Taking a chance, I said, "Why don't you join us?"

Her knowing grin widened, and she pulled her head back. "Really? You wouldn't mind?" She hesitated. "I shouldn't…"

I was about to respond when she continued, "I do feel a bit vulnerable. But are you sure your friends and the stag won't mind?" She winked.

"I'll go powder my nose and join you, then. Are you *sure* you don't mind?" she asked, elongating the word "sure" for emphasis.

Enthusiastically, I raised my hand in a stop motion. "Na, na, come on. It'll be a good laugh!" I struck a mock-defiant pose, pressing my right index finger to my cheek. "I won't take no for an answer!"

She threw her head back with a laugh, her hair cascading in glossy waves. Sliding gracefully from her seat, she briefly revealed the lacy tops of her stockings. She adjusted her dress, flashing the faint triangle of her thong as she moved.

I was breathless.

Does this happen on every stag weekend?

Chapter 5
Get Up

O n my return to the lads, Ally questioned, "Who the fuck is that?"

He pursed his lips and puffed out his cheeks.

"The girl from work—you know, the new secretary I was telling you about!" I replied. I'd told everyone about Joan.

"If you lot don't mind, she's going to join us. You see, she's on her own—her friend got sick."

My brothers simultaneously stroked their chins in a mock-pensive way, despite neither having a beard. They exchanged a knowing look and, like the Thompson Twins, said in unison, "We'll look after her for you!"

A tiny tinge of jealousy flickered in me, but I joined in as we all laughed.

Joan emerged from the restroom and strode effortlessly across the bar—those shoes! She introduced herself to the lads with a handshake and a peck on the cheek. When she reached me, she looked at Paul, pointed in my direction, and asked, "Would it be rude to kiss the groom? Or, in fact, would it be ruder not to?"

How did she know I was the stag? I wondered.

Paul sniggered. "Go ahead, kiss the guy. Might get his fucking chin off the ground and stop him drooling!"

I was still puzzling over how she knew when she planted her soft lips on mine. I wanted her to stop. I didn't want her to stop.

I couldn't tell how long she lingered—long enough for the lads to clap and cheer when we came up for air.

"Good, innocent stag party behaviour—NOT!" exclaimed Joe, grinning.

We all laughed, even Patrick—or Paddy, as the boys had now christened him. His hearty laugh put me at ease.

Joan threw her head back, her outline captivating. She lifted the glass of prosecco I'd brought her, sipped, and then looked at me with a lingering gaze before winking. The house DJ was playing Erykah Badu's "Next Lifetime." Joan began to sway.

Playfully, she extended her hand, shaking it dramatically, before taking mine. Despite my feigned resistance, she soon had her arms around me on the dance floor. There's only one way to dance to this song—intimately.

I placed my hand on her back, at waist level. She pulled herself close—very close—so her left leg nestled between mine as we swayed. She whispered in my ear, "Do you like that?"

I recoiled slightly, stammering, "As you said, I'm the groom."

The lads, including Paddy, were all whistling and giving me the thumbs up. That was all the encouragement I needed. Ignoring my earlier protest, I pulled her closer.

Joan bit—more than a nibble—on my earlobe and whispered, "You're not married yet. Do you like the feel of my suspender belt?"

I was turned on.

"You'll like that I took my thong off in the powder room," she murmured.

I was rocking. Oh my God, I was so turned on.

We glided across the dance floor. I found myself wishing the lads weren't there. Marvin Gaye's "Let's Get It On" followed. We nearly were. Joan pressed tighter against me, and I could feel her heartbeat through the firmness of her breasts as she skilfully teased my chest. She was no novice.

I was lost in her.

The DJ announced, "We'll follow that tune by Mister Gaye with another for the lovely couple giving us a show on the dance floor."

Joan smiled.

The DJ continued, "Mister Gaye sings: 'Sexual Healing!'"

"Get up, get up, get up, get up, let's make love tonight," the song began.

She nibbled my ear again. "Think someone's already up. But will we make love tonight?"

I hoped so.

She threw her head back—God, she looked incredible. Almost professional, the way she moved. Then, giggling in a girlish way, she licked her lips and echoed my unspoken thoughts, "God, I hope so!"

She placed my hand on her arse, and I felt the elastic of the suspender belt holding her stockings. She pressed tightly against me, swaying and teasing. At that moment, I'd forgotten all about the lads—even Paddy. Not that it mattered; they were chatting up a group of six girls and had long since lost interest in my escapades.

As "Sexual Healing" faded, Joan licked her lips again.

"Slippery when wet. I need a drink!" she declared.

She grabbed my hand and almost marched me to the bar. I was her lapdog.

As the night went on, Joan was brilliant. She blended in effortlessly, the life and soul of the party. She kept telling the lads they looked gorgeous, flirting shamelessly. They loved her.

She was easy to love.

The dance floor filled up, and the lads were doing well for themselves. Joan reached for her oversized handbag with one hand while sliding the other effortlessly between my legs.

She looked up at me, staring directly into my eyes. I was transfixed.

"Think we need to get a room," she giggled, clearly tipsy.

If only, I thought. I wanted so badly to ravage her. I laughed nervously and gently moved her hand aside as Paddy approached from her blind side. She kept staring at me.

Paddy lifted his glass and said, "Think I'm in here with these two!"

Joan smiled, glanced at the dance floor, and said provocatively, "You're not the only one!"

Chapter 6
The Phone Call

Joan fumbled in her bag, rummaging around in that absent-minded way some women do. Eventually, she extracted her phone. With a flick of her hair, she ran her finger up the screen, then stabbed at it alternately with her thumbs. **Pin code**, I thought.

She looked perplexed and suddenly exclaimed, "Oh. Em. Gee!"

I hate it when people say that. **By the way.**

I scratched the side of my face and asked nonchalantly, "Something wrong?"

She stood up, running her left hand down her side until it rested on her waist.

"It's Marie, my friend," she declared. "She's just texted to say she's on her way home. She's already at the airport!"

"She managed to get a flight home?" I asked.

"Must have."

She seemed so unconcerned, and yet I might have smelt a rat. She smiled, staring directly at me.

"All yours," she said with a playful smirk. "And now, it would appear we have *that* room."

I hadn't even noticed that my "team" had moved on. My phone buzzed with what I call "the Siobhan noise." I ignored it. But then it started pinging again, a flood of texts pulling my attention.

"Where the fuck are you?" Ally texted.

Stephen: *"Everyone's in Walkabout! Except the stag! Hope you're not being naughty!"*

Paul: *"Get your arse here!"*

I looked up from my phone just as Joan hitched up her dress, giving me a private view while adjusting her suspender belt. It was a deliberate onslaught.

She rummaged in her bag again and handed me a key card. "Room forty-three. The Hilton," she whispered.

"I'll see you there later." She winked. As she walked away, she added, "No rush. It's your big night, and I can entertain myself in the meantime!"

She threw her head back, the outline of her body sending a rush of blood to my head. I was dizzy. Purposefully, she strode across the bar toward the exit. I couldn't take my eyes off her. I wasn't alone in that.

She tugged the door open, took one step outside, slung her bag over her left shoulder, and glanced back at me to ensure I was still watching. I was.

She blew a kiss and mouthed, "Later."

I couldn't think straight—or walk straight, for that matter. I turned to the table, rested my head in my right hand, and, with my left, took a large slug of whisky. Always Jameson.

As I set the glass down, Patrick approached me, looking rather urgent. I was relieved he hadn't shown up five minutes earlier.

He pushed my left shoulder and pointed at the door with his free hand. "C'mon, for fuck's sake. Everyone's in Walkabout. Why are you here on your own?"

He glanced around, clearly looking for someone. It was a waste of time. He spotted the lipstick on my cheek and pointed.

"That one in the red dress, I take it?" he asked.

"Yeah, she gave me a peck before leaving."

I grabbed a napkin and began rubbing my cheek.

"She was giving you more than a peck when she was dancing, big fella." He raised an eyebrow. "I know you're marrying my sister in two weeks, but, man, I wouldn't blame you if you did. I'm a man of the world."

He smiled, and I was surprised at his apparent acceptance of my potential deviance. Still, I wasn't stupid—Siobhan *is* his only sister.

I brushed my left shoulder with my right hand. As I stood up, I grabbed my glass and gulped down the rest of my whisky.

I slapped my cheeks as we walked across the floor—partly to sober myself up, partly to make myself believe that what had happened hadn't. Shrugging, I walked through the door Patrick was holding open.

"After you, sir!" he laughed.

As we approached Walkabout, Patrick slung his arm around my shoulder. "Really, I wouldn't blame you!"

I wasn't sure if he was encouraging me or fishing for reassurance. I decided on the latter.

"No chance, Paddy," I said, using his new nickname. "I'd never do that to Siobhan."

He slapped me on the back. "Right answer!"

At that, I pulled out my phone to check Siobhan's messages. It was the same one repeated:

"I love you. Is everything going okay? Is Patrick behaving himself? Man of the world, you know—lots of laughs! xxxxxx"

I began typing my response, but Patrick grabbed my phone.

"Who are you texting?" he asked, sounding genuinely concerned.

"Your sister, if you must know!"

He glanced at the screen, sighed, and handed it back. "Go ahead, tell her I said hello."

I started typing again, as he'd blanked the screen:

"So much for not texting until tomorrow. With Patrick now—as I have been all night (a lie). Heading to meet the others. A domani! Xx"

I liked to throw in the odd Italian word or phrase. In my head, it made me seem more intelligent. My cousin Orla once said;

"Intelligent, complete bloody twat more like!"

We arrived at Walkabout and had our picture taken by the security camera. We paid our admission and made our way to the third floor. Each floor had a different music genre: the first floor played indie music, the second floor was rock music, and the top floor had dance, soul, and R'n'B. Jimmy, who had studied in Liverpool, assured us that the top floor was, to quote him, "where all the fanny went!"

As we walked through the door, I noticed all the lads standing at the bar. Everyone was in great form, and they spontaneously started clapping as I approached. Ally began singing, "The Lady in Red."

I rolled my eyes.

I went to the bar and ordered twenty-five bottles of beer. We clinked our bottles and laughed. Some of the lads had already coupled up—fast movers, I thought. Who was I kidding?

I looked around to get my bearings when my phone buzzed in my pocket. I didn't recognise the number. I opened the message, and there was Joan, lying on a bed wearing stockings, a black basque, and those shoes. She had something in her hand that I couldn't quite make out. She tagged the message with, "Thinking about someone, slippery, I have all night!"

26

I stared at my phone, mesmerised. Again, my distraction prevented me from hearing the alarm bells. She looked stunning! I tapped my trouser pocket to feel the room key, then began wondering how I could possibly get away. Patrick was sticking close.

"Colonel Abrahams," the track "Trapped," with its heavy bass line, was thumping out of the speakers. Jimmy tapped my shoulder and pointed at one of the speakers. Frank had sat down beside it and fallen asleep. We were laughing—not at Frank falling asleep (he always did that), but because the heavy bass was making his head bounce rhythmically against the speaker as he slept.

My phone vibrated. Two more photos. Wow, she was spread-eagled, her left hand between her legs, right hand obviously taking the selfie. She clearly doesn't like wearing pants of any description, I thought to myself, smiling. She was careful to show me just enough to whet my appetite but not everything. In the second photo, she had revealed most of her breasts, though not all, and was smiling innocently. I was transfixed.

My interest was piqued. I smiled. "That's a new name for it," I thought to myself.

I hadn't even considered how she had my number. I was too far gone to be rational.

I replied, "Joan, I've just saved your number as 'John from work.' I would love to be there right now, but I'm struggling. Her brother is sticking to me, and I may not get away anytime soon. Apologies."

My phone beeped almost immediately.

"No worries, I'm here all night and all weekend. I know we'll get more than one chance!"

Another beep.

"You know you want it!"

Beep! She was under what looked like a silk sheet, obviously naked, as her nipples were making an impression under the silk—awesome. My head was completely turned. My cock was bulging in my boxers. Patrick, my shadow, waved his hand in front of his face, mocking a drinking gesture. I nodded. My head was fuzzy—too much drink, shots, pints, bottles of beer, more shots, more shots. You know the drill. The lights were dancing on the floor and ceiling, intermittently licking the walls too. There was a heaving mass of bodies—men pursuing women in the traditional way, but also the new sport of the twenty-first century: women pursuing men.

Viva la liberta!

Disco classics like "I'm Every Woman" were spliced together with Northern Soul favourites. Frank Wilson blasted out, "Do I Love You?"

My phone beeped again—another photo. Those heels were sticking out from under the sheet, and she had added a tag: "It's cold when you only have shoes on!" She added a wink emoji.

"Do I love you? Indeed I do!" I danced with some of my mates, soul-stepping like crazy. Another relatively new sport: men dancing with men and no one giving a damn. Vive la liberta! Or vive la libation.

From the corner of my eye, I could see Patrick getting chatted up by the two women he'd been with in Tikki Joe's. I was delighted.

I tried to remain cool, but I was growing ever more frustrated with the inane chatter of my now drunken mates. There was a lot of white powder flying about, and I appeared to be the only person in there who didn't have a talc-like daub on the side of my nostrils.

"Competition Ain't Nothing," by Carl Carlton, filled the air, another Northern Soul classic. The boys all moved to the floor and started stepping—soul boys to the end. I noticed Patrick heading through the doors, a girl linked to each arm. "Back of the net!" I thought. I moved quickly to see where he was going. He was heading through the doors of the rock floor, and the two girls were obviously very into him. As soon as the door closed behind them, I was almost running down the stairs. The walls were festooned with brilliant photographs of some of pop's biggest icons. I even stopped to stare for a second at a superb photo of a very young Stevie Wonder, entitled "Fingertips." I shook my head and hurried for the door, slipping down the last four steps—a combination of sambuca and eagerness.

What was I thinking?

I wasn't!

I hailed a taxi and stumbled into the back. Through the intercom, the driver enquired, "Where to, friend?"

I hate that. I'm not his friend.

"Hilton hotel, please," I responded, settling back in my seat.

"No problem. You staying there?" he continued.

"No, no. I'm meeting some friends there for a nightcap."

I wanted him to keep quiet. I had no patience for his patter.

"You sound Irish?" he enquired.

"Yeah."

"Second Irish person I've taken to the Hilton tonight—no offence, the last fare was more my type."

I was intrigued. Joan?

He continued, "Red dress, some body, and the hair. She knew how to work every blessing God has given her. I couldn't take my eyes off her as she strutted to the door. Could even see the lace on her stockings."

Joan!

SEMI-DETACHED

We arrived outside the Hilton. I paid the £7.20 fare with a tenner and told the driver to keep the change.

Chapter 7
Indeed, I Do

We arrived at Walkabout and had our picture taken by the security camera. After paying our admission, we made our way up to the third floor. Each level had a different music genre: the first floor played indie music, the second was dedicated to rock, and the top floor featured dance, soul, and R'n'B. Jimmy, who had studied in Liverpool, had assured us that the top floor was, to quote him, "where all the fanny went!"

As we walked through the door, I noticed all the lads standing at the bar. Everyone was in high spirits, and as I approached, they spontaneously started clapping. Ally grinned and started singing, "The Lady in Red."

I rolled my eyes.

At the bar, I ordered twenty-five bottles of beer, and we all clinked them together, laughing. Some of the lads had already coupled up—fast movers, I thought. Who was I kidding?

I was taking in my surroundings when my phone buzzed in my pocket. An unknown number. I opened the message. Joan was lying on a bed, wearing stockings, a black basque, and those shoes. She held something in her hand that I couldn't quite make out. A message followed:

"Thinking about someone. Slippery. I have all night!"

I stared at my phone, mesmerised. Once again, my distraction prevented me from hearing the alarm bells. She looked stunning. I tapped my trouser pocket, feeling the room key, and started wondering how I could possibly slip away. But Patrick was sticking close.

Colonel Abrams' "Trapped," with its heavy bassline, thumped through the speakers. Jimmy tapped my shoulder and pointed at one of them. Frank had sat down beside it and fallen asleep. We weren't laughing at the fact that he'd nodded off—he always did that—but at how the bass was making his head bounce rhythmically against the speaker as he slept.

My phone vibrated again. Two more photos. Wow. In the first, she was spread-eagled, left hand between her legs, right hand obviously taking the selfie. I smirked—she clearly didn't like wearing underwear. She was teasing, showing just enough to whet my appetite but not everything. The second photo revealed most, but not all, of her breasts. She was smiling innocently. I was transfixed.

My interest was aroused. I chuckled. That's a new name for it— "my interest."

I hadn't even considered how she had my number. I was too far gone to be rational.

I replied:

"Joan, I've just saved your number as 'John from work.' I'd love to be there right now, but I'm struggling—her brother is sticking to me. Might not get away anytime soon. Apologies."

Almost immediately, my phone beeped again.

"No worries, I'm here all night and all weekend. I know we'll get more than one chance!"

Another beep.

"You know you want it!"

Beep!

She was now under what looked like a silk sheet, clearly naked, her nipples pressing against the fabric—awesome. My head was completely turned. My cock bulged in my boxers.

Patrick, my shadow, waved a hand in front of his face, miming a drinking gesture. I nodded. My head was fuzzy—too much drink. Shots, pints, bottles of beer, then more shots—you know the drill.

The lights danced on the floor, the ceiling, intermittently licking the walls. A heaving mass of bodies moved around us—men pursuing women in the traditional way, but also, in a sign of the times, women pursuing men.

Viva la liberta!

Disco classics like "I'm Every Woman" were seamlessly spliced together with Northern Soul favourites. Frank Wilson's "Do I Love You?" blasted through the speakers.

My phone beeped—another photo. Those heels sticking out from under the sheet. She had added a tag:

"It's cold when you only have shoes on!"

She'd even added a wink emoji.

"Do I love you, indeed I do!"

I danced with some of my mates, soul-stepping like crazy—another relatively new sport, men dancing with men, and no one giving a damn.

Vive la liberta! Or maybe, vive la libation.

From the corner of my eye, I saw Patrick getting chatted up by the two women he'd been with earlier at Tikki Joe's.

I was delighted.

I tried to stay cool, but I was growing ever more frustrated with the inane chatter of my now-drunken mates. There was a lot of white powder flying about, and I appeared to be the only one in there without a talc-like daub on the side of my nostrils.

Carl Carlton's "Competition Ain't Nothing" filled the air—another Northern Soul classic. The boys moved onto the floor, stepping in sync, soul boys to the end. I noticed Patrick heading through the doors, a girl linked to each arm.

Back of the net, I thought.

I moved quickly to see where he was going. He was heading onto the rock floor, and the two girls were clearly very into him. As soon as the door closed behind them, I was almost running down the stairs. The walls were festooned with brilliant photographs of some of pop's biggest icons. I even stopped for a second to admire a superb photo of a very young Stevie Wonder, entitled "Fingertips." I shook my head and hurried for the door, slipping on the last four steps—a dangerous mix of Sambuca and eagerness.

What was I thinking?

I wasn't.

I hailed a taxi and stumbled into the back. Through the intercom, the driver enquired:

"Where to, friend?"

I hate that. I'm not his friend.

"Hilton Hotel, please," I responded and settled back in my seat.

"No problem. You staying there?" he continued.

"No, no, I'm meeting some friends there. Nightcap."

I wanted him to keep quiet. I had no patience for his patter.

"You sound Irish?" he enquired.

I simply replied, "Yeah."

"Second Irish person I've taken to the Hilton tonight—no offence, the last fare was more my type."

I was intrigued. Joan?

He continued, "Red dress. Some body. And the hair. She knew how to work every blessing God has given her. I couldn't take my eyes off her as she strutted to the door. Could even see the lace on her stockings."

Joan!

We arrived outside the Hilton. I paid the £7.20 fare with a tenner and told the driver to keep the change.

Chapter 8
The Lift is Going Up

I hurriedly alighted from the cab and made my way unsteadily to the front door.

"Bet he's not staring at me!" I said to myself.

I walked through the generic Hilton hotel reception area and headed towards the lift. I pressed the button repeatedly. Eventually, the doors slid open and an automated voice announced:

"Doors opening."

"Really?"

I jumped in, and a blonde woman jumped in just as the doors began to slide closed. After what seemed like an eternity, the doors started to close again.

"Doors closing."

She smiled at me, and I pressed the button for the fourth floor. True gentleman that I am, I enquired:

"Which floor?"

"Seven, please," she replied.

She laughed.

"Nearly said four there! Freudian slip."

She winked. She was drunk.

"Going up!" she giggled.

She was gorgeous—blonde, petite, the antithesis of Joan. As I looked at her, I imagined going to the seventh floor with her.

Joan.

I flirted,

"You look gorgeous, something special on tonight?"

"Well, I was supposed to meet a friend from work, but she didn't turn up! So, I got plastered and now I'm going to bed!"

She held both hands up, about six inches either side of her face, a drunken smile, and stumbled. She grabbed my arm to steady herself. I placed my other arm on her shoulder and looked straight into her eyes. She was plastered, but I felt a connection.

"Fourth floor."

The voice seemed louder.

"Doors opening."

The doors slid open, and she stuck her face forward, pointing at her cheek. I leaned in and kissed her cheek.

"Good night."

I stepped out, and as the voice said,

"Doors closing, going up,"

the silver doors began to slide closed.

"Enjoy!"

I said awkwardly.

'I think I was in there,'

the voice in my head tried to convince me.

I was dazed.

Chapter 9
Room Forty-Three

I turned to the wall and read the directions. The third line down had an arrow pointing to the right, below which it said, "Rooms 28-55." I began walking. I passed 41 on my right, 42 on my left, and there I was, standing in front of 43. I paused for a moment, then slid the key into the electronic slot. The green light indicated that the door was open. I pushed the handle down and entered the dragon's den!

Joan was lying on top of the bed, with candles strategically placed around the room. I could make out her shape against the black silk duvet cover; she was naked, apart from those shoes. She slid down the bed and came towards me. She was as beautiful in the flesh as I had dared to imagine. Black silk duvet cover, in a Hilton hotel? Mmm... those alarm bells should have chased me out of there right away. Why the hell was I even here? What was I thinking? I wasn't thinking, and the only bells I could hear were party bells.

As I noticed the generic Hilton paintings screwed to the wall, Joan slipped her arms around my neck and rested her head on my shoulder. Through the flickering light, I caught her eye. Still transfixed, she nibbled my ear and whispered:

"Are we going to stand here all night?"

We fucked like our lives depended on it. I was having an out-of-body experience; I was enjoying this more than I'd ever thought possible. Fuck everyone! Yes, everyone!

She bit my chest and dug her nails into me as she jumped on top of me. I closed my eyes as she mounted my cock. In the same motion, she lifted a candle and drizzled hot wax onto my chest. Instinctively, I grabbed her wrists. She smiled down at me, undeterred, and as the searing heat relented, I submitted to Joan. She saw that I was in pain, but that I was starting to enjoy it. She writhed and screamed, and came. And again!

Either that, or she was good at faking it.

As soon as she was finished with me, she lit a cigarette from one of the candles and moved to the open window. She took two puffs, then reached out and nonchalantly let the fag end drop below. She didn't know or care where it went, nor did I, as I did the exact same. She made her way to the bathroom. I was back under the sheet when she returned, and when I went to speak, she simply put her left index finger on my lips.

I had a feeling we weren't finished.

She climbed into the bed, and without saying a word, she eased her head under the sheet and placed her mouth on my semi-erect penis. Two solid hours, without a word. What was there to say?

Eventually, I sensed that she was finished with me. I know I was struggling to keep up. Joan lit another cigarette and headed for the window. I rolled over and began to pick the scabs of wax from my chest. I walked to the window, took two drags on the cigarette, and puffed the smoke out of the window. There was a fifty-pound fine for setting off the smoke alarm, and we were trying to avoid that.

She coughed, and apart from the screaming and moaning, this was the first sound she'd made since she'd whispered:

"Are we going to stand here all night?"

As if the cough had broken the silence, she exclaimed:

"Wow."

As she came towards me, she declared:

"That was even better than I'd been dreaming about for weeks!"

I looked up as she spoke, but I was in such a self-congratulatory mood that I couldn't hear a word. I made my way to the bathroom.

After using the toilet, I turned on the shower, and as I stepped in, I felt the hot water cascade over me. My chest and back began to burn.

Despite the discomfort, I grabbed one of the miniature shampoos provided by the hotel and began to lather up. I was starting to get used to the burning sensation as the water poured over me.

Just as I was about to begin feeling some regret, I felt a soft hand on the small of my back. The same hand soon began caressing my chest.

I was lost again.

Joan started massaging soap onto my back, working her hands gently over the open skin, then onto my shoulders. She moved down to my waist, massaging the soap into me. She pushed me against the shower window, turned her back to me, and as the water rinsed me, I slid into her. We began rocking back and forth in unison.

When we finished, she showered while I towelled off, still in silence.

As I made my way to the bedroom and began getting dressed, the atmosphere shifted, and the silence was definitely broken.

"Where the fuck are you going?"

I was startled by the aggression in her words and the threat in the way she spoke. Panic set in.

"I... I have to go back to my hotel. My soon-to-be wife's brother is sharing a room with me."

"So you just fucking used me, you bastard. Fucking cunt!"

Silence.

After about ten seconds, she started to laugh.

"I'm only kidding! Fuck's sake, don't be so uptight. I'm having a laugh!"

She accentuated the last part.

"I'm having a laugh!"

I couldn't really see the funny side, but I smiled, pursed my lips, and replied, "Phew, you had me there!"

She threw her head back, and water dripped onto her duvet. I looked at her, and she smiled with her mouth but not her eyes.

I was fully dressed, and she slipped her key into the electric meter. She pulled on a bright red kimono with a large yellow dragon emblazoned on the back. She bent forward, ruffling her hair to disperse the water, then shook her head and effortlessly threw it back. She instantly looked stunning.

She lit a cigarette, opened the window wide, and sat on the edge of the bed as I slid my right arm into my jacket. Fully dressed, I motioned toward the door. She lifted the second key card and slid it into my pocket.

"Think you'll be needing that before this weekend is over."

It wasn't a question. She grinned and winked. I shrugged.

I just wanted to leave now.

I made my way to the door, sidestepping between Joan and the TV. I leaned in to kiss her, but she pulled her head to the side. I tutted, shrugged my shoulders, and tutted again as she raised an eyebrow. I nodded and made for the door.

Chapter 10
Room Twenty-Nine

I glanced at Siobhan's text as I walked through the lobby but couldn't muster the energy to respond.

"Love you, handsome. I'm awake—since four A.M.! Just think, this day in two weeks. Love you, good morning for when you eventually get this."

Before I knew it, I'd arrived at our aparthotel.

I hurried to room twenty-nine. I hadn't even thought about what I was going to tell Patrick. I pressed the lift button, and after what felt like an eternity, the doors finally began to slide open. That irritating voice declared:

"Ground floor. Doors opening. Going up!"

As I slouched into the lift, I noticed Patrick rolling through the sliding doors in the foyer. He was obviously plastered, and I prayed the lift doors would close before he figured out what he needed to do to get to our room.

I squeezed my eyes shut, waiting for your woman—"Doors closing." Eventually, I thought.

I was going up!

The lift shuddered to a halt, and the doors slid open. I was ready to choke her.

"Doors opening. Second floor!"

I squeezed out before they'd fully opened, quickly establishing that room twenty-nine was to my right. Groping in my pocket as I broke into a gentle jog, I tried to locate the plastic key card.

As I ran, I was removing my jacket and unbuttoning my shirt—I just wanted to be in the shower before Patrick got to the room.

I slid the key card into the slot.

Nothing.

Nothing.

I patted my trousers and felt another key card.

For fuck's sake—I was trying to open our door with Joan's card.

In my head, I could hear my mother: More haste, less speed!

Funny how I could hear her words of wisdom now and not when they actually mattered.

I slid the second card in—green light.

I practically ran into the room, slid the key card into the electric meter, stuffed my clothes into my suitcase and stumbled to the bathroom. Closing the door, I locked it and turned on the shower.

The sound of running water always made me need to pee. I stood over the toilet, shook the little fella, and then caught my reflection in the mirror. Grimacing, I baulked at the array of red marks on my chest.

"JESUS!"

I slid the shower door back and stepped under the stream. It was beautiful, even if it burned. I had to use my teeth to tear open the miniature shower gel.

Faint shuffling outside—Patrick was trying to open the door. He fell into the room, and I could hear him just beyond the bathroom.

"That you in there, Colin?"

"Who the fuck do you think it is?"

My confident response didn't match how I felt.

"You okay?" I added.

"What the fuck are you doing in the shower in the middle of the night?"

He obviously looked at his watch at this point and proclaimed:

"Holy fuck, it's nearly ten past eight!"

I stayed nonchalant. "I'll be out in a minute."

Silence.

I finished up and was relieved to see my T-shirt from yesterday lying in the corner. I towelled myself down, dried my hair as best I could, threw on the T-shirt and wrapped the towel around my waist, tucking it in so it wouldn't fall. Casually, I strode out of the bathroom.

Patrick was lying on the single bed, hands behind his head, not under the quilt.

"You okay?"

I broke the silence. He laughed.

"Yeah, I had such a night. Met two girls—we danced and drank like fuck until we got thrown out at half-seven."

He sat up so suddenly that he knocked over the Gideon Bible he'd placed on the bedside table between our beds. I turned my back, fearing he'd furnish me with every last detail. Time to circumvent the conversation.

"Here now, hey boy—spare me the detail. You can tell me everything you intend to tell Paula on Monday!"

Paula is his wife.

He laughed—still pissed.

I walked towards him and put my index finger to my lips just as he started again.

I glared at him. "P.A.U.L.A." I spelled out.

As I turned away, I noticed a pair of lacy knickers protruding from my jacket pocket.

"Oh fuck."

I moved towards the jacket, but Patrick had already noticed.

"Where the fuck did they come from?"

He was interested.

I laughed. "That fucking eejit Ally was wearing them on his head all night. He's put them in there, hoping I wouldn't notice—hoping Siobhan would find them."

I didn't dare look at him as I lied.

"Where the fuck did you go?" I deflected.

He bought the Ally story, so I added: "Don't fucking mention the knickers to Ally—let him think he's gotten away with it."

I winked. He nodded—very unstable—then rolled onto his bed. Kicking off his shoes, he mumbled:

"Here, your woman from work was some shape!"

I said nothing.

Then, barely audible: "What a night!"

He hugged his quilt and, within seconds, fell fast asleep, a massive grin on his face.

I couldn't help thinking: He's remembering.

I was wrecked.

I dived under the duvet, grateful we'd avoided any chat about the night before.

About Joan.

By the time Patrick woke, I'd have a story concocted, and Ally would corroborate it.

For now, I just needed sleep.

I was nodding off, staring at the trees in the painting above my bed.

The room was stuffy.

My phone buzzed.

"Hey, sexy... what a night. Reprise soon? Miss you already!"

I went cold.

Then, another message—from Siobhan was sent while I was in the shower.

"Hope you're having a good time, FIANCÉE. Soon-to-be husband. Miss you. Cannot wait to hear all the details on Sunday! Love you, handsome. Phone me,

(sad face) YOUR Siobhan. Xxxxxxxx"

"All the detail?"

I think not.

I texted Joan back:

"Hey sexy, we'll have to play it by ear. Xxxxx"

I pressed send—then panicked.

I'd sent the message to Siobhan.

She replied immediately:

"What do you mean, 'play it by ear'? And 'sexy'? You're getting very frisky! Remember, handsome, we agreed—no sex for six weeks before the wedding! We agreed! I want our wedding night to be so special! I know you do, too!"

Joan texted as I was reading Siobhan's message.

46

"???????????????"

I forwarded my accidental message to Joan, then hastily began composing my response to Siobhan.

*"Sorry, gorgeous! 'Play it by ear' is kind of the running joke of the weekend—everyone's saying it at the end of each sentence. Like, if I say to Ally, 'Want a pint?' he says, 'Play it by ear.' Everyone laughs.

And by the way—you are a sexy!"*

I thought that covered my tracks—last night had been a blur, but it had kind of happened the way I remembered.

Siobhan texted back:

"Very funny, enjoy your day, handsome. I'm off out with Donna and a few of the girls—we're going wedding clothes shopping, then a few cocktails in Hell Cat Annie's before glamming up and heading to the Errigle to see The Untouchables. I'll text you later. Love you... or should I say 'play it by ear'—I'm literally laughing out loud! Xxxxxx"

Tracks covered. I replied:

"Very funny, enjoy! Meeting some of the lads shortly—we're heading up to Anfield to soak up the atmosphere before the game. Laters. Play it by ear, sweet cheeks! Lol lol, xx"

My phone buzzed again:

"Ok... but if I nibble your ear, would that work? I'm heading into town—few cocktails, bit of shopping, might even buy myself a toy! I'll see you somewhere tonight. Guarantee xxx"

I rolled over. Patrick snored beside me. I used my breathing technique and dozed off.

I was woken by loud thumping at the door. Patrick was still comatose.

Ally shouted through the door:

"For fuck's sake, it's twelve o'clock!"

I slouched over and cracked the door open an inch, squinting as I tried to wake up properly.

"Alright, dirty dick in the red dress?" Ally smirked.

I put a finger to my lips and silently raged.

"Thought we were going up to Anfield?" he asked.

"We are, we are! I'll jump in the shower now—see you in the foyer in ten minutes. Oh, and for fuck's sake, get me a bottle of beer! Or two!"

Ally nodded and moved away. I closed that door and opened another—there's a metaphor for my life if ever there was one.

In the shower, I found myself belting out The Horslips' Sideways to the Sun. Book of Invasions—best concept album in the history of the world, I thought, as the hot water ran over me. The warm, sweet breath of love...

Thump. Thump. Thump.

"Hurry up to fuck, I need a piss!"

I reached over and released the latch.

"Will I leave the shower running for you?" I asked as he drowned in the toilet.

"Why, what time is it?" he mumbled, still half-pissed.

"It's gone twelve."

"Fuck, really?" He flicked his cock back and forth. "Aye, leave it on then!"

As I stepped out, he stepped in. I brushed my teeth as he showered, then moved into the bedroom, which was fully lit. I noticed the candle wax marks on my chest and puffed out my cheeks. At that moment, I was glad of Siobhan's six-week rule.

Deodorant under my pits, Aramis on my cheeks, a dollop of wax through my hair. Patrick stumbled out of the bathroom, rubbing his head.

"What a night! My head is fucking thumping!"

I nodded in his direction. Paragon of virtue that I was.

"You better hurry up, mate. The lads are meeting in the foyer in ten minutes—you'll miss the game."

He frowned. "I'm not going to watch the Scouse scum!"

I flipped him the middle finger. He was one of the thirteen in our group who weren't going to the match. As Ally had said on the plane:

"The ones not going to the game are either Manchester United fans, or they know fuck all about football—which is the same as saying Manchester United fans!"

We laughed then, and I laughed again now.

Patrick suddenly lurched forward, dizzy. "Shit, tell them to wait for me—I won't be long."

I shrugged on my coat, grabbed a packet of shortbread from the hospitality tray and bit through the plastic wrapping as I shouted:

"See you down there. Quick as you can, mate."

From the bathroom, I barely heard his muffled reply through the running water:

"No worries."

"See you in five. For fuck's sake, get me a beer!"

I yelled back that his key card was in the electric metre and left.

"Ground floor, doors opening."

49

I stepped into the lobby.

"Ole, ole, ole!"

Cheers erupted. Ally handed me a beer, and to rapturous applause, I downed it in one. A large burp.

Ally threw an arm around my neck in a playful headlock, dragging me towards the others. He whispered:

"Whatever you need, son—your tracks are covered."

I grinned up at him and joined in the raucous chanting of You'll Never Walk Alone.

I sat beside Ally as the craic continued. He told me he'd met the love of his life last night—she was from Lurgan, worked in Liverpool, and was moving back home next week.

"She's my plus-one for the big day!" he cheered. We all joined in.

I gave him a brief outline of my night and begged him to cover for me—no matter what Patrick asked.

He agreed instantly.

"Patrick will be here in a minute."

Ally sipped his beer, waved a hand dismissively, and burped:

"He's solid. I like him!"

Then, grinning, he added:

"I'll cover you, mate, don't worry. Sure, we'll just play it by ear."

I laughed, and the others joined in. A chorus of "Play it by ear!" rang out across the lobby. Even John shouted:

"Aye, your ma plays it by ear!"

The place erupted.

It was always play it by ear when we were on the sauce.

Chapter 11
The Game

Patrick was the last to arrive, strolling in casually before sinking a beer. Within minutes, we were outside—heaven itself, or Anfield, as the heathens called it.

Thousands thronged about. "Hats, flags, scarves!" rang out from every corner. Badges for sale, all sorts of memorabilia. The air was thick with the smells of fried onions, dead beef, beer, and smoke. In my state, it was a heady mix.

I was wretched.

All twenty-five of us made our way to the ground, even though only twelve were actually going in. We naturally split into factions again, agreeing to meet outside the Albert pub at 1 p.m. for a pre-match pint.

I couldn't wait to get to the Albert. I'd heard so much about it—I needed to see inside for myself.

A few of our Manchester United lot started singing "Red Army!"—risky, I thought.

We reached the pub, and I went in to get six pints. The moment I stepped inside, I was taken aback.

This old Victorian pub was a shrine—every inch of wall and ceiling draped in football memorabilia. Flags from all over the world. Liverpool banners celebrating their countless European victories. Not a blank spot in sight.

I caught the barman's eye, still trying to take it all in.

"Six lager, please!" I shouted over the din.

The pints were already poured. On match days, they brought in extra staff to do nothing but pull pints. The barman handed me a tray and called out:

"Twenty-one, our kid!"

He held up two fingers on his left hand and one on his right. I handed him a twenty and a fiver, waving off the change.

"Sound!" was his only reply.

I grabbed the cardboard carrier with four pints, managing to balance the other two in my right hand. Half-focused on not spilling, half-absorbed by my surroundings.

I handed two pints to Joe—an Everton supporter who was going to the game anyway.

"For the spectacle," he'd said. "What the fuck else am I going to do?"

Pints distributed, we broke into songs. The old favourites rang out, and other groups joined in.

I was loving it.

Glancing at my watch—1:20 p.m. No sign of the others, including Stephen, who, unbelievably, had the tickets.

First pint down. Paul nudged Joe.

"Come to the bar with me? Need a hand carrying the next round."

Joe necked the last of his pint and followed.

The others trickled in, the craic flowing as fast as the beer. Everyone had a story from the night before—or, as Jimmy put it:

"Sexploits!"

Frank turned to me, eyes narrowed.

"Where the fuck did you go?"

I shrugged. "Back to the room. I was fucked, had about thirty shots."

He looked at me, incredulous. I just wanted him to drop it.

Patrick piped up:

"He was in the shower this morning when I got in!"

Holy fuck—Siobhan's brother was my alibi. How perfect.

I am not sure Frank believed him, but the subject changed.

Beer was flowing. Songs were flowing. The piss was flowing—so much so I had a once-in-a-lifetime experience as a man.

A queue for the toilet.

The eleven of us (minus Stephen) going to the game finally got our tickets. We skulled the remnants of our pints, said our goodbyes, and headed for the ground.

Frank had organised ten-pin bowling for the others.

No, thank you.

Our tickets were from the local supporters' club, meaning we were all sitting together—except Patrick. I was beside Ally, which suited me. It gave me a chance to explain last night.

Not that Ally was interested. Fanatical Liverpool supporter that he was. He only cared about the game. Frankly, I was relieved.

It was my secret.

Well… mine and Joan's.

At eight minutes to three, the teams emerged for the usual pre-match formalities.

The opening notes of You'll Never Walk Alone fell from the stadium speakers—not that we needed any encouragement. The whole ground erupted in full voice.

I looked around, taking it in. Martin stood there, eyes closed, singing at the top of his lungs.

Liverpool v Manchester City. The game of the season, they'd called it.

Six minutes in, Fabinho scored a wonder goal.

We leaped for joy.

Seven minutes later, Andy Robertson floated a sublime cross onto Mo Salah's head—goal! The place exploded.

"Mo Salah, Mo Salah, running down the wing…"

The entire stadium roared as the little Egyptian took a bow before being mobbed by his teammates.

The Robertson chant followed right after.

We jumped for joy.

It was unreal. But six weeks ago, I'd been at Croke Park watching Tipperary hammer Kilkenny in the All-Ireland hurling final. Wall-to-wall excitement.

Liverpool 2-0 up at half-time.

I hit the toilets, grabbed two burgers on my way back.

Six minutes into the second half, Jordan Henderson curled a perfect cross onto the head of Sadio Mané—goal.

Game over.

Ten minutes from the end, Silva pulled one back for City, but it was a consolation goal at best.

Full-time: Liverpool 3 – Manchester City 1.

The plan was to regroup at the hotel, then head to Concert Square for 8 p.m. We'd agreed to sort ourselves out for food in smaller groups.

Me?

I just wanted to lie down.

Chapter 12
"John from Work"

As soon as my head hit the pillow, my phone made the "Siobhan noise." I flipped it open and saw that I had also received messages from "John from Work." I read Siobhan's first. It was simple and direct:

"This time in two weeks, handsome, we'll be man and wife. I can't wait to marry you! Xxxxxxxxxxxx."

My reply was just as straightforward:

"Me too. Heading out shortly—see you tomorrow, beautiful! X"

She didn't respond.

I looked at my phone again. Three missed calls from Joan. Then a text:

"Can you phone me, please? Something really mad has happened in this hotel."

The exact same message had been sent twice. My phone buzzed again as I was reading.

"Please, please, please, can you fucking phone me?"

Why should I? I thought to myself.

Patrick was in the bathroom, so calling Joan wasn't an option. The phone buzzed again:

"I fucking know you're receiving these. Can you please, for fuck's sake, phone me?"

The phone rang—just once. I declined the call as quickly as I could.

"Can't talk in company. Will phone ASAP."

I knew that wouldn't placate her, and sure enough, another message came through immediately:

"I'm out of my mind, don't know what to do. We've been told to find somewhere else to stay—someone was murdered in this hotel in the middle of the night."

I panicked—but still failed to see how this had anything to do with me.

Patrick emerged from the bathroom and said he was heading down to get a beer. He asked if I wanted one.

"Get me two. But if the boys are there, enjoy the craic—no rush."

As soon as the door closed, I rolled onto my side and phoned Joan, already doubting my decision.

"Hello!" she blurted through tears. Then silence, just sniffling.

"Jesus, what the fuck happened? Are you OK?"

"I'm OK," she whispered, her voice shaking.

I could smell fried onions.

"I don't know what to do," she continued.

Neither did I.

"How long have they given you to get out?" I asked, babbling.

"I'm not sure. They want to interview everyone before we leave to get all our details. I suppose to see if we heard or saw anything."

I panicked again. She'd have to tell them I was there. They'd definitely have CCTV footage of me arriving and leaving.

Joan spoke again, more assertive now.

"Colin, I'll have to tell them about you being here."

I froze.

"I could say I met you and didn't know who you were, but CCTV will show we came in at different times."

She seemed to be enjoying this bit.

I ran my fingers through my hair, exhaling heavily.

"Tell them the truth. Just... discretion, please."

She chuckled. What the fuck was funny?

"I'll get you out of this, but then you owe me, lover-boy. I'm getting excited."

I tried to think fast.

"We'll find somewhere for you to stay here."

Patrick.

What the fuck was I thinking?

"OK, but I don't plan to sleep much. I'm hyper."

What a mess.

I slid the phone closed just as Patrick returned, handing me two beers. He made his way to the bathroom without a word. I alternated sips of beer and whiskey.

What a fucking mess.

Patrick whistled as he towel-dried himself.

"Who put the cream in your bun?" I asked.

"You know those two cute ones I wasn't allowed to tell you about this morning?" he said, spraying deodorant under one arm.

"Aye. What about them?"

"One of them texted me while I was getting beers. I'm meeting them in Concert Square in twenty-five minutes."

It was only half six.

He sprayed his other armpit and pulled on a navy shirt—it suited him. Carefully buttoning it, he smoothed the front with his palms, inserted his cufflinks, and grabbed my aftershave, using far too much. He rubbed his hands together, slapped his face, then rubbed his wrists before patting behind his knees.

60

Weirdo. Who the fuck does that?

Without looking at him, I asked, "You'll hardly be back here tonight?"

"If things go according to plan, I'll be getting devoured by two young cuties." He winked. "Don't wait up."

I went cold at the thought—but it didn't deter me.

"Tell you what—text me as soon as you know what you're doing."

He scrunched his eyebrows. "No bother. And sure, what does it matter where I sleep?"

I reminded him about Paula. "Paula might care."

He inhaled sharply.

"That hurts." Then he winked.

"What time are you lot leaving tomorrow?" he asked.

"We need to be gone by two in the afternoon, but even with late check-out, we're out of here by twelve."

He brushed imaginary dust from his shoulder, stared at himself in the mirror, ruffled his hair—trying to hide the fact he was balding at thirty-two—turned sideways, grinned, and then blew me a kiss.

"I'll see you in the morning!" he called as he left.

He hadn't even taken his key.

Gone.

I texted Joan:

"Are you OK?"

Immediate reply: "Yeah, I think I'm covered. Can you talk?"

I phoned. She answered instantly.

"Hiya Just finished with the police—it was pretty straightforward, nothing accusatory. Seems the CCTV is decent in this hotel."

She continued.

"I told them about you being here, but I explained the sensitivity—said you have a girlfriend back home."

I asked if they wanted to speak to me. She confirmed they did.

Without thinking, I said I'd be there in ten to fifteen minutes.

Joan said she'd packed but hadn't found anywhere to stay.

"I'll get that sorted," I assured her.

She giggled.

I didn't.

I grabbed my jacket and both keys, rushed to the lift, and was so beside myself that I didn't even notice the annoying voice from the intercom in the partitioning window.

"Where to?"

The driver asked.

"Hilton," I replied.

His eyebrows lifted slightly.

"There was a murder there last night. Pretty bad—young blonde woman, strangled."

I froze for a second. Was it her?

"Yeah, I heard. I'm just going to get a friend to bring her to our hotel."

What was I thinking?

Again, I wasn't.

"Do you want me to wait for you?" he asked, his tone generous.

"No, you're all right. I was there last night—the police want to speak with me."

He let out a short laugh.

"Friend, you say?"

I decided that was the end of our conversation.

The hotel loomed ahead, cordoned off by police tape, patrol cars flashing red and blue, vans parked haphazardly near the entrance. As we pulled up, I shoved a tenner into his hand.

"Keep the change."

I stepped out, the night air thick with something unspoken. The officer on duty at the entrance studied me carefully before allowing me through.

Joan stood in the lobby. Her hair cascaded over her shoulders that tight black dress clinging in all the right places. The five-inch heels made her look taller and sharper. Impossible to miss.

She waved before pointing towards a woman in uniform sitting at a makeshift station by the foyer.

I took a deep breath and approached.

"Hi."

The officer looked up from her notes, her gaze flicking between Joan and me—our hands briefly clasped. Her lips pressed into a thin line.

"Sir, I take it you're Colin? Joan's filled me in."

Not everything, surely.

"How can I help?"

I just wanted out of there.

"Just a few formalities—information, details, that sort of thing."

She gestured to the yellow leather chair across from her. I sat.

"Full name?"

Her eyes locked onto mine.

"Colin Francis Hill."

"Address?"

"4 Lennox Drive, BT8 8LA."

She nodded.

"Occupation?"

"Same firm as Joan—Smith & Company, Accountancy. Six May Street, Belfast. Sorry, don't have the postcode handy."

I patted my coat pockets as if searching for a business card, then reeled off my phone number.

"You can contact me anytime."

Her pen scratched across the notepad. I forced my voice to stay casual.

"Do you have any suspects?"

She glanced up.

"There are one or two we're looking at."

After the necessary questions, she turned a laptop towards me. A grainy video played—a figure leaving the victim's room.

"Did you see this person enter or leave the building? He left around the same time as you."

I kept my eyes on the screen just long enough before shaking my head.

"No, nothing."

I focused on the framed painting behind her—counting the pebbles in its abstract sea.

In the back of my mind, something stirred. A memory, indistinct but there. But I needed to get the fuck out of here.

She studied me, then closed her notebook.

"You're free to go. I have your number if I need to follow up."

She stood, offering her hand. I shook it.

Then, with a smirk, she added,

"Girlfriend at home?"

Her gaze flicked to Joan.

I ignored her and walked towards the lobby, signalling Joan to follow.

Outside, I pulled out my cigarettes and offered her one. She accepted. I slid one between my lips and tapped the box for my slim-line lighter to slip out. Being a gentleman, I lit hers first, then mine. The first drag hit deep.

"This wasn't the weekend I had planned," I muttered, raking a hand through my hair.

Joan laughed.

I didn't see what was remotely funny.

Fuck, she looked incredible.

The silence stretched. I couldn't stand it.

"What happened? Did you hear?"

She looked at me blankly.

"What do you mean?"

I furrowed my brow.

"The girl who was killed. What the fuck do you think I mean?"

I stared at her.

"Oh, right. Strangled, apparently. Concierge told me."

She paused, then added, "I mean, fuck's sake—I was in the same hotel. That could've been me."

She giggled.

I couldn't get my head around how unaffected she seemed.

If this had been Siobhan, she'd be in bits.

SEMI-DETACHED

The details of the murder reminded me of another case—a woman killed just outside Belfast a few weeks ago. I mentioned it to Joan. Her eyes lit up.

"Should we tell the police?"

She reached for my hand. I shrugged and turned away.

"Taxi's here. I doubt it's related."

As I opened the taxi door, she murmured,

"Mind you, it was the talk of our Ballymoney office."

I turned to her.

"That's right—you worked in Ballymoney before?"

She nodded.

"Yeah, transferred about a month ago. Got promoted."

I stubbed my cigarette out in the ashtray, watching as Joan flicked hers to the ground and crushed it beneath her heel in a slow, deliberate circle.

I hated when people didn't use the ashtray.

I told her as much.

She just smirked.

The driver loaded her bag into the boot.

I slouched back in my seat. Joan perched on the edge, her dress riding up just enough for me to catch the faintest glimpse of lace at the top of her stockings. She knew I saw.

And she was loving it.

When we reached the hotel, I handed her one of the room keys.

"Room twenty-nine. I'll be up in ten minutes."

She tilted her head.

"Discretion, yeah? If anyone's on the corridor, walk past."

She winked.

Chapter 13
Room Twenty-Nine Too

As she moved towards the lift, I perched on a bar stool and ordered two glasses of red wine and two bottles of beer.

What was I thinking?

Again.

If my own brothers found out, they'd kill me. Siobhan's would do worse.

I downed the first beer in one go, flicked open my phone, and scrolled through the messages.

Buzz. Buzz. Buzz.

Same thing, over and over.

"Where the fuck are you?"

I was about to reply, then decided it'd be easier to call Ally.

He picked up after two rings.

"Went for a walk to clear my head. I'll be there in an hour."

Ally never asked questions. That's what I liked about him.

"No worries, I'll let the others know. You should see Patrick—pinned between two belters, grin on him like he's died and gone to heaven."

He laughed.

"Hurry up, heavy hole."

I hung up.

Lifting the drinks, I headed for the lift.

The room door clicked open, and there she was.

Underwear. Those shoes.

I froze.

Not just at the sight of her—but at the weight of what I was doing. The cost if I got caught.

I closed the door quickly.

She had it. And she knew it.

I set the drinks down beside the TV, and we tore into each other.

For me, it was over embarrassingly fast. Only then did I notice the sheets.

Black silk.

The same ones that had been on the bed the night before.

A cold wave ran through me.

I handed her a glass of wine and lifted my beer. As we clinked glasses, I sighed.

"I'll have to go soon—meeting the lads in Concert Square."

She shrugged.

"I knew that. I'm happy here. Got everything I need."

She patted her suitcase.

"To entertain myself."

I was still trying to convince myself this was doable and that it made sense. It had merit.

"Might pop down to the lobby for a drink. But I'll be here when you get back."

She winked, exaggerated.

I made my way to the shower room. She followed.

The shower cubicle was too small for two.

Part of me was relieved.

She perched on the toilet, watching me as I lathered up. Reaching for one of the small hotel toiletries, she pulled out a shower cap and tucked her curls in neatly, all the way around.

We laughed. It felt natural.

It was anything but.

"Leave the water running," she said, peeling off her underwear and shoes.

Completely bare except for the ridiculous shower cap, she still looked phenomenal.

As I stepped out, she ran a hand down me, slow and deliberate. I was ready again, and she knew it.

Bent over the bath, hands splayed against the wall, she took me. Again, for me, it didn't last long.

She smiled, lips curling.

"There'll be a lot more of that later."

Then she dropped to her knees, lips parting.

Before she could take me in, she changed her mind, standing instead and stepping into the shower.

I dried off and got dressed. As I slid on my second Chelsea boot, she strutted out of the bathroom, a small towel wrapped around her midriff.

It barely covered her.

And barely didn't.

I moved to kiss her goodbye.

She shook her head, grabbed the back of my neck, and whispered against my ear,

"Later, big boy."

I felt nothing.

I just needed to leave before Patrick and the others suspected anything.

She pouted as I slipped into my jacket. I caught my reflection in the mirror.

"You're gorgeous," she murmured.

"Have fun. But not too much."

I smirked and said nothing.

And left.

Chapter 14
Patrick's Plus Two

As I arrived at Concert Square, I raised my right hand to shield my eyes. I phoned Ally but could barely make him out over the noise. I only caught his last two words:

"Tikki Joe's!"

That was all I needed. I turned in that direction.

The "Ole, ole's" started as soon as I walked in, followed by loud cheers. I grinned, dancing my way across the floor as the noise grew louder, applause breaking out.

"Where have you been, dirty hole?"

Frank was always the first to ask. To deflect, I smirked.

"Trying to stay sober," I said before adding, "Shots, everyone!"

"Yeeeoooooo!" came the collective response.

Quick headcount—nine of us in Tikki Joe's. As I made my way to the bar, I spotted Patrick with his arms around the two girls from last night. He winked.

Patrick barged in beside me at the bar, grinning.

"Leaving soon," he said. "The girls are dying to get me back to their hotel—dying for a threesome."

"Lucky bastard!" I laughed.

He said he'd ring me in the morning but needed a favour. Their hotel was way out near the airport, and his flight back to London was later than ours. Could I gather his stuff and drop it at reception?

I agreed, relieved he wasn't suggesting bringing them back to our room. Mind you, I had a feeling Joan might've been up for it.

74

"Ring me in the morning, sure."

Patrick nodded and disappeared to the toilets. Just then, Ally tapped my shoulder. I caught his eye in the mirror, running the length of the bar.

He pulled me close in a bromance kind of way.

"We alright over here, dude?"

I forced a smile.

"If only you knew."

He squeezed me tighter.

"Sure, we can chat about it tomorrow!" He winked at me in the mirror, then started passing out shots.

We rejoined the lads. Through the crowd, I glimpsed the back of Patrick, a girl on each arm, making his way outside.

I rationalised that I wasn't as bad as Patrick. Who was I kidding? The night dragged. And dragged. And dragged. I kept searching for an opportunity to slip away but was failing miserably.

Then my phone buzzed.

Joan. Naked on the bed. Something was moving between her legs.

Caption:

"I'm entertaining myself until you get back! xxxxxxxx"

That was my cue.

At fourteen minutes past one, I finally escaped from the Walkabout. I sprinted to our hotel, breathless as I reached the lift—then spotted Joan in the lobby bar, entertaining a group of five men.

Does she ever stop?

I waved. She stood up slowly, making sure all five got a glimpse of something. Then she giggled and almost broke into a jog, grabbing my arm.

"Wait until you see what I've got planned for you!"

"Doors opening! Going up!"

And we were. Or at least, I was.

As soon as we burst into the room, she kissed me hard, ripping at my clothes. Then I noticed a full bottle of Jameson on the sideboard, two shot glasses beside it.

I pointed. "Where did that come from?"

"Bought it today. It's your favourite, right?"

I smiled. It was indeed.

Now undressed, she handed me a glass of whiskey, her hand sliding down to fondle me. Within seconds, I was standing to attention.

She hitched up her dress. No knickers. A bright red suspender belt, stockings straining against their elastic.

She turned, and I slid in. We fucked, almost violently. Too quickly for Joan's liking. I groaned as I finished.

She stood up. "Nice starter, sir!"

She winked. She always winked.

I threw back another shot. She shoved me onto the bed—I was happy to comply.

From her case, she pulled out a pair of handcuffs, locking one around my right wrist. With surprising ease, she pushed my arms above my head, securing the cuffs around the headboard bar. My left wrist followed.

She disappeared into the bathroom. Seconds later, she returned—wearing the most incredible red basque, her tits practically pushed up to her chin.

I exhaled. "Wow."

She held a dildo in her hand, sliding it seductively between her legs as she began to writhe.

That's what was in the photo she sent me earlier! I thought.

I couldn't take my eyes off her as she slowly penetrated herself, her body shuddering. With a deliberate motion, she withdrew the dildo.

"Just three things purchased today—whiskey for you, this for me," she murmured, running her tongue along the tip.

Then, with a smirk, she traced her hands down the basque over her stockings.

"And this for both of us. You like?"

I nodded.

Her expression was strange—almost vacant—but I didn't mind. She lifted the whiskey bottle, took a long swig, and then bent towards me. As our lips met, she passed the liquor into my mouth.

I liked this game.

At the same time, she moved the dildo to my cock, the buzzing sending waves of sensation through me. In a flash, her mouth engulfed me, her head bobbing rhythmically, her right hand pressing firmly against my chest.

Without warning, she straddled me, guiding me inside her. She rocked gently at first, her eyes rolling back as she found her rhythm. Then she picked up the pace, moaning louder, losing herself in it. A sharp cry escaped her lips, but she didn't stop. Another scream—then suddenly, she collapsed beside me, breathless.

SEMI-DETACHED

I was relieved.

She lay there, motionless for what felt like an age. My wrists ached—I wanted the handcuffs off. At first, she refused, but when I asked again, she relented.

We sat, sipping whiskey.

I took a shower. Just as I was rinsing off, I felt her hand slide between my legs from behind. She bent over the sink, waiting. I didn't hesitate. My hands gripped her hips as we rocked steadily, my moans echoing in the steam.

Through the mirror, she watched me. I was loving this.

After, I pulled on a pair of shorts. We sat in silence, drinking whiskey, just staring. At that moment, I wished I'd booked her another room. This was reckless. But even if I had, would she have gone?

Eventually, we rolled into bed. She curled up tightly against me.

I snored. It was almost half five. Just after seven, I woke to the warmth between my legs.

Joan's head was under the covers, her mouth wrapped around me. She was ravenous, insatiable. It was impossible to keep up, so I surrendered to it and let her take full control.

When she was done with me—when there was no doubt who was in charge—she slid out of bed and disappeared into the bathroom. I heard the shower switch on.

Ten minutes later, she emerged in faded jeans and a tight white T-shirt, a dark green leather jacket thrown over her shoulders. Her dark green Doc Martens Chelsea boots completed the look. Even dressed down, she was sex on a stick.

She pointed her thumb towards the shower. "Your turn."

I did as I was told.

78

As I finished rinsing, she popped her head around the door.

"That's me away. I've stripped the bed—can you put their bedclothes back on? My flight's at 10:30, taxi's at the door. See you at work tomorrow. Key's beside the TV. Ciao, baby!"

And just like that, she was gone.

The door clicked shut as my foot touched the bathroom floor.

It had been a whirlwind. A wild, reckless, exhilarating whirlwind.

Chapter 15
Nice Starter Sir

As soon as we burst through the door, she began to kiss me passionately. She was ripping my clothes off when I noticed a full bottle of Jameson sitting on the sideboard with two shot glasses. I pointed at it.

"Where did that come from?"

"I bought it today. It's your favourite, right?"

I smiled—it was indeed.

Undressed now, she handed me a glass of whiskey and began to fondle my penis. She soon had me standing to attention. Hitching up her dress, she revealed a bright red suspender belt and no knickers. The stockings were straining on the elastic. She turned her back to me, and I slid in. We were fucking almost violently. I finished again rather too quickly for Joan's liking. I groaned as I did, and she stood up.

"Nice starter, sir!"

She winked—she always winked.

I grabbed another shot, and she shoved me onto the bed. I was happy to comply.

She took a pair of handcuffs from her case and adeptly wrapped and locked one around my right wrist. She pushed my hands above my head and slid the cuffs around a bar on the headboard. My left hand was then locked in too. She went to the bathroom and, within seconds, returned wearing the most amazing red basque that pushed her tits up towards her chin.

"Wow," I breathed.

She had a dildo in her hand as she seductively slid it between her legs and began to writhe.

"That's what was in the photo she sent me earlier!" I thought.

I couldn't take my eyes off her as she penetrated herself. She shuddered and slowly withdrew the dildo.

"Just three things purchased today—whiskey for you, this for me," she said, running her tongue along the tip, "and this."

She ran her hands down the basque and onto the stockings.

"And this for both of us. You like?"

I nodded my approval.

She had a strange, almost vacant look on her face. I didn't mind. She lifted the whiskey bottle and took a large swig. Moving towards me, she bent to kiss me and exchanged the contents of her mouth.

I liked this game.

Simultaneously, she moved the dildo to my penis. The buzzing soon had me aroused, and in a flash, her mouth engulfed my erection. Her head bobbed up and down rhythmically. She put her right hand on my chest and, as she removed her mouth, straddled me. She began to gently rock up and down. Her eyes started to roll in her head, and she became a bit more enthusiastic in her movements. She let out a scream and continued. I could feel the wetness. She let out another scream and rolled off.

I was glad.

She lay there motionless for an age. I wanted her to take the handcuffs off. Initially, she refused, but when I asked again, she gave in. We sat sipping whiskey.

I showered, and as I did, I felt her hand slide between my legs from behind. She bent over the sink and waited for me to insert my erect penis into her. I obliged. We rocked steadily, and I moaned as I finished. Joan looked at me through the mirror as I withdrew.

I was loving this.

I put on a pair of shorts as we sat, stared, and drank whiskey. In that moment, I wished that I had enquired about another room for her—this was so risky. Eventually, we both rolled into bed, and she snuggled in tightly. Not sure she would have gone to another room if I had booked one.

I snored. It was almost five thirty.

I was awakened just after seven. Joan's head was under the covers, and I could feel the warmth of her mouth between my legs. She was ravenous—it seemed impossible to satisfy her. I went with the flow.

When she was finished with me, I was in no doubt that she was in charge. She removed herself from the bed and went to the bathroom. I heard the shower being turned on, and ten minutes later, Joan emerged wearing faded jeans and a tight white T-shirt. She also had a dark green leather jacket on and a pair of dark green Dr. Martens Chelsea boots. Even dressed down, she was like sex on a stick.

She pointed with her thumb towards the shower, and I did as I was told.

As I was just finishing rinsing, she popped her head round the door.

"That's me away! I've stripped the bed—can you put their bedclothes back on? My flight's at 10:30, taxi is at the door! See you at work tomorrow. Key is beside the TV. Ciao, baby!"

With that, she was gone. The door closed behind her just as my foot hit the bathroom floor.

It was like some crazy whirlwind.

Chapter 16
Twenty Quid, Is That All?

I got dressed and started to pack my bag and Patrick's. Joan had left about twenty minutes earlier when the bedroom door was gently tapped.

"Had she forgotten something?" I said to myself as I pulled the door open.

A rather angry Patrick stood there, asking to borrow twenty pounds for his taxi. His "friends" had handcuffed him to the bed and disappeared with his wallet. I instinctively tapped my back pocket—wallet intact. I withdrew it and was about to hand him a twenty-pound note when I saw how bad he looked.

"Go get a shower. I'll sort your taxi," I said.

"I'm fucking raging, mate! If I could get my hands on those two fucking slappers, I'd fucking kill them! Not a word to Paula—she would fucking kill me. I can't believe how fucking stupid I've been."

I asked, "How the fuck did you get out of the cuffs?"

My own wrists were still a bit sore from my experience.

"Night porter. I was going apeshit shouting, and another resident phoned to get me quietened. He laughed—seems it's not the first time he's had to do this. So fucking embarrassing! I think that bastard might be in on it!"

I shook my head and, in an act of sympathy, patted him on the back.

As I made my way to the lift, I congratulated myself on my timing. The room was in good shape, and any womanly smell was covered in a mix of Jameson and aftershave.

When I got back, Patrick was standing with a mug in his hand—tea, I thought. More like Jameson.

"Thanks, pal, you're a lifesaver. I'll pay you back! My sister is a lucky girl marrying a guy like you. To be honest, I was half expecting that doll from your work to be here with you! You've some willpower—not sure I'd have resisted!"

Disaster avoided.

He took his cigarettes out and offered me one. I pointed out the fine for smoking in the room, and he put them away again. I gave him another sixty pounds to get home as he filled me in on the finer details. When he was finished, he began ringing his bank and credit card company to cancel all his cards—it took ages.

In between calls, I went down to reception to see if anyone else was about. A couple of the lads were sipping coffee and eating bacon sandwiches. I got some coffee and a sandwich and joined them. Everyone had a story to tell, and they were still buzzing. As time rolled on, more joined us, and the conquest stories and near-misses were rolling off their tongues.

I listened.

We agreed to meet at a quarter to twelve. As the lift doors slid open, a beautiful blonde girl stepped out. As she walked past me, Frank shouted over, "Our Ally look after you okay, gorgeous?"

She blushed, bowed her head, and made for the exit. "Walk of shame" suddenly made sense as I watched it in the flesh.

Paul asked, "Here, Col, I was pissed when I got back last night. Couldn't be sure, but I would have sworn your woman from work was here getting chatted up by about six lads!"

His lips turned downwards. I shrugged and said nothing.

"Go, Ally!" I whispered as I stepped into the lift.

This was the girl from Lurgan. He wasn't wrong—she was stunning.

Patrick was calmer when I returned. I heard him say, "I know, love. I think he would have stabbed me if I didn't hand it over!"

He pointed at the phone and mouthed, "Paula!"

He continued, "Waste of time, love. It was dark, and I have no description. Yes, yes, I have cancelled all my cards. Thank God you said to leave my licence at home! Cards will be returned to me in seven to ten working days. Colin was just behind me when it happened, but by the time he got there, they had scarpered. We did give chase, but they had vanished. He has given me the money to get home. I will talk to you later. Love you, darling!"

He hung up and grimaced.

"By the way, you found me shaking and terrified just after I was held up!"

I nodded in compliance. I was hardly in a position to argue.

At eleven forty, we did the sweep of the room and made our way to the foyer. Everyone was assembled apart from Ally and Stephen. For Ally, this was unusual, but Stephen had an excuse. For him, this was normal. Thankfully, when he handed out the tickets on Friday, he also gave us our return tickets—no panic today.

I phoned Ally, and he answered immediately.

"We're just leaving now!"

Stephen was with him.

Patrick was saying his goodbyes and talking about how much he was looking forward to the wedding and seeing them all again. Not all of them were invited to the reception, but those who weren't were coming to the evening party. Ally and Stephen stepped from the lift, and we trudged towards the doors.

We got in the taxis, and there was no drama at the airport.

Subdued.

The flight home was uneventful. No one wanted to drink, and most were sleeping. Stephen Mulcahy was our attendant again. As he passed me, he leaned in and said, "Yous are awful quiet, so yous are!"

I nodded. "Big weekend. Not much sleep!"

He gave me a knowing look.

"LEST WE FORGET!"

In bold capitals.

A chill came over me as I closed the door with a kick.

We landed safely. As we walked through arrivals, I saw Siobhan jumping with excitement. When she spotted me, she ran towards me and, from about two feet away, jumped into my arms, giving me a slow kiss.

"I love you!"

She took my hand, and we made our way to her car.

I was glad Paul and Joe were with us on the journey home— they did all the talking. From what they said, it appeared that I had been with them all weekend.

After dropping them off, Siobhan drove to the house I was staying in. It was to be our marital home, but Siobhan refused to live with me before we got married. She was quaintly old-fashioned like that. Besides, I had floors to sand and painting to do. Siobhan wanted the house "just so" for our return from our honeymoon in Italy.

She wouldn't come in.

"I'm too excited to see you back safe. I think if I went in, I would break my six-week rule!"

I feigned protest and gave her a long, slow, passionate kiss. I was glad— I just wanted to sleep.

I got out of the car with Siobhan blowing me lots of kisses and saying, "I love you, Mister Hill."

I stood and waved her off. As I opened the front door, I lifted the mail. Bills and letters for the previous occupants.

One envelope simply said "Colin."

No stamp.

I opened it.

A print of Joan's green Dr. Martens.

Several prints of her naked.

The tag simply read:

Chapter 17
On The Road

THREE WEEKS EARLIER

Siobhan smiled as she stuffed her suitcase into the boot of Sheila's Nissan Juke. She trotted around to the front passenger seat—riding shotgun was her privilege. It was her hen weekend, after all.

Eight girls.

Two cars.

Four bottles of champagne (though Sheila doubted that would be enough).

Eight massages.

Six facials.

Two manicures.

Two nights' bed and breakfast and one evening meal.

The girls were buzzing. A nice, wee, sedate spa weekend at the Galgorm Country Club and Spa. Siobhan placed her phone into the cradle and hit play on her weekend playlist.

Song one: "Dancing Queen" by ABBA.

Typical Siobhan, Donna thought—but they all joined in anyway.

Donna wasn't just Siobhan's cousin; she was her best friend. They had all booked a special deal that included two treatments. Everyone had opted for the massage, and for their second, they had chosen individually.

They had just rolled onto the M3 when Donna unzipped her oversized handbag, extracted a chilled bottle of Villa Maria Sauvignon Blanc, and pulled out three plastic wine glasses.

Siobhan lifted her phone to text Colin:

"On the M3 now, love. Hope you survive this weekend without me! Xxxx Don't miss me too much xxx"

They all cheered—except Katie, who was driving.

Sheila held the glasses, handing the first to Siobhan before holding the other two steady as Donna poured. Donna screwed the lid back on and returned the bottle to her bag. Teresa handed her a glass. A pointless, noiseless "clink," and then—

"Cheers, girls! This is going to be such a good laugh!"

And laugh they did.

"Give It Up" by KC and the Sunshine Band blared as Siobhan turned the volume up.

Donna started the ball rolling.

"What's the worst chat-up line you've ever had to endure?"

She paused for a second, then blurted:

"Me first!"

She continued, *"I'm not a photographer, but I can picture me and you together!"*

They all over-laughed.

Sheila even spat a drop of wine onto a hanky as she laughed, tapping Katie's shoulder in apology. Katie was too busy giggling to care.

Katie went next. *"Do I know you? Because you look an awful lot like my next girlfriend!"*

They were still laughing when Siobhan joined in.

"When Colin—"

They all roared with derision.

"Stop it!" Siobhan frowned. *"I love him!"*

The roars of laughter only got louder.

"Well, he once said to me, 'You must be a magician because when I look at you, everyone else disappears!'"

Katie yelled, *"Yeeeeeuccck!"* dragging the word out for emphasis. She continued, *"Oh, boke! You could turn milk sour with a line like that!"*

The laughter continued as they passed Patsy's car, where the other girls were traveling.

They were laughing so much in Patsy's car that they hardly noticed Sheila's—until Stella, sitting in the back seat, slid the window down and raised a glass. More giggles.

Siobhan's phone buzzed. She opened it excitedly, only to find a message from Mary—Maz for short—who was in the other car.

"Paula and I were wondering—should we have dinner tonight or tomorrow night? We're easy. What do you lot think?"

"The Look of Love" by ABC was playing now.

Siobhan read the message aloud. The vote was unanimous— Saturday was the better option.

Sheila added, *"Sure, we won't even arrive until near seven o'clock!"*

Siobhan replied:

"I'm afraid it's unanimous in this car—tomorrow night is the best option!"

Paula had already begun typing back:

"We think tomorrow night too—after our treatments, we'll all be ready for a lovely three-course meal!"

It was settled.

Siobhan replied, *"Okay, see you all there shortly!"*

At 6:53, Katie slid her car into a space close to the reception doors. She grabbed a used coffee cup and, through the open window, casually slung the remnants onto the ground.

She turned to Maz. *"Bartender, please!"*

They all laughed.

Maz poured.

Katie gulped.

Siobhan tapped her phone—left thumb, then right.

"We have arrived safe and sound. Hope all okay in our new home xxxx"

Still nothing from Colin.

They soon climbed out of the car, and as they moved toward the boot, it began to open automatically.

Patsy pulled into the space beside them. More hugs, more laughter—everyone talking at once, no one making sense.

The weekend had begun.

Chapter 18
Pop Your Cork

Bags in hand and suit bags slung over their shoulders, they bumped and jostled their way to reception.

The receptionist took a good five minutes filing paperwork before she even looked up. Katie had to stop herself from tapping the bell that sat in front of her.

Eventually, the woman peered over the top of her pound-shop reading glasses.

"Yes, please, how can I help you?"

Siobhan stepped forward.

"Hi, we're here for the spa weekend—four rooms booked under the name Lowry."

She handed over the printout of their confirmation email.

"Let me see..."

The receptionist, whose badge read *Hilda*, flicked through some papers. Siobhan noted the name and thought to herself, *What an awful name.*

For a moment, Hilda looked confused. Then, suddenly, she nodded.

"Ah yes, here we are. Four rooms together on the first floor— 113, 114, 115, and 117."

She smiled at Siobhan.

"There was nearly a problem, you see—a rugby team from Cork booked up a lot of rooms. But we managed to keep you ladies as close together as possible!"

Siobhan smiled, thanking her before presenting her credit card for the deposit and to secure the key cards. She liked that it had both her and Colin's name on it.

Hilda handed over the key cards, two per pouch, as the girls had already sorted out their room pairings.

"Reception is open 24/7," Hilda added. *"We suggest leaving your key here when you go out. There's a £20 charge for lost cards."*

She smiled, though it felt more like a warning.

As they made their way toward the lift, a crowd of rather large men with thick Cork accents passed by. One whistled. Another winked. The guy at the front simply nodded and said,

"Evening, ladies."

They giggled and pushed their way into the lift.

"He's lovely," Donna sighed dramatically, pressing a hand to her forehead as if about to faint.

They all laughed as Katie hit the button for the first floor.

"Going up," she announced.

"If I have my way!" Teresa shot back.

"Going down!" Sheila added with a smirk.

Siobhan tutted in mock disapproval while the rest burst into laughter.

Once they reached their floor, they agreed to meet in Siobhan and Donna's room in half an hour for a glass of bubbles before heading into town. Taxis were pre-booked for 8:30 p.m. to take them to Ballymena.

As they approached their rooms, Sheila quipped in an innocent voice,

"Why are we going into Ballymena when we have a chance of a big up-and-under right here?"

She kissed her fist for emphasis.

More laughter.

They separated into their rooms. Showers were had. War paint was applied. Outfits were put on—some squeezed into more than others.

Siobhan caught a glimpse of herself as she passed the full-length mirror outside the bathroom. She hesitated.

She should be more confident.

Tall—five foot eight. Slim—almost too slim. Beautiful, thick, natural blonde hair styled in loose curls. That little black dress—the one that had rocked Colin backwards the first time he saw it. She smiled, remembering how he'd actually said *"Wow!"*

Makeup? Perfect.

Killer heels? Almost four inches—but comfortable enough for dancing.

She had always been told she was pretty, and in her quieter moments, she sometimes believed it.

This was one of those moments.

She smiled at herself.

Then she checked her phone.

Still nothing.

Her heart sank.

The others were just as dazzling. They were all at—or near—their 'wedding weight.' Hair perfected, faces painted, and no shortage of cleavage on show.

Just before the others arrived, Donna turned to Siobhan with a mischievous grin.

"Are you wearing knickers?"

Siobhan shot her a look of disbelief.

"Of course I'm wearing knickers!"

She pulled a disgusted face and made a childlike sound of revulsion.

"Yeeeeuuuugh."

"Mine's too tight for knickers," Donna shrugged, heading to the bathroom to brush her teeth.

When the others arrived, corks were popped, and the giggling began.

Maz, ever the show-off, slowly stroked her hips and ran a hand through her hair. She had undone three buttons on her blouse, revealing her ample cleavage.

Paula pointed.

"They look amazing!"

Maz smirked, squeezing her breasts together for effect.

"If I'm having no luck later, I'll just open another button. Wouldn't mind tackling a big hooker tonight!"

The rugby reference had them roaring with laughter.

Siobhan rolled her eyes. *Incorrigible.*

Bubbles were poured, glasses clinked, and a Tesco bag appeared—Stella had brought crackers, cheese, and pâté.

As they spread their snacks onto crackers, a dozen different conversations overlapped.

Northern Soul classics played through the Bluetooth speaker.

SEMI-DETACHED

"I picked a few that remind me of Colin," Siobhan said softly.

"Fuck me, boke!" Sheila laughed as Lamont Dozier's *"Fish Ain't Bitin'"* filled the room.

Of the group, five were single. Siobhan was engaged. Stella was married. And Paula... well, Paula was recently reacquainted with Jamie.

None of the others agreed with the *re-acquaintance*, but Paula was too besotted to see Jamie's controlling nature.

The others could. Sheila had even said as much.

After about twenty minutes, Hilda called up.

"Your taxis have arrived."

Coats were hurriedly thrown on, an assortment of designer bags were grabbed, and the *clacking* of heels echoed against the laminate floor as they strutted toward the lift.

Mock confidence masked real insecurities—insecurities that couldn't always be covered up by short skirts and war paint.

"Doors closing. Going down," the lift announced.

Sheila clapped her hands loudly, laughing exaggeratedly.

"Maybe I will!"

They burst into laughter again.

"Doors opening."

As they stepped into the lobby, they saw them.

The rugby team.

About thirty men, all wearing matching hoodies, milling about near reception.

Time to strut.

Even Siobhan.

Keys were left at reception.

A cascade of whistles and shouts followed them.

Hilda tutted. She'd seen it all before—too many times to count.

"See you later, ladies!" one of the rugby players called out.

Stella laughed.

"Wishful thinking, boys!"

They smiled as they walked out to the taxis, ready for whatever the night had in store.

Chapter 19
The Front Page

They went in the same groupings as they had arrived at the hotel.

"Where to, love?" asked the driver of the first car as he winked at Donna, who was in the front seat beside him.

"The Front Page," offered Maz from the back seat.

He lifted his radio and spoke clearly to the driver of cab two.

"Front Page, Mervy."

He replaced the radio in its cradle without waiting for a response.

As they drove, the driver was full of chat. He was talking about the woman who had been murdered.

"Strangled to death in her own bed, she was. Just two days ago!"

Siobhan said that she had heard it on the news, and the others agreed.

"Be careful, girls. He's still out there, and you girls look good enough to draw attention to yourselves. Just saying, like."

Donna paid for both taxis out of the kitty of seven hundred pounds, one hundred each. Siobhan was excused.

As they pushed open the door of the mock Tudor façade, it was like a scene from a Wild West movie.

Ballymena didn't know such glamour!

Everyone in the bar went silent and just stared.

Donna strode to the bar and, with confidence, ordered eight mojitos.

The barman immediately kicked into the Tom Cruise character from the movie. Donna thought it was funny that his name badge said Brian, Ballymena.

Brian hadn't a clue why she thought this was relevant.

He lined up eight cocktail glasses and crushed the ice, which was inside a bag, with a hammer.

Mint leaves pressed, he began to measure rum and brown sugar. He was vigorously shaking two cocktail shakers. He liked making mojitos, and every now and then, he would toss one in the air, twirl, and catch it again.

The girls clapped. It was impressive.

Donna asked if the kitchen was still open, and he nodded as he poured the drinks.

He looked at the clock and said, "For ten more minutes."

"We just want burgers, please."

She checked with the others—six chicken and two beef burgers—but Paula patted her tummy.

"Wedding weight."

They all laughed.

"Two portions of chips will get us a few chips each!" They all nodded in agreement.

Donna went back and said to Brian, "Six chicken burgers and two beef burgers, please. Can we just have two portions of chips? I know they're included, but we are watching our figures!"

"You're not the only ones, love," said a stocky middle-aged man who was perched at the bar.

Donna felt uncomfortable.

They moved to a table that had been set up, as Maz had booked. They clinked glasses, and Katie commented on the silence that had ensued when they arrived.

"Eerie!"

After about twenty minutes, the burgers with salad trimmings arrived. Two portions of chips were passed around, one on each side of the table. Katie, Stella, and Patsy didn't take any chips at all.

They laughed, and the craic began.

"Who is going to tackle the big six-and-a-half-footer from Cork?" began Stella.

"I'm glad I have Jim at home. I don't even have to think about it!" She laughed.

Sheila giggled and said, "I'd be up for that, too right. Might be walking funny tomorrow, but I think he'd be some ride. And just think—'going down' wouldn't have to be that far!"

They were all laughing.

"Rugby is a game played by men with odd-shaped balls!" added Paula.

"I'll confirm that for you tomorrow!" Katie threw her head back.

They all laughed.

Patsy joined in.

"Wonder if his," she pointed between her legs, "is proportionate to, you know, his height?"

Sheila shouted, "I refer you to Katie's last answer."

They were having a ball.

Donna called Brian to the table and asked him to take the orders for drinks. She liked being in control of the kitty.

The Front Page was a bit of a disappointment, and Sheila suggested, "We drink these, eat our burgers, and go back to the hotel."

Siobhan wanted to stay for at least one more drink or maybe try somewhere else.

Just then, the strange stocky man returned from the toilet and stared in their direction. Stella confidently opened a button on her blouse and, looking directly at him, said, "See enough?"

He blushed and turned to face the other direction.

Drinks arrived, and Siobhan was acting 'mummy,' making sure everyone got exactly what they ordered. Mind you, it was four vodka and slimline tonic, three gin and slimline tonic, and a Jameson with one ice cube. Siobhan drank the odd whiskey after Colin had introduced her to the flavour, and she liked it.

The locals were all commenting to Brian about the 'strangers' in their pub.

Gentle music played in the background.

Sade's greatest hits. "Is It a Crime?" slid effortlessly into "The Sweetest Taboo."

It was the epitome of easy listening.

The bar started to pack up, and everyone, no matter what age, seemed to know everyone else.

It was a strange atmosphere.

The main, no, the only topic of conversation was the murder. Everyone had a theory and even spoke indiscreetly about the woman who was dead.

"She was a slapper," said one quite heavy girl in an accent that sounded almost Scottish.

She was wearing very overstretched leggings that were pulled so tight they were semi-opaque, and it was easy to read the tattoo at the top of her thigh through them.

"I'll sleep when I'm dead!"

"How do you make that out?" came the response from one of the younger lads.

The heavy girl became instantaneously aggressive.

"Well, you've slept with her, and so has every other man in the greater Ballymena area!"

The tension was palpable.

Siobhan felt uncomfortable. She simply didn't like confrontation.

She motioned to Donna, making a phone sign and mouthing the word, "Taxi."

Donna did as she was told.

Within minutes, Brian shouted over, "Your taxis are out front, ladies."

Donna moved forward to settle the bill, and the rest gathered their coats and bags.

The guy at the bar looked at Donna again. He was just lonely, she thought to herself.

Chapter 20
Still Nothing

Sheila asked Mervy, "Where's the best place in Ballymena for a girl like me to meet," she paused, "a boy like you?"

She hoped that the modicum of flirting would elicit his best response.

"Well, there's The Moat or The Coach, but they say the best night to be had in Ballymena on a Friday is Gillie's Bar in the Galgorm, hey."

They decided to try The Moat and jumped in the cars.

When they arrived, they liked the atmosphere, and the crowd was quite friendly. Donna ordered drinks. Everyone got the same as before except Siobhan, who had moved onto white wine.

Sheila could see why they were liking this bar, but she was itching to get back to the Galgorm to "hook up" with the rugby team.

After a brief discussion and a few locals chatting them up, Siobhan eventually gave in.

"Galgorm it is!"

Sheila yelped.

Taxis were ordered again.

Mervy winked at Sheila and said, "Told you so, hey!"

The taxis sped to the Galgorm, and the ladies strutted into reception.

Hilda was still there. Donna asked if there was any entertainment on.

Hilda pointed towards the door and said, "Up the lane to the left. Gillie's Bar always has live music on a Friday night!"

Donna thanked her and said, "Goodnight!"

"Oh, I'll be here when you get back."

Donna smiled.

They squeezed out the door and linked arms as they teetered up the hill.

"Hope the rugby boys are here!"

Laughed Sheila. The rest agreed.

Donna commented that she was cold.

"That's because you're not wearing any knickers!"

Siobhan was quite pejorative in her tone.

Katie laughed, and Sheila joined in.

"You mean you ARE wearing knickers?"

Siobhan was appalled.

She flicked up her phone and was struggling to hide her disappointment that she hadn't even heard once from Colin. She said to the others.

Susan looked over at her and gave her a reassuring smile.

She texted him again.

"Is everything ok, love?"

She could tell by the ticks on WhatsApp that he hadn't even read her previous two messages, even though he had looked at his phone an hour earlier.

"Wise up," said Stella. "You're as good as married. Next time I speak to Jim will be Sunday when I get home! And that's if he isn't down at the bar."

This didn't reassure Siobhan.

As Patsy pushed open the door, "When I Kissed the Teacher" by ABBA was blasting out of the speakers. Not live music but a DJ in the corner—it was 70s night. The mobile disco lights revolved and bounced off walls and ceilings.

They all variously danced to a booth that was empty and sat as Donna said, "Same again?"

They all nodded as Siobhan reminded her that she was on the wine.

"YMCA" by the Village People cut across ABBA, and Sheila, Patsy, Katie, and Maz almost ran to the dance area. They were joined by some of the rugby boys who had filled two booths on the other side of the room.

Siobhan laughed and pointed as Katie did exaggerated Y.M.C.A. arm movements.

Paula went up to the bar to give Donna a hand. As she nudged in beside her, she felt a presence right behind her.

She was unnerved.

She turned and was staring right at the sternum of the guy Sheila had been talking about.

He was even taller close up.

He spoke with a lilt as he offered to get her a drink.

Paula was flattered, but she remembered what Jamie had said and refused.

Sheila came rushing over and introduced herself.

"Sheila Prentice."

She reached out her right hand. He took hold, and she gasped at just how big his hand was. She giggled.

"You got big feet too?"

He blushed and said, "Size seventeen."

Sheila, all of a sudden, was quite flushed.

"Tomas O'Brien."

He said, "I play with this mob." He gestured over his right shoulder with his thumb.

Sheila, keen to keep the chat going, asked, "What has you up here?"

She ran her hands slowly through her hair.

Tomas was polite.

"We play for Cork Con. We play Ballymena in the All-Ireland League tomorrow at two o'clock if you girls are at a loose end?"

Sheila laughed.

"Spa day!" she declared.

She was an international netball player and looked at her watch as if to say, Game tomorrow and you're in a pub at this time?

Donna Summer was singing "Enough is Enough." Siobhan and Paula were dancing.

"We are heading now. Curfew is 11.30 p.m. But tomorrow night, we have a wee function in the big room next door," he motioned towards the hotel.

"Why don't you ladies join us? It will be good fun—few drinks, finger food, and a dance."

Sheila knew that they had planned their meal in the hotel for Saturday night.

On behalf of the others, she said they would.

Tomas smiled.

Errol Brown of Hot Chocolate was starting "You Sexy Thing." Sheila loved this song and thought Errol was one of the sexiest men who ever lived. She winked at Tomas. As she was leaving, she looked down at his feet.

He laughed.

As Sheila returned to the table, Stella was finishing a story about a girl she used to work with who thought that the singer was actually singing, "I believe in Malcolm, you sexy thing!"

Maz and Patsy laughed.

Sheila told them about the function on Saturday night and their invite. Patsy, Donna, Teresa, and Maz were delighted.

They were just nodding in agreement.

"Anything would be better than that bar tonight!" offered Siobhan.

It was agreed.

Sheila rubbed her hands.

The rugby players, all eleven who had turned up, trudged out, gentlemanly saying, "Good night and goodbye" as they passed.

The girls reciprocated.

Tomas winked at Sheila.

She gasped and looked at his feet again. He shushed her and left.

"I'm Every Woman" by Chaka Khan blared out, and they all danced.

The DJ spliced this with Michael Jackson's "Don't Stop 'Til You Get Enough!" They stayed up.

They were having a ball.

Disco classic after disco classic, they danced for hours.

They all sat down when the DJ put on Kraftwerk's "She's a Model!"

Patsy pointed at the Latino-looking woman in the short red dress who was effortlessly floating about the floor in killer heels. She had a magical figure, and Patsy said,

"Think that song might be about her."

They all looked over. She was gorgeous.

Men were drooling over her and nearly queuing up to dance with her.

"Men are suckers for short dresses and big tits,"

offered Maz as she opened a fifth button and crossed her legs.

They all laughed.

Siobhan had 'gone to the rest room' during the Michael Jackson song, but really, she was outside ringing Colin. By the time she returned, the bar was starting to empty, and they were the last people there.

They gathered themselves up and went back to Donna and Siobhan's room for a nightcap.

Stella opened the fridge and took out the snacks. After a few drinks, they were glad of the nibbles. Donna produced two more bottles of Sauvignon Blanc from her suitcase and refilled the flutes that had been drained earlier. They chatted, nibbled, and sipped.

Music was playing in the background: Terence Trent D'Arby's "If You Let Me Stay!" Patsy was dancing just like Mister D'Arby had in the video, hair throwbacks included. She was a good dancer, and they all admired her.

After one drink, Stella said goodnight and wandered off to bed. Paula, who was sharing with her, followed suit.

Siobhan wanted them all to go but couldn't actually say that.

She yawned.

Katie took the hint and nodded at Patsy. They said their goodnights and left.

Sheila and Maz were always the last to leave a party, and half an hour later, Siobhan handed them three-quarters of a bottle of white wine and asked them to finish off in their room.

Maz grabbed the wine and the Bluetooth speaker. Sheila lifted their coats and bags.

Air kisses goodnight.

"See you in the morning."

Siobhan stretched as Donna emerged from the bathroom, ready for bed.

As the door closed, Siobhan flipped open her phone to check the time—2:38 a.m. She was more concerned to see whether Colin had responded to her goodnight message.

He hadn't.

Siobhan got ready for bed and slouched under the quilt.

Donna could hear what sounded like gentle sobbing from the other bed. She was tired but knew she had to ask,

"Everything alright over there?"

Within an instant, Siobhan sat rigid against the headboard and turned on the light beside her bed.

Donna sighed and sat up to listen.

"I haven't heard from Colin all day. He hasn't even read some of my messages!"

She upturned her palms.

Donna said,

"There will be a simple answer. Maybe his phone died. Maybe, with you away, he took the chance to get fully drunk and fell asleep?"

Siobhan continued,

"I love him so much, and sometimes it hurts when I think about him! He's everything I have ever dreamed of—tall, handsome,"

Donna nodded in agreement. He certainly was handsome.

"Funny,"

Siobhan continued.

"Smart, well-educated, funny,"

"You said that," replied Donna.

Siobhan laughed as she said this, remembering his 'funny face'—the one he reserved only for her.

"I worry sometimes that he doesn't seem to have the need for me that I have for him. Why has he not contacted me all day? We're getting married in five weeks, for goodness' sake."

Donna sighed. She couldn't explain it, but she had always thought that Siobhan, her cousin, was the luckiest girl in the world the day she met Colin Hill.

Donna had actually spotted him first, but he had made a beeline for Siobhan. People had always said they looked like sisters—someone once even asked if they were twins.

Donna was pretty, but her hair wasn't as luscious as Siobhan's, and everything seemed to take a little more effort for Donna.

Siobhan had gotten out of bed, and as she returned, she handed Donna a cup of tea she had made at the hospitality tray—just the way Donna liked it, strong and black,

"Like her men," she used to joke.

The conversation—monologue—continued.

"Am I doing the right thing? I know he's my man, and he does it for me, but I wonder… does he even love me? He does really nice things, and he's kind and sweet and can be very loving. He's generous to a fault, and he's hardworking… but does he love me? I sometimes think of that song, 'Do I Love You,' and sometimes I think of Colin and wonder—he doesn't. You know what I mean? I want Colin to be as excited to be getting married to me as I am to be getting married to him."

Donna wanted to scream. Siobhan had everything Donna wanted—a beautiful new home, a honeymoon in Italy, that vintage sports car she had always dreamed of—the one Colin had bought her for her birthday and as an early wedding present—a lavish wedding to prepare for, a future, and COLIN HILL!

Siobhan continued,

"I really hope I'm doing the right thing! I love him so much. I'll phone him first thing. Sorry to bother you, but I hate doubting myself."

Donna countered,

"No worries. Happy to listen."

She sipped the last of her tea, turned out the light, and rolled over before Siobhan had the chance to start again.

Chapter 21
The Giant Rope Bridge

Saturday was all planned. Siobhan had insisted that, since they were so close, they should visit the Giant's Causeway and the Carrick-a-Rede rope bridge.

"I always loved the Giant's Causeway when I visited as a child!" she declared before adding, "When I have kids, I'm going to bring them there too! It is a UNESCO World Heritage site, and I always loved when my daddy told us the story of Finn McCool and how he built the causeway so he could fight with a Scottish giant called Benandonner. Colin can do the same for our kids."

She had said this on Wednesday night when they met to finalise the plans.

As Donna woke, she noticed it was almost 9:45. Breakfast finished at ten.

Siobhan emerged from the bathroom, decidedly chirpier than she had been at 3 a.m.

"You seem in better form," Donna offered, as Siobhan hummed something that sounded like "You're Beautiful" by James Blunt.

"All sorted," said Siobhan in a rather high-pitched and frankly quite annoying tone. "Colin texted me at 3:33 a.m. to say that Stephen had commandeered his phone because he didn't want Colin on it all night texting me. Colin was laughing, saying something about it being his last night as a free man in Belfast."

She sounded quite self-assured as she said this.

At times, Donna didn't really like how prissy Siobhan could be.

Donna hopped out of bed and tied her hair back with a scrunchie. She threw on her gym clothes, and they hurried to breakfast just in time.

She was starving.

The others were dotted around the breakfast room, and Donna made her way to the self-serve area. She always took canned fruit and natural yoghurt when she stayed in a hotel—a kind of breakfast starter. Siobhan followed suit.

They sat, and the waitress brought them the tea they had ordered, accompanied by a rack of toast.

They went back to the self-serve area to get something cooked, agreeing that if they ate well now, they would manage until dinner.

One sausage, one bacon, one black pudding, two fried eggs, and a spoonful of mushrooms that were very watery from sitting under the bain-marie.

There was a din in the breakfast room as the rugby players were just finishing their pre-match meal. As they began to shuffle out, they were very polite again.

"Morning, ladies. Have a nice day. See you later!" were just some of the comments.

Tomas O'Brien winked at Sheila. She felt her cheeks redden as she winked back and stared at his feet. Maz burst out laughing, and Teresa joined her.

Breakfast consumed, they agreed to meet in the foyer at 11 a.m.

"We haven't got all day," said Stella, pointing out that her massage was at 2:30.

She looked at her watch.

They made their way to their rooms, got cleaned up, and put on their day clothes, including sturdy walking boots.

Donna quickly showered; the others had done this before breakfast.

Siobhan walked into the bathroom to brush her teeth. She couldn't help admiring how well Donna looked in the flesh, and she said as much.

Donna smiled.

They got into their respective cars just as the coach taking the rugby players to their game pulled up.

When they arrived at the causeway, Siobhan couldn't contain her pleasure.

Weird, thought Sheila.

They parked as close as they could to each other in the car park, and Donna went to pay the entrance fee from the £422 left in the kitty.

They walked down the steep decline towards the causeway, some huddling together as it was cold.

"It's always fucking cold here," said Katie.

At the causeway, Siobhan climbed over the basalt columns and posed as the others joined her one by one. Stella was the last and had to settle for a selfie.

They walked around the strangely shaped rocks, taking various photos on their phones. Only Patsy had actually brought a camera.

They spent the best part of an hour there, laughing as Sheila stood on a high column and shouted out at the sea,

"Tomas. Tomas, wherefore art thou?"

Siobhan even laughed out loud at this.

They made their way to their cars and drove the short distance to Carrick-a-Rede. After a long trek to the rope bridge, only Katie, Maz, and Siobhan were brave enough to go down the very steep steps and cross. The others made their excuses, while Sheila and Paula sat on a rock and lit a cigarette each.

When the others returned, Stella pointed at her watch.

"Ten to two, ladies, we'd better hurry—it's nearly SPA o'clock."

They laughed.

Back at the Galgorm, the ladies gathered their gym gear and swimsuits—in Sheila's case, a bikini.

At the thermal spa reception, they all giggled as they confirmed their treatments. All eight had booked a massage. With only four masseurs on duty, Stella, Paula, Donna, and Siobhan went at 2:30, while the others were booked for 3:30.

Maz and Sheila, like the first group, had also booked facials and went with the beautician for their treatment. Katie and Patsy went in the opposite direction for a manicure.

The treatments lasted about forty minutes. During the swap-over, they all agreed they had never felt so relaxed.

When the treatments were over, no one felt like going to the gym, so they ordered a bottle of champagne and sat in the oversized Jacuzzi.

"This is the life," offered Stella. They nodded and smiled.

"Hush, I can hear footsteps," said Sheila. She added, "Loud enough to be Tomas!"

Katie choked on her bubbles as they all laughed.

Spa time over, they returned to their rooms. Siobhan asked if it was okay to meet in Stella and Paula's room at seven for a pre-dinner drink.

They all agreed and went to get ready.

Siobhan seized the chance to send thirteen photos to Colin via WhatsApp. She added to the last one:

"Having a ball, can't wait to see you tomorrow! Xxx This six-week pre-wedding agreement will be tough, but it will be worth it. Xxx"

To her surprise, Colin texted back immediately.

"Glad you're enjoying. Heading out shortly with a number of the lads."

He didn't specify how many or who, which infuriated Siobhan.

"I'm leaving my phone at home. Last night I thought Stephen was going to drop it into a pint of Guinness! Chat tomorrow when I see you. Enjoy your night. Love you xxxxx."

Siobhan smiled contentedly.

Chapter 22
Ladies Night

They began to assemble in Stella and Paula's room, glasses filled.

Katie said, "Fuck me, we look even better than we did last night."

They all studied each other and agreed.

The music was blaring from the Bluetooth speaker, but tonight it was Maz's choices—Bon Jovi, Springsteen, AC/DC, The Cult. They all gently rocked as they listened to Ian Astbury blasting out L'il Devil!

At about twenty-five past seven, they headed for the lift.

"Tonight's the night!" laughed Sheila. She looked stunning. She was ready.

Wine was ordered for the table—two Sauvignon Blanc and two Merlot.

Glasses were filled, and the menus were being studied. Different options were discussed.

"It all looks lovely," Patsy said, putting her reading glasses back in their case just as Stella asked to borrow them.

"Vanity isn't as proud as it used to be!" Katie laughed. They all laughed.

The waiter was summoned, and they placed their orders. More wine was poured, and they chatted across each other. In another closed-off section of the restaurant, they could hear raucous laughter.

"Big Foot and the Hendersons!" Sheila laughed, pointing with her thumb over her shoulder at the temporary partitioning wall.

They didn't have to wait long for the starters to arrive, and with all the chatting and wine drinking, before they knew it, they were sipping Irish coffees.

The waiter told them the coffees had been sent over by a rather tall man from behind the screen.

"Big Foot!" laughed Sheila. She was allowing herself to get even more excited now—the prospect.

By the time they were finishing, it was quarter to ten.

"I'm stuffed!" Donna pushed her chair back and went to pay for the wine.

"Two hundred and fifty-three quid left," she volunteered as she sat down again.

They all thought that was good, and she and Katie said as much when the waiter returned with two more bottles of wine that Donna had ordered.

They poured and waited for instruction.

Tomas could read the signals and moved in.

"We are heading next door. There are lots of people in the other room. Join us?"

They graciously accepted.

As they went through the door, they could hear live music. A big banner behind the band read: THE UNTOUCHABLES.

They were playing until 11:30, followed by JEMS Disco. The noise made it hard to make out a word, especially with Tomas' lilting Cork accent.

They had drinks, so Tomas walked in front of them to the table he had set aside. The lead singer recognised Patsy and waved over as he sang. He even interrupted the song to say,

"Evening, ladies. Looking good!"

Patsy blew him a kiss as they settled themselves. Tomas went to get his pint from the table his mates were sitting at. They spontaneously applauded. The girls laughed.

The band finished, and they had all been dancing together through the last few songs.

When the DJ started, he quickly summed up the situation. He knew if he could keep the good-looking girls dancing, it wouldn't be long before the rugby players had enough drink in them to join in.

Kool & The Gang—Ladies' Night!—was a good starter, and he followed one floor-filler with the next.

The girls were all dancing to Thriller by Michael Jackson when Sheila suddenly said,

"Fuck this!"

She turned on her killer heel and headed straight for Big Foot. She grabbed his hand and marched him to the dance floor.

He was a bit gauche to begin with, but he soon loosened up.

The other players gradually made their way to the floor, moving in and out through the women without even asking.

Patsy paired off with a tall, dark-skinned, muscular player. Before the rest knew it, she was snogging him in the corner of the dance floor. Maz laughed.

Sheila motioned for Tomas to lean down, grabbed his neck, and planted her lips on his. He didn't resist.

Sheila took one more look at his feet.

"The last time."

She smiled. So did Tomas.

One guy took a shine to Siobhan and leaned in for a kiss.

"This is my bloody hen night!"

Siobhan was disgusted. The poor lad went from hot to very cold in six cutting words. Siobhan left the floor.

Donna was dancing with another of the guys. She really liked him, but she didn't really fancy him. However, she did fancy the lad Siobhan had just knocked back.

She hated Siobhan in that moment.

Siobhan was checking her phone, even though she knew Colin hadn't brought his out with him. Still, she decided to send him a text that he would get when he got home. She couldn't believe she had been giving off an "available" vibe.

"Hi, handsome. Hope you had a good night. Love you loads! It's good fun here—think Sheila and Patsy have 'coupled' with a couple of rugby players from Cork. This time in five weeks, you'll be my husband, and I can't wait. Love you xxxx."

She was satisfied.

It was after one, and she just wanted to sleep. She waved at Donna and said,

"I'm going to head up."

Donna shrugged. She was still feeling lucky.

As Siobhan got out of the lift, she heard giggling coming from Room 101. Sheila, no doubt.

She smiled and thanked God for Colin. She wasn't long in bed before she was fast asleep.

Meanwhile, Donna had managed to get the attention of the guy from earlier. After some quick thinking, she worked out that if she convinced Maz to sleep in Room 113, she could have their room to herself—Sheila was otherwise occupied, after all.

Negotiations complete, key cards were exchanged, and Maz, Stella, and Paula made their exit. Patsy was still working her magic in the corner, but Donna was focused on Paul—she'd finally found out his name. Holding up the key card, she pointed toward the exit. She couldn't wait to devour him.

The man that wanted Siobhan? A plus one, maybe?

As soon as they entered the room, Donna pulled him close and started undressing him. There was little resistance.

He slid her dress over her head and ran his hand between her knickerless legs—she was wet.

He pushed her onto the bed, but she stopped him.

"Condom?" she asked.

He quickly reached for his jeans. From inside his wallet, he pulled out a condom—another one fell to the floor. He ripped the corner open with his teeth, and with skill and precision, slid it over his erect penis.

Donna was ready.

They went at it from all angles—Donna on top, on her hands and knees, him on top, from behind. When they finished, Donna was glad he had another condom, because she certainly wasn't done.

Sheila was having the time of her life. She wasn't sure about rugby being played by men with odd-shaped balls, but she had a sharp intake of breath when Tomas dropped his shorts.

She giggled and looked at his feet. So, it is true.

He made a gesture that indicated he had heard it all before.

Sheila was fascinated. She muttered something about Saint Patrick and snakes as she took his cock in her hand and felt it stiffen.

He quickly removed all her clothing and produced his own extra-large condoms.

Sheila didn't know what to think.

She placed her hands on the bed, standing on tiptoes, and felt him slide into her. Her eyes rolled back as she let out a quiet scream.

She had never felt anything like this before.

She loved it—she moved with his rhythm, loving the fact that he was tall enough to caress her nipples as he rocked in and out of her.

She came.

And then again.

And again.

She had to muffle her screams by biting down on the bed sheet.

Tomas eventually finished, and they showered together.

But this wasn't over—not by a long chalk.

Sheila smiled at the thought.

Long chalk.

They rolled onto the bed, and Sheila decided to take a closer look. She was fascinated. She took the tip into her mouth, and Tomas moaned. Before long, she was on top of him again, riding his erection, writhing, moaning—coming twice more.

Tomas was finished. Definitely finished.

He wrapped his massive arm around her waist, and she fell asleep beside him.

But she hated this.

As soon as she knew he was sound asleep, she gently lifted his arm and slipped out of bed.

When Tomas woke in the morning, Sheila was already gone.

In fact, all the copulating pairs had separated.

At 9:30, they all began to rise from their slumber.

Siobhan asked Donna if she was awake and was surprised when Maz's head poked out from beneath the duvet.

Room phones were hastily called, and they all scrambled back to their own rooms.

It was like musical rooms—without the music.

Showered and changed, they just made it in time as the rugby players were heading out, and breakfast was closing in five minutes.

Numbers were quickly exchanged, and kisses accompanied the goodbyes.

The girls grabbed what they could from the buffet—the rugby players had put a big hole in this morning's offerings.

As Sheila made her way to the table, she exaggerated a limp.

The girls burst out laughing.

"True what they say, you should see the size of his socks!"

They all laughed, even Siobhan.

Donna sat with a satisfied grin that made it clear she'd had fun too.

"And why wouldn't I?" she protested. "I'm single!"

No one had even asked her a question.

She caught herself before continuing, "Think I have my plus one sorted!"

Siobhan was happy for her.

Patsy, however, remained tight-lipped in the corner.

After the initial excitement, they settled into quiet conversation about the day ahead. Some were planning a steam and Jacuzzi session, while others couldn't face it.

Their final stop before heading home was Sunday lunch at the Crawfordsburn Inn, a fitting goodbye.

They agreed on times and went their separate ways. Some took a walk around the grounds, while others opted for an hour's rest.

Since the rugby team had left so early, Hilda had extended their checkout time to 1 P.M., a relief for Patsy and Katie, who were driving.

The two still decided to indulge in a steam and Jacuzzi, though no one was sure if it made much of a difference.

At five to one, they gathered in reception. The bill was settled, keys were returned, and final goodbyes were exchanged.

Hilda wished them well, smiling as she said, "Sure, I'll see you here in five weeks for the reception!"

Siobhan grinned.

Hilda glanced at a piece of paper, adjusting her glasses before adding,

"Next time I see you, sure you'll be Mrs." She paused, double-checking. "Hill!"

Siobhan nodded, beaming.

And with that, they left.

Chapter 23
Sunday Night/ Monday Morning

I sat with a cold beer, carefully peeling the label between sips.

Sunday night. A Sunday night laden with memories—or, as Ally put it, mammaries.

I flicked through the images, and as I did, I could feel a presence.

I looked around me and even went to the door again. It felt like I was being watched.

I listened to Michael Kiwanuka and sipped more beer. I poured a whiskey chaser.

My nerves were shattered. I had done what I did. I enjoyed it, but now I was panicking blindly. I couldn't sleep. I kept hearing noises. I kept checking.

What the fuck? What if she's here? I could hear something but couldn't see anything.

What if Siobhan finds out?

Ronnie? Her dad? He'll fucking kill me.

I was so tired. My nerves were frayed, not just at the edge. I tried to sleep, but I couldn't.

Tiredness overcame me, and I fell into a drunken sleep. I woke on the sofa at 5:33 A.M.

I went to go up to bed, but it was pointless. I was coming off a drink-fuelled weekend—and then some. No way I'd sleep now.

I heard the gate.

No one used the gate.

What the fuck?

I ran to the front door. It was 5:41 A.M. I could see taillights. One set. I checked round the back. Nothing.

As I passed my car, I noticed something hanging from one of the side mirrors. I lifted it. A black thong.

For fuck's sake.

I heard myself. I looked around as I lifted the bin lid and chucked it in.

As I moved inside, I slammed the door. I put the coffee on and walked into the downstairs toilet.

I poured myself a mug of thick, black coffee. My hand was shaking as I drank it. I took a deep breath, exhaled loudly, and said, "Calm the fuck down, Colin!"

I gulped the coffee as I made my way to the spare bedroom on the first floor, almost enjoying the pain of the burn.

I removed my navy pinstriped suit from the wardrobe and laid it out flat on the bed. I took a light blue shirt and selected a plain red tie with a matching handkerchief. My black belt was rolled up inside one of my brogues, and a pair of black socks were folded in the other shoe. Boxers selected. All of the day's clothes were on the bed.

I showered.

While dressing, I hungrily drank the coffee. With just my socks and trousers on, I went to the kitchen for a refill.

Outside, I heard a loud bang and raced to the door in time to see next door's cat scuttling off our bin.

I was relieved.

On returning to the bedroom, I completed my dressing regime by tying my laces and made my way downstairs, sliding my arms into my jacket.

More coffee. I stood at the back door, pulling on a cigarette.

Having finished my third coffee and second cigarette, I made my way to the downstairs bathroom to brush my teeth.

When flossing, I looked straight into my own eyes.

No recriminations. It is what it is.

I squeezed the atomiser on the aftershave bottle and made my way to the door.

I received a large bonus and a promotion last year. This enabled me to buy Siobhan the vintage sports car she had always wanted, and I upgraded my company car to an S-Line A5 Audi.

I pulled out of the driveway and was nearly rammed from the side.

The car that was now sitting on its horn had one occupant. Joan.

She waved in her rear-view mirror as she slowed at the first red light. Reluctantly, I waved back.

We arrived at the staff car park almost simultaneously. I saw more than I needed to as she slid out of her Mini Cooper.

"Nice car. Love the colour!" she smiled.

I tried not to.

"What the fuck are you playing at? You do know I'm getting married Saturday week?"

I was about to walk away when she nonchalantly said, "Good weekend?"

"As if you don't know."

I was raging as she giggled.

I could hear her heels clicking as she made her way towards me, and we walked to the lift together.

Silence.

Joan didn't appear to be too happy. I was anything but.

"What the fuck is your problem?"

She had gotten aggressive in the sanctity of the lift.

"No problem. Good weekend. In fact, great weekend. But it stops now."

I was assertive and dismissive in the same breath.

"We'll see about that."

I panicked, momentarily, as the lift stopped.

The lift shuddered open, and she strutted out ahead of me into the open-plan office space.

Fuck, she looked amazing, and she knew it!

She went to her desk, and I made my way to my private office. It came with the bonus and the promotion.

I removed my jacket, hung it on the stand, and stabbed the power button on my computer as I slid my office chair under my desk. I took my phone from my shirt pocket, and as soon as I did, it started to beep. I slid my thumb up the screen to see what the four loud beeps were about.

"John from work!"

I looked over my shoulder before opening the messages.

I shivered.

Four photos of me in bed, asleep—Joan, topless, had taken selfies.

"Oh fuck!"

I looked at the seating plan in front of me. I wasn't even sure if I knew her last name. I certainly couldn't remember it.

I was tapping the plan when I came across her name.

Joan Sanders.

I'd never forget that again.

I lifted the receiver and pressed 6-0-1. She answered promptly.

"It's Colin Hill. Can you come into my office now, please?"

"Right away, sir."

She giggled as she replaced her receiver.

She strutted across the room, and some of the guys were straining from behind their screens to watch her.

Slowly, she opened my door and stood as if waiting for me to ask her to sit down.

My phone made the Siobhan noise. I ignored it.

I shoved my open palm towards the chair opposite me. As she sat, she hitched up her dress and crossed her legs.

As tempted as I was to stare, I looked away.

She began.

"How can I help you, Mister Hill?"

"We need to talk."

I was staring at her, trying not to look at her breasts, trying not to remember the weekend.

"Yes, but not here. We can meet at mine after work. It's Monday. Siobhan goes to Zumba on a Monday."

"How the fuck do you know that?"

I stuttered.

She leaned in and whispered.

"Careful, Mister Hill. We don't want everyone to hear, now do we?"

I shifted uncomfortably in my seat, leaned back, and tried to regain some control.

She continued.

"I normally go to a class myself on Mondays, but today, there are more important things to sort out."

She smirked.

I shook my head.

"I live in Number 7, Knock Apartments. I live alone, so we won't be interrupted."

With that, she stood and opened the door, throwing an exaggerated glance over her shoulder.

"Will that be all, Mister Hill?"

I nodded.

She was gone.

I spun around in my chair and stared out the window.

Siobhan's dad already fucking hated me. He would be glad of a reason to call the whole thing off.

I turned back to my desk and busied myself with our new account, wondering how the fuck I was going to make this go away.

At eleven I went to the tea room and was greeted by some of the lads and Mister Smith, as he liked to be called, the owner. He was a short man, balding and, as my mother would say, heavy-set.

Questions were being asked about the weekend, and my colleagues laughed when I told them about my mate falling asleep against the speaker, his head bouncing with every beat.

One of the younger lads asked, "Did you get up to any madness? Or should I say badness?"

Joan had just arrived.

"You must have had a good time."

She smiled at Mister Smith, who grinned as his eyes strained to take her all in. He was putty in her hands.

"Not long until your wedding," she continued. "I'm sure you can't wait."

All the men just listened and stared.

I stared too.

I couldn't believe how brazen she was.

She grinned and left.

I was overcome with panic. I wanted control.

She had it.

I returned to my office and slouched in my chair.

Seven Knock Apartments.

I repeated it over and over again.

What was I thinking?

In the afternoon, as I sat at my desk, my phone rang. I lifted the receiver and pressed the internal phone button.

It was her.

"Mister Hill, I have a dental appointment this afternoon. I need to leave at four-ish. I can make the time up some evening after work, but next week, not this week. Hope that's okay. And I'll see you later, I mean, tomorrow."

She giggled again.

"Good. See you tomorrow, then."

I was trying to be brief and evasive.

She hung up.

My phone beeped.

"See you at mine after work."

She included two heart emojis.

I noticed her leave just after four, and I worked on leaving on the stroke of five.

Chapter 24
Up Them Stairs

The shortest route to hers was past my own house, so I took a lengthy detour to be safe. I parked my shiny red Audi in one of the two spaces that had a number seven plaque on the wall.

Tentatively, I made my approach. I used the stairs, figuring most people would use the lift, and I wanted to avoid anyone if possible. The door was ajar, but I knocked and stood waiting for her to open it.

When she came to the door, I almost lost my breath. She wore a white dress that clung tightly to every curve. Her hair cascaded over her shoulders, and she had on open-toed slingback heels.

"Wow!"

She glided through the small hallway into her living space and gracefully sat on one of the two dining chairs that had been removed from the small dining table in front of the window. The chairs had been placed facing each other. I sat confidently and glanced around the room. The apartment was small from what I could see. The open-plan kitchen was modern and bright. Looking over her shoulder, I noticed the bedroom door was slightly open, revealing just enough. Two more doors—I assumed they led to a second bedroom and a bathroom.

I noticed two paintings adorning the walls on either side of her. They were a matching pair, both featuring a girl in different poses, painted in a mixture of dark and light rust, holding what appeared to be a champagne flute.

I liked them.

Apart from these, the place could have been a showroom.

My attention returned to Joan. She was being more discreet with her leg positioning than she had been before.

"So," she began. "A drink?"

I declined.

I simply said, "Let's get this over with."

She feigned a sad face as my phone made the 'Siobhan noise.' Without looking, I turned it off.

"Slow down, cowboy. This is only starting."

"Can we please just pretend this never happened?" I continued. "I've made an awful mistake. I think you're amazing, and you are stunning, but I'm marrying my childhood sweetheart—the love of my life—in just two weeks. Please."

I pleaded.

She smiled.

"Not that easy, I'm afraid."

I clenched my hands at my side.

"I want you. We can do this. You just need to stay focused."

She was so calm, I panicked. In a rage, I blurted, "You can't fucking do this! I'm getting married in two weeks—less, twelve days. I made a mistake, a big mistake. You fucking seduced me! There was never a fucking friend called Marie. You went to Liverpool with one thing in mind."

I grabbed my head with both hands.

"How could I have been so fucking stupid? You won't ruin this for me. I'm fucking warning you!"

She cut across me in a very calm and measured way.

"You weren't that difficult to seduce. And let's face it, if I broke this now, I'd be doing Siobhan a big favour!"

134

I stood up.

"Why the fuck would you want to do that? I made a mistake! It will never happen again. This whole thing was premeditated. You set out to get me! There's something fucking wrong with you. You are fucked up. I wouldn't be surprised if your transfer to our office was part of this shit. You didn't even fucking know me then!"

She calmly smiled.

"Maybe not. Maybe I did. Oh, and I think this"—she waved her index finger between us—"will continue, you know."

I was speechless.

She went on.

"The only way Siobhan—or anyone else—doesn't find out about this is if it continues."

She looked incredible.

She stood up and walked to within two inches of me. Fuck, she smelled good.

She took my hand. I attempted to pull back, but who the fuck was I kidding?

Before I knew it, she was leading me into the bedroom. Within minutes, we were both naked and fucking on her bed.

It was over very quickly.

I was hypnotised.

She finished—or rather, I did—again. She lit a cigarette.

"It will be okay," she said as she leaned over to get an ashtray.

I wasn't so sure as I lay on yet more black silk bedclothes.

The wall at the foot of the bed was a mirror, giving the illusion of a massive room. But I had a feeling that wasn't the reason it was there.

Exhibitionist.

I lay staring at the elaborate, over-ornate chandelier, which seemed incongruous in this ultra-modern apartment. She had a thing for chandeliers—I had noticed one in the living area too.

She had a smug grin as she said, "So, this continues!"

In that moment, I wanted to kill her. I also wanted her on top of me again.

I had no choice. As I looked at my watch, it had gone six, and Siobhan was due at our 'marital home' before seven.

Joan began to caress my penis again. I resisted—I needed to get home.

"We can talk about this again, but I'm, as I'm sure you can imagine, very busy the next few weeks. It will have to wait until after the honeymoon."

I was trying to buy some time.

I just wanted out of this.

I was getting dressed when she nonchalantly commented, "So, twelve days until you get married, then the honeymoon and all the razzmatazz that goes with it, and we take up where we left off after you get back?"

She was beginning to sound irrational. I glanced at her as she pushed herself forward in the bed.

"Do you really think that's going to satisfy me?"

I couldn't see how this was going to work, and I said as much.

She threw her head back and, laughing, announced, "Where there's a will, there's a way!"

I didn't even attempt to kiss her as I ran downstairs. Crossing the car park, I pressed the button to open the car, jumped in, and sped home.

I rushed into the house, grabbed the envelope from last night, and went to the bin outside to rip the contents into shreds. Good riddance.

I quickly showered and put on my painting clothes. I was rolling the hallway seconds before Siobhan walked in.

A deep, passionate kiss. No sex.

She had brought some food to heat in the microwave, and as I joined her at the marble breakfast bar, she was keen to hear about the weekend.

I brushed it off as quickly as I could.

"You know, the usual—get drunk, get up, football, get drunk, get up, quiet flight home."

I continued, "It was really uneventful, apart from the Frank story."

She asked, and I told her.

"Did none of your single friends meet a nice girl? Did our Patrick behave himself?"

If only she knew.

"Ally met a nice girl. Gorgeous-looking, the others were saying. She's living in Liverpool but moving back to Lurgan soon."

"Oh, that's good. At least now he might have a plus-one for the wedding."

I agreed and told her that Patrick was on great form and that all the lads loved him. She was pleased.

As I was finishing, Siobhan said something that made my blood run cold.

"Colin, about five weeks ago—no, six—it was before the hen party," she corrected herself. "A new girl joined our Zumba class. In fact, she goes to most of my classes."

She smiled.

I didn't.

"She wasn't at the class tonight, so when it was over, I texted her. She said she wasn't feeling well. She lives in an apartment off the carriageway. She asked if I would call up with some food. I have another portion of that lasagne in the car."

I tried to stay calm.

What the fuck?

Siobhan continued.

"She's called Joan. I don't even know her second name."

I did.

"So, I'll nip up and throw the food in—won't be long. Then we can get stuck in and finish the hall."

I waited until she was well away and let out a primal scream.

Within twenty minutes, Siobhan returned. As she tied her hair back, she said, "That girl Joan is stunning. Even tonight, when she's not well, I nearly fancy her myself. I think I'll invite her to the evening do. You never know—one of your single friends might get lucky! She's lovely. She doesn't even know how good she looks."

Siobhan smiled as she popped the lid on the gloss paint.

I was dying inside.

I tried to stay calm as we chatted, painted, and listened to music.

When it reached half ten, Siobhan, as she always did, downed tools and kissed me before leaving. As she turned the latch, she said, "Oh, I texted Joan about the evening do. She said she'd love to go. I'm excited—I hope one of your mates takes a shine to her. She's just moved here from outside Ballymena and doesn't really have any friends. I also told her about coming to Mum's this Saturday night for our girlie night. She's going to come—I like her."

Siobhan had, unbeknownst to herself, dropped a bomb on my lap.

I tried to remain nonplussed as I waved her goodbye from the driveway, but like a duck calm on the surface, under the water, its feet were flapping like crazy.

I felt like I was underwater.

As soon as I closed the door, I collapsed in a heap on the floor. When I gathered myself, I made for the kitchen—a stiff whiskey was required.

The doorbell rang.

I wondered why Siobhan hadn't used her key.

Joan was standing there. She offered me an empty Tupperware box.

"I wanted to give this to Siobhan."

My nosey neighbour was standing in his driveway, and though he didn't know it, he was saving the day.

"She's not here."

I reached out my hand to take the box, but she tightened her grip. In that instant, she stared directly at me, then let go and walked away. Her Mini was parked across the driveway.

I quickly closed the door and returned to my whiskey.

One gulp.

A second glass.

Holy fuck.

Chapter 25
New Bed

I had booked Tuesday and Wednesday off as Siobhan and I had wedding shopping to do—presents for the best man, bridesmaids, and parents, new shoes, and God knows what else.

I was glad of the relief.

We shopped, we painted, we talked, we kissed—no sex.

'John from work' texted three images on Tuesday and four on Wednesday.

As we were heading to the car after our shopathon on Wednesday, Siobhan announced that she was meeting Joan in Hell Cat Annie's.

"Why don't you come too?"

She was almost insistent.

"Nah, it's a girlie thing. You go and talk weddings. I'll go home and get started on the painting—need to get our bedroom finished before Friday. The new super king-size bed arrives Friday."

She smiled and kissed me before departing with the words,

"I will probably not call this evening, as I won't be much use with a few glasses of Chardonnay inside me."

I nodded. At least I knew Joan was occupied too.

I had a free night, and I was glad when Ally parked his car outside mine, as it would deter unwanted callers—or so I thought.

10:43, my watch said when I heard the doorbell.

I looked at Ally and was tempted to ignore it. He stared at his watch as he stood to go see who it was.

It was pointless. I was feeling the noose tighten around my neck. I was about to crack when I heard Siobhan's voice.

"I forgot my key!"

She was pissed.

"Just wanted to see my man before I go home!"

Ally gave her a peck on the cheek as he shouted towards the kitchen,

"That's me away, Col. See you Friday night."

We always played five-a-side football on a Friday night. It was our thing.

Siobhan stood and stared at me, doughy-eyed and tiddly. I put my arms around her waist and calmly asked,

"Where's your friend?"

"Wouldn't you like to know? She's gorgeous. Oh, here—she works in your place! She told me tonight. What the fuck? Do you know her? Some coincidence! Do you fancy her? Is that why you didn't let on?"

In panic, I fobbed her off by saying she was drunk and didn't know what she was saying.

I also shrugged to feign a lack of any kind of knowledge of Joan. Siobhan was too pissed to notice either way. She continued,

"You're bound to have noticed her. She's gorgeous!"

I looked as disinterested as I could.

"Joan, you say? Never connected. The new girl? The guys are getting out of shape, okay, but I only have eyes for you, gorgeous!"

This pleased her, and she slurred,

"Right answer. Now I'm a wee bit worse for wear—could you leave me home?"

Thursday and Friday were uneventful at work. Some picture messages from Joan—varied states of undress, never nude and leaving anything to the imagination.

Constant messages from Siobhan:

"180 hours to go, handsome! Xxxxxxx"

"177 hours to go! Can't wait. Missus Siobhan Hill—has a nice ring, don't you think? I'm looking at my engagement ring now! Xxxxxx"

"176 hours! Can't wait to take your name. Xxxxx"

I looked out my window as Joan was passing.

I played football as normal on Friday and, as usual, went to the best little pub in Belfast, as Ally called it—the Parador Lodge. A few pints, a takeaway meal from Bengal Brasserie, and home for ten.

Perfect.

I was excited to get home to see the new bed. Siobhan's mum, Peggy, had let the delivery men in today, and I was looking forward to my first night alone on my new bed.

No such luck. The delivery guys were supposed to assemble the bed. Instead, I was met by four cardboard boxes and a mattress inside a sheath lying on the floor.

I was hungry and thirsty and said out loud, "Fuck that—I'll do it tomorrow."

In the kitchen, I splashed the rice and the Jalfrezi onto a plate and stuck it in the microwave for two minutes, which was just enough time to open a nice bottle of Malbec.

As I looked around, I was happy with the floors and the painting. It was going well. The house looked good, and with Siobhan, Donna, and their mums all going shopping on Saturday, I was sure I'd get it finished.

Ally said he would lend a hand all day Saturday, and my brothers were coming over too.

My phone beeped and made the Siobhan noise almost simultaneously. I didn't even look at the messages. Instead, I turned my phone off, ate my food, drank my wine, and listened to The Cult—very loudly.

I woke on Saturday morning with a thumping headache and a thumping door. Ally, Paul, and Joe were on time. I wasn't.

I had made a list of things that needed doing, and once the coffee was put on, we set to work.

It went well, and at one-thirty, I made a big fry-up.

"Thank fuck—I'm starving."

Joe was rubbing his hands as he made his way to the sink to wash them.

He was always good craic.

Brunch was a laugh.

"This time next week, you'll be married, ya fucking rocket."

Paul sounded like a Siobhan text, but he laughed, and the others joined in.

"Don't know what you three are laughing about—you have speeches to make."

Ally and Paul were groomsmen, and Joe was to be the best man. He added,

"I know—I'm shitting myself, but in a strange way, I'm looking forward to taking the piss out of you a bit too!"

"I've seen some of it," added Paul. "It's very funny."

"Did you hear the one about the two guys in the poetry competition?"

Joe had started. He was brilliant at telling other people's jokes.

"Two guys get to the final of a poetry competition, and they're given the word 'Timbuktu.' They have to come up with a poem using that word.

The first guy stands up at the mic, an erudite wordsmith, and says,

'Slowly cross the desert sand Tracked the lonely caravan Men on camels Two by two Destination—Timbuktu.'

Massive round of applause.

The second guy is a wee bit more agricultural. He says,

'Me and Tim a-hunting went Met three girls with a pop-up tent They was three We was two So I bucked one... And Tim bucked two!'"

We laughed our heads off.

I was clearing up and filling the dishwasher when I asked if we could all go to the main bedroom to make the bed up.

We did.

It took all four of us to make the bed and lift the huge mattress onto the top of it. The others moved to do their specific tasks, and I started to dress the bed. I wanted to lie down there and then.

I was hanging like a bat.

My phone beeped—Joan in that white dress. There was something about Joan in that dress.

I had just finished making the bed when Siobhan phoned.

"Hiya, handsome."

"Alright, love. How are you?"

"All good. We're nearly done. How comfortable was the new bed?"

"They didn't make it up, so the four of us have spent the last hour assembling it. I'll be looking for a refund—they were supposed to do that. I'll sleep on it for the first time tonight. I can't wait."

"I can't wait to 'christen' the bed next Sunday!"

She giggled.

"Take a photo and WhatsApp it, please."

She continued,

"We're heading for something to eat—oh, and guess what? We bumped into Joan in Topshop. She's coming with us for food. Think my mum has fallen in love with her."

My stomach turned.

"Oh."

She went on,

"Don't forget to remind the boys that the rehearsal time has changed for Tuesday!"

"Holy fuck!"

I mumbled as I hung up. Ally heard and asked if all was okay. I nodded.

"We going for beers after this?"

Paul always knew when to change the subject—it was like a gift.

I answered,

"Aye, I've a big pot of chilli made. I'll drop you boys off to get showered and that, then pick you up again. We can come here, eat, and have a drink before we get a taxi to the Cathedral Quarter."

"Way ahead of you, brother," Joe winked. "We have our pulling clothes in a bag in the car, so we'll shower here."

He looked at his watch.

"It's after four—any beer chilling?"

They laughed.

I returned with four bottles of Rockshore. The lids were removed, we slugged, Ally burped, we laughed.

Siobhan had left specific instructions about the placing of pictures, mirrors, and lampshades, etc. She also made it clear that she only trusted Paul to complete this task. He was putting the finishing touches on when Joe came in from the garage.

"That's me done, I'll go shower!"

We nodded.

"I'll join you!" I offered.

"Fucking sure you won't." His eyes widened.

We roared—he knew I was going to the en-suite.

We all showered, dressed, and splashed on products and aftershave.

We were gorgeous!

I opened a bottle of Malbec and poured three glasses. Joe refused to do red wine, but luckily, there was a half-bottle of Chardonnay in the fridge door. We ate, drank, and laughed.

Unexpectedly, Siobhan turned to check on Paul's handiwork. He was so excited he jumped up to take her around the house. Siobhan motioned for me to follow. I couldn't be fucking arsed, but I trudged behind them. I left Ally and Joe in the conservatory and moved through the kitchen into the dining room.

It was painted blue—Siobhan called it azure. I still called it blue.

Siobhan was gushing over the new placement of the paintings as I looked down at the floor. I had spent hours sanding it, and I was pleased with the sheen of the varnish covering the mahogany stain.

The floor contrasted well with the expensive glass table and leather chairs that Siobhan had insisted on buying.

I looked up, and they had moved on. I followed their voices to the living room. The floor was exactly the same as in the dining room. Siobhan continued to gush over the paintings and mirrors like she'd never fucking seen them before.

I loved this house.

This huge living room had my print all over it—leather, a massive corner sofa, bespoke shelves that housed my large vinyl collection, and my sixty-inch plasma. My victory sat proudly in prime position. Siobhan hated this TV, but I insisted—it was, after all, the way to watch live football.

I was still grinning about my victory when they moved into the hall. I heard her comment on the mirror that ran the length of the hallway, and I held back until they were far enough up the stairs that I could mosey into the conservatory unnoticed.

"Want to just go to the Parador?" Ally always did this.

"My last Saturday night as a free man? I think not."

A taxi was ordered. Paul and Siobhan returned, and she was happy to lock up as we got in.

We headed for the Spaniard.

"Always great music in here," Paul said, nodding at the doorman.

He wasn't wrong—R.E.M. were losing their religion as we arrived, loud enough to hear but not so loud as to be intrusive.

"You always get good-looking women in here." Ally rubbed his hands.

Drinks were ordered, and we squeezed onto the end of a table.

The boys worked their magic. I was looking at the records and album sleeves. The two girls were giggling—my brothers are very funny.

We said our goodbyes as soon as Joe noticed they were both wearing wedding rings.

We went upstairs. The décor on the first floor always fascinated me—so many different artistic incarnations of Mary, the mother of Christ.

We left after one drink and went to the Harp Bar to listen to some good live music. One man and a guitar—he was class.

"Weller, Oasis, Stone Roses, all the classics!" I said, and we loved him.

We did the rounds, but we were tired and decided to get a taxi home at twenty to one to beat the rush. I was the last drop-off, and we agreed to meet for breakfast at Graffiti on Sunday morning. I was so looking forward to my new bed.

I stumbled slightly up the drive, and as I stabbed the key into the keyhole, I heard a familiar clicking. My heart stopped, and I jumped slightly as Joan emerged from behind the chimney wall.

"Hiya, sexy!"

She looked great.

"What the fuck are you doing here?"

I was raging and quickly ushered her into the hallway before anyone saw her. She removed my hand from the small of her back and, cool as a cucumber, said,

"Calm down, will you?"

I wished she would just disappear, but I also wanted to see what she had under that coat.

Nothing.

WOW.

She moved towards me. I didn't even really want to kiss her anymore. She took my right hand and placed it gently between her legs—so wet.

After a couple of seconds, she lifted my hand to her mouth, and in a drunken haze, I was following her to my bedroom.

Our bedroom.

She pulled a litre bottle of Jameson from her pocket and, in the same move, slid out of the coat.

I was already undressing. She handed me the bottle, and I took a long slug.

It began.

I climbed onto the new bed, commenting on how comfortable it was.

She shushed me as she eased herself onto the bed and towards me. She teased my penis with her tongue before climbing on top and staring down at me.

I finished very quickly.

She tutted, rolled over, and began to vigorously rub herself.

I watched. I drank more whiskey and slid my head between her legs, returning the favour before slowly moving upwards to lick and bite her nipples. I moved towards her mouth, and she turned her back to me. I arched my back and slid in.

We violently fucked.

She screamed.

She was finished.

Coolness personified, she calmly got up and put her coat on.

She made for the door and headed downstairs. I followed as I was pulling my dressing gown on.

From the top of the stairs, I saw the back of her as she closed the front door. I lingered.

My phone made the 'Siobhan noise.'

"I can't sleep. Just think, this time next week we will be spending our first night as Mister and Missus Hill! xxxxx"

This was really getting up my nose now.

She continued,

"You never sent me a photo of the bed!"

She knew I'd seen the message, so I quickly took a photo and sent it.

She came straight back.

"Can't wait to christen that bed next Sunday, handsome. xxxxxxxx"

Already done.

I just wanted to sleep.

Chapter 26
Countdown!!!

I woke, head fuzzy, mind fuzzy. I rubbed my open palms up from my chin and over my aching head. My phone was flashing—I had two messages.

Siobhan: "Morning, handsome. This day next week will be my first full day as Mrs Colin Hill."

Fuck, she was now dropping her own name. This countdown was frying my head.

She continued, "Hope you enjoy your golf today. Mind you, I hope you've the house finished before you go. You're going to have to learn to take orders! LOL. Looking forward to our spa day. Mum is a geg. Yesterday she took to your colleague Joan so well that she invited her along today. I'm secretly glad—I think Joan and I could be really good friends. We have a lot in common!" Some of her texts, at times, resembled a novella.

More in common than you fucking think, I said to myself as I staggered out of bed, rocked to the adjoining bathroom, peed, and stepped into the shower. I walked from the en-suite naked, poking and circling a cotton wool bud in my left ear, then turning it to do my right. I slumped on the bed, threw my aching head back, and spread my arms wide either side.

I studied the ceiling before shaking myself and lifting my phone.

Second message—John from work: "Hope you enjoy your golf today. So you know, I'm going to back off for the next week to give you some space. You won't even know I'm about. I've even booked the middle of the week off. Anyway, got to rush—big spa day to get ready for. Peggy, your soon-to-be mother-in-law, invited me yesterday. Seemed rude to resist. Should be a good day. Siobhan even asked me to go to extra classes at the gym with her. She's lovely—really like Peggy."

Another fucking novellaist.

No matter how much I rubbed my face, and no matter how roughly, the pain was still there. The more I thought about all of this, the less sense it was making. I shook myself again. Nothing was working.

"Fuck it, time to get going." I had left my golf gear in the spare room yesterday. As I made my way down to put the coffee on—and fuck, I needed coffee—I was putting my dressing gown on as I descended the stairs. I had just turned towards the kitchen when the doorbell rang. Loudly. Very loudly. I wretched. I felt sick. I dreaded opening the door.

Ally was standing there, pulling on a cigarette—he refused to smoke in his car. "Ah, for fuck's sake, you late again?"

I shrugged. "I need coffee. I REALLY need coffee!"

Ally pushed past me. "Get you dressed, I'll make the coffee!" I smiled.

I pulled my baby pink golf T-shirt over my head and put the collar up. I was wearing matching pink and black checked trousers and a pink and black argyle sweater. I looked in the mirror. I knew this get-up was just me and that it would give the boys a laugh.

As I headed into the kitchen, I grabbed a coffee and a cigarette and headed to the back garden to join Ally, who was sitting at the patio table.

"What are you like? You'll be late for your own funeral. Saw your woman from your work heading up to Siobhan's as I got out of the car. Friendly girl. She's going to a spa day, she tells me, with Siobhan and her ma and the rest. You comfortable with that?" He squinted as smoke went into his eye while he drew on his cig.

Comfortable? Fucking comfortable? I was a nervous wreck, but this had gone too far and too deep to even confide in Ally.

I smiled to look disinterested. "Sure, what does it matter?"

Ally raised his left eyebrow and gave me that knowing look. What else could I do?

"What are you like? Those clothes and the weird way you wear your collar up. Anyway, always gets a laugh. Finish that coffee—we need to get going." He looked at his watch and continued, "Tee's booked for nine thirty-seven. That's only thirty-four minutes." He stood and lifted his cup as he stubbed out his cig on the patio. I said nothing.

We left.

The craic was good. All the boys were gathering near the first tee. Joe had organised the golf day. "Your last as a single man," he had said.

They all laughed at my get-up. I didn't care.

I was first to tee off, and just before I stepped onto the tee box, Frank said, "What about your woman from last weekend? Fiona. My wife tells me she was chatting to Siobhan, and she works in your place." I looked at him. "Sure, I said that last weekend."

"Not to me, you didn't!"

I shrugged and moved to the tee box. Howls of laughter accompanied my first drive, which was sliced out of bounds. Frank had put that in my head deliberately. I reloaded and fired a golf ball straight down the middle of the fairway.

We were off—me, Paul, Joe, and Ally.

As we approached the tenth tee box, my phone beeped and made the Siobhan noise again almost simultaneously.

"Popular man!" Ally glanced over his shoulder as he shook his head. And for the first time, they said virtually the same thing.

Siobhan: "Hope golf is going well, handsome. Spa day is class—really like Joan, she's so easy to be around. Six days! This is such a nice way to start OUR wedding week. Xxxxxxxx." Typical Siobhan, I thought.

John: "Hope golf is going well, sexy. Loving Siobhan and her cousin Susan—they're such good company. Spa day excellent. Just what the doctor ordered at the start of a wedding week!" No kisses. Typical Siobhan, I thought again. What the fuck?

Golf completed, we headed for the locker room, got showered and changed, and made our way to the table in the clubhouse that was set for eighteen. Only sixteen played golf, but Jimmy and Stephen, who never played, were keen to join us for food and drinks. I ordered four pints, and as I did, I said to the barman, Paul, "Make it five, mate!" He did. I necked the first pint in one go. I just needed the cure.

All assembled after golf, the meals had been pre-ordered, and they started to appear. Wine, courtesy of Paul, also appeared. I nodded my approval in his direction.

The craic was ninety, as we say, and we were eating and skulling pints to our hearts' content. The waiters were clearing the table when Frank, always full of his own self-importance—or self-impotence, as Stephen once put it—stood to speak and announce the winner. Nobody really cared, but they let on that they did. I was declared the winner, which surprised me. As I made my way to collect my prize, I was surprised by how heavy it was and why first prize was wrapped in wedding paper. I opened it and, with a smiley laugh, I looked at the table and said sarcastically, "You guys!"

A ball and chain.

They were laughing and backslapping. Cars were abandoned at the golf club as we made our way in taxis to the Parador.

Pints were flowing, but soon the boys started to fragment. I was one of the last to leave. I walked home, as I only lived up the road. Ally walked with me, as he lived round the corner.

We were quiet until Ally broke the silence. "Do you know what you're doing, ya fucking header?"

I hadn't a clue. I was so far out of my depth, and the ball and chain weren't even close to representing the restriction and constriction I was feeling.

"Course I know what I'm doing, mate! I'm marrying the love of my life!" I skipped and looked at him to try to reassure him. I didn't even refer to Joan, and he didn't pursue. I reassured myself that he wasn't certain, but inside, I knew. He wasn't convinced.

Neither was I.

Chapter 27
Besties

Mister Smith had given me the morning off, and I was glad of the lie-in. I was, however, shocked that I hadn't heard from Joan or Siobhan. I checked my phone again.

Nothing.

I texted Joan, "How'd you get on yesterday? Not sure what you're playing at!" Then Siobhan, "How'd you get on yesterday? Only five more days." I played her game, although I knew she could probably tell me how many minutes.

Instant responses.

Joan: "Couldn't text you last night as Peggy insisted I stay at her house. We were pretty drunk. See you're not in today. Everything okay?"

This was becoming too normal.

Siobhan "Hi, handsome, 7,317 minutes to go!"

We were getting married on Saturday at noon. It was three minutes past ten. I didn't check, but I was sure it was 7,317 minutes away. Her text continued, "Joan is lovely. Mum even insisted that she stay at ours last night! Think she could become my new 'bestie'. If I could, I'd invite her to the whole day on Saturday. Hope you enjoyed your golf day—last one as a free man!!!"

She attached three laughing emojis and six heart ones. Then I didn't even count the x's.

My blood ran cold. The noose was tightening. I was struggling to breathe.

I texted Joan, "What the fuck are you playing at? You need to back off!"

Immediate response: "Make me!"

I texted Siobhan, "Morning, gorgeous. Glad you enjoyed. Weird how your woman Joan has become so reliant on you and yours. Be careful—you don't know much about her!"

I was trying to plant a seed. I would have preferred to drive a wedge, but I settled for subtlety.

Siobhan didn't bite.

Nonsense. She is lovely. She is going to class tonight. I will bring her round to give her the guided tour after—you can get to know her outside a work setting. I think you'll like her. She is really looking forward to seeing the house... She says she dropped the Tupperware off. You never mentioned. Not important. Gotta run. 7,312 minutes now! Xxxxxxx

A part of me died inside.

I took my time readying myself for work. I simply couldn't be bothered. I rang Mister Smith's direct line, and he answered straight away—I was his blue-eye.

"Colin, my boy, what's up?"

"Morning, Mister Smith. Thanks for the morning off—much needed. Okay if I go straight to our new clients this afternoon? I'll be in the office first thing tomorrow."

He chuckled. "With your numbers, my boy, you know what you're doing. I shall see you tomorrow. Go get 'em, tiger!"

He hung up.

I got dressed and drove to my mother's house. Joe and Paul were there too. They were younger than me and still lived at home.

We chatted about everything. My mother was so excited to be planning a wedding. I think she actually loved Siobhan more than she loved me! Though, really, she loved her three boys, who were her rock after the death of my father ten years earlier—massive heart attack.

Joe asked about Joan. My mother perked up.

"Joan!" She looked over her glasses directly at me. "Hope you are behaving yourself. I'll kill you if you are messing about!"

I flashed Joe a disdainful look, and when my mother averted her gaze, I mouthed the word "wanker" in his direction. He smiled.

Mother made lunch even though all three of us insisted we weren't hungry. A good pre-wedding atmosphere had returned, and we all laughed and joked.

"Your Aunt Rose left that in yesterday," she said, pointing at a box wrapped in wedding paper and sitting under the big Belleek lamp. "Says it's delicate!"

I was guessing it was something Belleek. It was her go-to, and it was where Mum got her lamp.

I left with the box, carefully carried to the car by both Joe and Paul. I meandered home and phoned our three new clients to touch base.

I was doing the last of the tidying up when I looked at the clock. Ten to seven. They would be here soon.

The car made a rattling sound as Siobhan pulled into the drive. I noticed it through my despair.

Siobhan burst through the front door, Joan in tow. She kissed me.

"Five more sleeps."

She stood back to reveal Joan.

"You know Joan? She works in your office, though she did say that you keep yourself to yourself. Thank God, with a hottie like that running about."

Joan said, "Och!" and waved her right hand in Siobhan's direction in mock disapproval.

"Mum made food for the three of us. I'll stick it in the oven. Would you take Joan up and start the tour?"

I froze.

Siobhan was so happy. She danced down the hall and through the dining room that led to the kitchen.

Joan winked. "Stay cool!" she whispered. I could feel her breath on my ear.

Cool and me were distant relatives at this stage.

I slowly started for the stairs. Joan playfully smacked my arse as I walked in front of her. I looked back and glared at her. She got the message.

I had done the tour of the three bedrooms, and Joan had twice tried to grab between my legs. I was furious.

I heard Siobhan ascend the stairs as I pushed our bedroom door open.

"Ah, the master bedroom," Joan declared as Siobhan joined us.

Awkward.

Siobhan grabbed my arm and said, "No master in this relationship." She leaned in to kiss me, and Joan winked at me from behind her before raising her eyebrows.

"You're shaking." Siobhan playfully nudged me as she hopped onto the bed. "First time!" She giggled. "Try it!" She gestured to Joan, who didn't need a second invitation.

There they were, both of them, bouncing about on my new bed. I walked out.

They joined me in the kitchen. Siobhan took out the food and dished up three plates. Joan stared at me across the table and even tried to lift her green Chelsea boot between my legs.

We were eating when Siobhan asked Joan if she wanted to come and look at the mirrors and pictures that had been mounted by Paul. Joan frowned in my direction and reluctantly agreed as Siobhan grabbed her arm and led her away. I cleared the table and went to the garden for a smoke.

They joined me. Siobhan hated that I smoked. I offered Joan a cigarette. She lied that she didn't smoke.

What the fuck is her game?

Siobhan said they were going to Joan's house for some bubbles and asked if I wanted to join them. I declined. She shrugged and said she would see me at the rehearsal tomorrow night.

Siobhan leaned in and kissed me. "I love that the pictures are up! Feels more like home." She kissed me on the lips.

Joan leaned in, winked as she did, and kissed my cheek. I was cold.

Very cold.

Tuesday at work was a non-event. Joan was off.

Three messages from Siobhan, all simply the countdown:

At ten o'clock: "5,880 xxxxx."

At three o'clock: "5,580."

At five minutes to five: "5,465 xxxx."

This was starting to really grate on me.

Ally, Joe, Paul, and I arrived at The Good Shepherd together. Everyone was already there. I was known for being late. The priest looked at his watch.

I quickly scanned the room and was relieved to note that Joan wasn't there. I asked as innocently and sarcastically as I could, "No Joan?"

Siobhan smiled. "She's back at the house with Auntie Flo making sandwiches."

My mum rubbed my left shoulder and kissed my cheek. "I'm so proud of you," she whispered.

If only she knew.

Rehearsal complete, we made our way back to Siobhan's mum and dad's house. Ronnie was all over Joan. Siobhan liked that her mum and dad both liked her new friend.

She sidled up to my mum, who smelt a rat and didn't make much effort. Joan sensed the uneasiness and backed off.

Soon after, Joan announced her departure to calls of derision.

She laughed. "Sure, I'll see you all on Friday night!"

They had invited her to the "night before" party? Holy fuck!

She was gone in a flash. Five minutes later, my phone beeped. My mother looked at me disapprovingly.

"John from work..."

"I sensed your mother was on to something, and we don't want to draw attention to ourselves just yet."

Just yet, I thought. Fuck me. She continued, "I love a challenge. See you Friday, big boy!" No kisses.

We returned to normal. Ronnie was actually being nice to me. I called it the Joan effect—he was as smitten as everyone else.

People started to make their way home. I made my excuses and left. As I did, I noticed the presents piled up in the front room. I upturned my palms and raised my left eyebrow.

"I know!" said Siobhan. "We'll have fun opening all of them after Italy. Four more sleeps!"

I kissed her and left. I walked home.

Chapter 28
Siobhan Who??

The next three days at work were pleasant enough. Joan had booked Wednesday off and phoned in sick on both Thursday and Friday. I was glad.

Ally called for me, and we walked to the O'Neill house together. People had already started to appear. It was a pleasant evening, and some were standing in the front garden smoking and chatting.

I nodded a greeting and made my way in.

Fuck. Joan looked fucking stunning. I hadn't even noticed Siobhan.

Joan was wearing the red dress—the one she wore the night we met. She was tanned. Her deep red lips and perfectly manicured nails complemented the dress, and her black heels accentuated her long legs.

Fuck, I was staring. My mum was chatting with her. She was winning her own challenge.

It was an open house, and people called to leave a gift if they hadn't already given one, had a drink, and left. It was pleasant.

Siobhan stood with me. I hardly noticed her.

The night drew on, and people were all talking about the wedding.

I didn't care.

Eventually, it reached five to twelve, and Siobhan was insistent that I leave before midnight. "Bad luck to see the bride on the big day before the wedding. Only 725 more minutes, if I'm on time, that is."

I forced a smile as I thought, More worried about me being on time.

Joe, Paul, and Ally were all staying at mine. I opened the door, and in the kitchen, I handed each of them a bottle of beer and poured four glasses of single malt.

Siobhan and I had purchased them three suits with shirts, matching ties, hankies, shoes, and belts. I handed them their wedding gift. It was how Siobhan wanted it—silver cufflinks. One had the letter T, the other the letter U.

"It stands for 'thank you,'" I had answered when Joe enquired.

We finished our drinks and made for bed.

Chapter 29
Hanging Like A Bat

I slept through the alarm and would have missed the wedding if Ally hadn't banged on my bedroom door and shouted, "Up you get, it's your big day!" I answered, "Grand," and rolled over.

Big day, with a big hanging head. I just wanted to sleep!

Joe was whistling as he passed my door. I knew it was him because he was always insanely happy first thing.

"I'm showered and ready," he hollered as he made his way downstairs, then added, "I'll make coffee and put the pan on."

I had no choice. This was happening. Reluctantly, I got up.

I opened the drawer in the bedside cabinet and plopped two effervescent Co-Codamol into my water glass. I went to the toilet, and by the time I returned, they had dissolved. I drank the liquid and grimaced at the bitterness.

Paul tapped the door and slowly opened it. "How you feeling?" He always had a kind word.

"I'm okay. To be honest, bro, I'm hanging like a bat!" He chuckled and moved towards me with his arms open. I accepted the hug. It felt good.

"Time you were showered. I think you've something important on!" He winked and turned, saying, "I'll give Joe a hand. A hearty breakfast for the condemned man!" He laughed again.

"By the way, did I hear the door in the middle of the night? Could have sworn I did."

I nodded. "Couldn't sleep, went for a wee dander." I had called to see Joan for a pre-wedding hug.

I felt condemned.

I did my ablutions and headed to the kitchen. I could hear the laughter. They were in great spirits. No wonder—the Buck's Fizz was flowing. Ally handed me a glass as I walked through the door. We clinked glasses, and Joe toasted, "The groom!" The others repeated the toast.

Sausages, bacon, mushrooms, and tomatoes were being fried as my mother arrived. She couldn't stay away. She cooked, we ate, she hugged us all. She left to get ready with the immortal words, "Your big day, son. I hope it's all you hoped it would be!"

She headed to her house to get ready.

We drank more fizz. I sipped from my hip flask and commented on how well they looked. They laughed, and Paul said, "Aye, for clones!"

I had my suit trousers and waistcoat on. My new shoes were a bit tight, and I was glad I had packed older shoes in my overnight bag, which had been left off at the Galgorm during the week. I had become fed up with our weekly drive to Ballymena for fine-tuning. Siobhan insisted.

My phone made the Siobhan noise. I had been expecting it.

I sighed. The others laughed.

Siobhan, unsure if the bride should speak to the groom before the wedding, texted instead: "Phone me ASAP!" That was all it said.

I did.

"Holy God!" She was hysterical. I thought she had changed her mind and I asked that.

"Don't be silly, though I will need my make-up touched up."

"What's wrong, then?"

Ronnie took the phone.

"Do you know Joan, who works with you?" he questioned. My heart sank as I asked, "What the fuck has she done?"

"What are you talking about? What has she done? Why would you ask that?" He paused. I panicked and added, "You said it was about her!"

"It is. The girl in the apartment next to hers was strangled in her sleep last night. Joan has just arrived here. She's in an awful state!"

I went very cold.

"Why did she go to yours?" My planting of seeds hadn't been working.

"Where else would she go? Poor girl doesn't know anyone else in Belfast." He put his hand over the phone, but I heard his muffled voice: "C'mere, love, don't worry. Sure, just come to the wedding. We'll look after you!"

He removed his hand as I heard a distant Joan say, "Really? You don't mind? I don't want to be alone!" She added that she had to go to the police station the next day, as they needed to question her.

Siobhan then said, "I'd be glad to have you!"

I was sucking hard on my hip flask.

Ronnie then added, "Can you get your Joe to ring the Galgorm and get one more place added to your Siobhan's Auntie Flo's table? It would be a big help!"

I said, "Sure," and hung up.

Joe was instructed. Joan was going to my wedding.

Ally said, "Wasn't there a girl strangled near Ballymena a couple of months ago? And in Liverpool on your stag weekend? That's just fucking weird!"

We all agreed. What could we do? I was filled with a sense of fear and dread. I needed air and went for a walk round the block.

I phoned my mate Sean in the Ballymena office, and he laughed, saying something about my wedding and that he would see me tonight. I subtly enquired about Joan and her backstory.

"Fuck me, mate. She's a man-eater. Why would you worry about her? It's your wedding day, and Siobhan is fucking stunning!" He was no help. He added, "Gotta run, things to do, see you tonight." He hung up.

When I returned, we continued to sip bubbles as the clock raced towards eleven thirty.

The car arrived. Siobhan insisted on limos. I laughed as she said it was her only demand. Bridezilla had nothing but demands. My only job was to turn up. Siobhan had even picked the light grey suit I was wearing. She wanted it to contrast with the other suits in the wedding party. Her dad was wearing exactly the same as the three amigos, as was Patrick.

"Be nice for the photos," assured Siobhan.

We all nodded, clinked again, and Paul added, "To the church!"

Joe laughed. "The hangman awaits!"

We got out of the car, and an awful lot of the guests were milling about. It was a beautiful day for late November.

I paused at the door, looked at my watch—eleven forty-eight—one last smoke.

Joe was carrying my cigs. He handed me one and the lighter. I lit up and dragged heavily as I handed the lighter back to him.

We moved to one side, and he handed me the hip flask. I drank.

When finished, we made our way to the front of the chapel. Although solemn, people were nodding and greeting us.

All of a sudden, I was nervous.

I heard the clicks and looked round. Peggy arrived with Patrick, Paula, and Joan. I nodded as they took their seats. Joan was dispensed in the pew beside Siobhan's Auntie Flo. Peggy hugged me and wished me luck. Patrick shook my hand.

I caught Joan's eye. She winked through the lace veil that covered the top half of her face.

I was so incensed. Joan in fucking white at my wedding. How the fuck did this happen?

Ally simply commented, "Fuck, your woman Joan looks even better in white than she did in red!"

I tried to look disinterested. I was about to be married.

Susan waved at me and winked too.

The singer and organist were belting out, All Things Bright and Beautiful.

Chapter 30
Ta-Do Ron Ron

Siobhan was hyper; her big day had arrived. Her father was immensely proud of his only daughter, and he said as much as he hugged her.

The car that had taken Peggy, Patrick, Paula, and Joan to the church had returned to collect the last two people. The car that had taken us had already returned to collect the three bridesmaids: Donna, Sheila, and Katie.

Ronnie took Siobhan's hand as he headed out the door and smiled. As they sat in the back of the car, Ronnie helped himself to a glass of bubbles from the cool box in the back of the limo. He offered Siobhan a glass to steady her—she was a bundle of nerves. She declined, saying, "Jesus, who would drink before their wedding?"

Ronnie looked at his daughter. "You don't have to go through with this, love. I have paid for everything, and I would happily lose everything rather than see you unhappy."

Siobhan wiped a tear from her eye—it was a tear of happiness—and reassured her father. "I'm marrying the only man I have ever loved or will ever love. I've never been more certain about anything!"

Ronnie had his reservations but held his tongue.

They arrived, and as they got out of the car, a number of the guests spontaneously broke into light applause before heading to their seats inside.

The three bridesmaids assembled as rehearsed. The usher, Stephen, nodded at the organist. Mendelssohn's Wedding March began.

Siobhan grabbed her father's arm tightly as she steadied herself before the walk up the aisle. Everyone turned to look at the back door—everyone except Joan, that is. Colin caught her eye. She winked again and was just turning to look backwards when Colin's mum, who had seen him stare, gave a disapproving look in his direction and mouthed the words, "Fucking concentrate."

Colin stood out from his pew as the bridesmaids passed. Reluctantly, Ronnie handed Colin his daughter's hand. Colin smiled and nodded at him.

"All Things Bright and Beautiful" rang out again as the priest reassured the couple he was about to marry. The service began with the priest inviting everyone to take a seat.

Paul and Katie walked to the altar, bowed, and went to the lectern to read—Katie first. She read from 1 Corinthians 13:4-13. She began, "Love is patient, love is kind..." I wished this bit was over. What the fuck is your woman Joan playing at?

Psalm 103, In Praise of Divine Goodness, was sung. It seemed interminable. Siobhan held tightly to Colin's hand. Colin sighed.

Paul stepped to the lectern. 1 Peter 4:7-11. He began, "The end of all things is at hand..." I couldn't help wishing he was right. More panic.

Finished, they both walked past us as we sat in the wedding chairs on the altar. The priest moved to the lectern and kissed the lectionary before raising his hands to indicate that all should stand. "A reading from the Holy Gospel according to John."

"On the third day, there was a wedding in Cana, in Galilee, and the mother of Jesus was there..." He looked at us and smiled. He went on to tell about water being turned into wine. He finished and indicated for all to sit. He then banged on for what seemed like an hour about the sanctity of marriage and how God had bound these two together. I tuned out. I couldn't get Joan out of my head—and not naked Joan!

The next part was the actual marriage. We stood before the priest, flanked on either side by the wedding party.

Joe had the rings.

For once, I was glad that I knew the priest doesn't actually say, "If anyone knows of any reason that these two should not be wed, speak now or forever hold your peace!" We exchanged vows. Siobhan had demanded that we use the traditional church vows. I didn't care enough to argue. The priest, who made us call him by his first name, Father Peter, was droning on. I was trying to count how many angels had been carved into the marble wall behind the altar.

Marriage over, Father Peter announced that I could kiss the bride. I lifted the veil. Siobhan had a tear in her eye. I leaned her back in a tango hold and bent in to kiss her. Everyone applauded.

We were married.

"Bind Us Together" was belted out as the congregation moved forward in lines for communion. This was followed by "Give Me Joy in My Heart."

Siobhan had carefully selected all hymns and readings— another one of her demands.

The ceremony over, the wedding party, accompanied by Ronnie, Peggy, my mum, and Patrick, made their way to the sacristy to sign the register. "Guide Me, O Thou Great Redeemer" was playing to the congregation.

When the choral music was over, we had arranged for one song each to be played over the church speakers. My choice was The Blue Nile's "Saturday Night." It begins, "Who do you love?" As it progresses, the unmistakable tones of the wonderful Paul Buchanan utter the immortal words, "I love an ordinary girl who makes me feel alright!" Simple and poignant. Siobhan picked Stevie Wonder's "I Just Called to Say I Love You." Now, I love Stevie Wonder, but to my mind, this was hardly even close to his finest moment. As it rolled to the chorus, we could hear everyone join in.

Legalities complete, the others left, and after a minute, Colin and Siobhan Hill began their exit to rapturous applause.

We nodded and smiled as we left the altar. Joan winked. Siobhan winked back. As we exited the chapel, our family and friends began to spill out of the church. Hugs and congratulations ensued.

I grabbed a cigarette from Joe and lit it.

Joan looked immense as she approached. Siobhan giggled in that girly way as she hugged her like she'd known her for her whole life.

I caught my mother staring at me, and I awkwardly shook Joan's hand, even though she had leaned in to kiss my cheek.

Everyone started making for their cars. I shook my head in disbelief as Ronnie turned to Joan and announced, "There's room in our car."

She smiled and, feigning disbelief, scrunched her face and said, "Really? You don't mind?"

"Our pleasure, love," interrupted Peggy. "After everything you've been through today! We'll get you a nice glass of something for the journey." Joan hugged her.

Fuck me—she was in one of the wedding cars.

Unfuckingbelievable.

She hugged Siobhan again and left.

We got into the car, and the photographer did all his best-choreographed shots. We were the last to leave the church grounds. I poured two flutes of bubbles from the icebox. Siobhan smiled and announced, "Missus Colin Hill!" I smiled. We kissed.

"Six weeks is a long time!" she winked. "Tonight should be fun—and the christening tomorrow!"

She now had competition, even though she had no idea.

She talked the whole way to Ballymena—lovely service, apparently, great guests, everyone looked well, Joan was gorgeous even though she had no idea she was going to a wedding, the singing was great, lovely when everyone joined in with Stevie Wonder, can't wait for the honeymoon... Palermo... yadda, yadda, yadda... I could hear her, but I wasn't listening.

Chapter 31
The Bouquet

I was glad when we got to the Galgorm as I located Joe, took my cigarettes from him, stepped outside, and sparked one up.

I looked to my left, and Joan was standing, laughing and chatting with Mister Smith and his wife. They walked towards me.

"Didn't know your new wife was friendly with Miss Sanders. You kept that quiet!"

Thank fuck that was all he didn't know!

His wife cut across him. "Sorry we were so late for the service." I hadn't noticed. "Stanley"—she pointed her right thumb at her husband—"had some urgent business at the office. Here now and looking forward to a good day." She leaned in to kiss me. "You were always his favourite. Think it's because you have the same high moral values that he does."

They left just after Siobhan arrived to announce I was needed for the photos. Joan smiled. Siobhan hugged her again.

The champagne reception was in full flow, and Joan had begun her charm offensive.

Photos were once again choreographed, and there were all sorts of combinations of people. On numerous occasions, the photographer pointedly asked us all to smile. Apparently, I wasn't.

Photographs over, we returned to the foyer of the hotel.

Everyone clapped.

Siobhan tossed the bouquet over her shoulder. It was caught by Katie. She asked Joan to hold it while she adjusted her dress. Joan stared at me as if to say, "She may have the ring, but I have you by the balls!" My heart pounded.

I grabbed a pint as Hilda announced, "Could everyone please make their way to the Ivory Pavilion and be seated as the reception is about to begin."

When seated, Siobhan and I entered the room after the master of ceremonies had announced, "Ladies and gentlemen, please be upstanding to greet Mister and Missus Hill!"

As we entered, Paul Weller, ably assisted by Mick Talbot, blasted out, "You're the Best Thing." This was my choice. My hero had to be included. We rocked and danced through the crowd, stopping to hug some of our guests. Siobhan actually hugged Joan again, and as brazen as you like, Joan winked at me from over Siobhan's shoulder.

We had decided to do the speeches before food, and everyone had been warned to keep it brief. Father Peter had been invited, and after the speeches were over, his job was to say grace.

The MC announced each speaker in turn, and the usual platitudes were rolled out. "Beautiful couple, welcome to the family, love of her life..." Again, I was hearing but not listening.

Then the MC said, "I would like to call upon Colin to say a few words!"

I stood. People clapped. I hadn't really prepared a speech. I thanked Ronnie and Peggy for allowing me to marry their daughter, thanked the wedding party, mentioned how gorgeous the bridesmaids were, and turned to Siobhan. With all the sincerity I could muster, I said, "You, Missus Hill, have just stepped onto my rollercoaster. Enjoy the ride!"

Everyone laughed—except Ronnie and my mum.

I continued, "The most beautiful girl in the world has just made my life complete." I raised my glass in the direction of the guests and said, "Thank you."

I leaned in and kissed Siobhan.

She smiled.

I sat.

The MC announced the best man, and Joe stood up.

Everyone laughed and clapped. Some heckled. I heard Frank shout from the floor, "Keep it short, you big eejit!"

"It'll be short, alright," retorted Joe. "I'm busting for a pee."

Everyone laughed.

"Unaccustomed as I am to public speaking, I shall begin!" He was using a squeaky, exaggerated Belfast accent. People were roaring with laughter. "I felt honoured to be asked to be best man today. As one of only two brothers Colin has, the competition— well, it wasn't that stiff." He had walked behind Paul and ruffled his hair. He continued, "Colin assured me that if I do a good job today, I can do his next wedding too!" The place was rocking.

"I know it's a sad day for all the single men out there, now that this beauty queen is no longer available." He had his arm around Siobhan's shoulders. She looked back at him and smiled. He put his hand on my shoulder. "And among the single women, not even an eyelid was batted!" More laughs.

"I would like to thank the most important people here today." He paused. "The bar staff." He was on a roll. He did the usual thanking of the hotel and all the parents and commented on the beauty of the bridesmaids. Think he had his eye on Katie as he winked at her when he said it.

He continued, "To be honest, there was a time when I thought Ronnie wouldn't approve of this union." Ronnie nodded. "But he's here now, and it's too late."

He raised his glass. "All the best. I love you both!" He took a swig and added, "Mum made me say that."

He told the story of me bed-wetting, and I was cringing. It was even worse when he announced, "And he was seventeen at the time!" More laughs.

He finished by saying, "Can you all stand up quickly and raise a glass to the bride and groom? Hurry up before I wet myself too!"

They laughed. Toast made, he made an exaggerated exit, holding his crotch.

They laughed more.

Speeches over, grace said, we tucked in. I couldn't really eat, and I was looking into the guests when I noticed Joan hugging Mister Smith.

The first song was announced by Brian Giffen of The Untouchables, and Siobhan and I made our way to the dance floor. Bryan Adams' words, "Look—"

"Into my eyes," emitted from the speakers—her choice. I fucking hate Bryan Adams.

The wedding party joined us halfway through. Ronnie was dragged to the floor by Peggy, and Patrick graciously danced with my mother. The party continued. We had booked The Untouchables for the live music and JEMS disco for the evening. We both loved them, and Siobhan laughed as she said they'd both been playing there on her hen weekend. Ally had his new love on the floor, and there were even a few Cork accents in attendance.

Joan had men queuing to dance with her again, and every so often, she would catch my eye and wink.

I was waltzing with my mother when I saw Joan approach Ronnie for a dance. Funny, he wasn't so reluctant this time.

Joe was getting on well with Katie—very well—and they smooched closely when the DJ played the slow set. Phyllis Nelson moved closer and morphed into Marvin Gaye. Joan made a beeline for the top table, looked at Siobhan, and held her hand in my direction.

"May I?"

Siobhan was more than happy and said as much.

I got up, and as I moved past my mother, Joan said, "Our song!" My mother looked ferocious.

"Sexual Healing, it's good for me," Joan whispered as she pulled me close and began to sway.

How come Siobhan and her family were so trusting of this woman? I was swaying but nowhere near as close to her as I had been in Liverpool. My mother looked on. I turned my back and angrily said, "We are being watched, and my fucking mother heard you say our song!"

She laughed and tried to pull me closer. I resisted.

The sense of relief I felt when Ally cut in almost floored me.

As I made my way back, my mother stood and strode towards me. She held out her hand for a dance. I couldn't refuse and was waiting for the lecture.

We waltzed to Clapton singing Wonderful Tonight. I told my mother she looked wonderful.

"You're not getting past me that easy, big fella. Who the fuck is your woman, and how come you and her have a song?"

I was shaking, and my voice trembled as I responded, "She works in our place—the new girl I told you about. I didn't know, but she goes to the same gym as Siobhan. They're like best fucking mates or something. The song thing is a running joke at work. We all say that's our song when any Marvin Gaye song comes on!"

She looked at me in disbelief but said nothing more. She was marking my card. I got the message.

The evening crowd had arrived, and I was at the bar with Sean when Joan approached. She hugged Sean.

"Long time, no see!" she declared.

He winked at me over her shoulder, pointed at the dance floor. "Dance?"

She nodded.

"One, two, three, four," OutKast were belting out the start of Hey Ya! She danced gracefully without moving her feet.

"My baby don't mess around because he loves me so, and this I know for sure," she looked in my direction.

Sean was a brilliant dancer and did an exaggerated soul-step all the way around her. She kept rotating so she could see him.

"Shake it like a Polaroid picture!" was ringing in my ear when Donna tapped my shoulder.

"Penny for them?"

I shook my head and laughed. "I'm just realising how happy I am!"

"This here's for that ice-cold Michelle Pfeiffer..." was being belted out by Bruno Mars. I made my way to the floor. I noticed Joan kiss the first two fingers of her right hand as Bruno sang, "Gotta kiss myself, I'm so pretty!" She had a point.

The night progressed, and just after ten, Siobhan approached me and asked if we could go to the room. She winked.

I said, "In a while, Missus Hill!"

That got a laugh and bought me some more time.

I went to the bar with Ally and Paul. Joe was invited, but he was too busy. We traded shots—six each. I was fuzzy.

Six more. I was lost.

We were staggering from the bar when Siobhan caught my arm.

"Bedtime, Mister Hill?"

I shrugged. I didn't want to go to bed, but I was too drunk to come up with another reason not to.

Joe ran to the microphone as he sensed we were leaving and started to sing.

"We know where you're going!"

He pointed at the back of the hall. Everyone looked at us and joined him in song. I was waving furiously as Siobhan hauled my ass out of there.

Everyone clapped.

We headed past reception, and I noticed Joan at the front door, smoking and holding Sean's hand.

We arrived at the bridal suite, and Siobhan turned nasty.

"What the fuck are you playing at? Dancing with everyone but me? Even Joan said to me—"

My blood went cold, and I nearly sobered up.

"For fuck's sake, do you have to go on?"

I was staring out the window that overlooked the River Maine. I wanted to storm out and confront Joan. I knew I couldn't.

I was still staring when Siobhan started again.

"And look at the fucking state of you. Six weeks I've waited, and you couldn't get it up even if you wanted to. You do want to?" she questioned.

Momentarily, I considered divorce.

I attempted to calm her down. I turned to face her.

"I'm sorry, Siobhan. I have never gotten married before, and I never will again!"

She smiled.

"Can I have a hug, Missus Hill?"

She made a sad face but moved towards me nonetheless. We hugged. She stripped. She had bought 'wedding night' underwear, and she was beautiful.

She got into the bed and pulled the covers up to her chin before reaching down and removing her knickers.

I stripped and joined her.

She lay on her back, as usual, and no matter what I did, I couldn't get my penis to play ball.

We slept.

We managed to consummate our union the next morning. Siobhan was happy. As she moved to the shower, I attempted to join her, but she put one arm across her chest and the other hand between her legs and shooed me out of the bathroom.

Chapter 32
The Spare Bed

We got ourselves ready and made our way down for breakfast. As we approached the breakfast room, we could hear loud laughter, as most of the guests had stayed over. I noticed Joan floating about. She was wearing THAT red dress.

Siobhan laughed. "I love her. She looks amazing. My dad loves her. What the hell—everybody loves her! Wonder where she stayed last night."

Joan approached us, and Siobhan asked her. Joan was speaking very loudly when she answered. "Oh, your mum and dad had a single bed in their room. They insisted. I wanted to get a taxi back to Belfast, but your dad wouldn't hear of it. He's even offered to go to the police station with me this afternoon when he brings me back up the road. He's so sweet. I love him!"

Joan hugged Siobhan, then turned to me. I stared through her and walked towards the bain-marie.

Panic had given way to desperation. I couldn't see a way out of this. Joan needed to disappear.

Joe was sitting happily with Katie, Donna, and Paul. He was mopping up brown sauce with a hash brown as I walked towards them. We smiled. Everyone was in such a good mood, considering they were all hanging like bats.

In a wee wedding bag Siobhan had delivered to each room, she had included a miniature alcohol-free bottle of bubbles and four effervescent headache tablets. They had obviously been consumed.

Joan was sitting with Ronnie, Peggy, Patrick, and Paula. Siobhan joined them. We laughed and joked. The manager weaved among tables, asking if we had been pleased with everything. Apparently, they were.

After breakfast, we dispersed—some to the spa, some to the car.

We were heading back up the road for a more intimate wedding dinner. My mother had booked the back room in the Parador. She insisted on paying for something.

It could only accommodate forty-five, and we had trouble getting down to that! There was absolutely no way Joan could get squeezed in, despite Ronnie's protestations. Peggy also pointed out that he wouldn't have time to go to the police station. She was beginning to get slightly irked by Ronnie's zeal in his desire to include Joan in absolutely everything.

The meal was set for four p.m., and we were all meandering up the road to make sure we got there in plenty of time.

Siobhan and I 'christened the bed' as soon as I had carried her over the threshold. She insisted.

The 'christening' was uneventful.

I was the only man she had ever been with, and she proudly told everyone that she was the only woman I had ever been with. I did nothing to disabuse her of this notion—though Joan did laugh out loud when Siobhan said it on the Sunday at the spa.

Dinner in the Parador was the usual. The food was always excellent—standard fare, but always good.

I loved the Michael Carlin originals that adorned the walls. He had a way of capturing iconic Belfast and Irish scenes.

Siobhan was talking to Donna about the honeymoon and how she was looking forward to Sicily, Procida, and even the day trip to Capri.

"Bit of Italian island-hopping." Donna said she was jealous.

"I wonder how Joan is getting on at the police station?" Ronnie couldn't let it go.

Peggy was at the loo. Siobhan reassured him and added, "I'll phone her when we get home and let you know."

Ronnie nodded.

Wine was flowing, and we had to leave about eight, as the taxi taking us to the bus station was booked for five a.m. We were getting the five-thirty bus to Dublin Airport.

We walked home.

As soon as we got through the door, I opened a beer. Siobhan tutted and lifted her phone. I was getting so stressed by how quickly the ubiquitous Joan had become almost essential in everything that we did now.

"Hiya, how did you get on with the police?" I was glad I could only hear one side of the conversation.

"Really?"

"No way!"

"Did you see him?"

"You're too kind. I couldn't possibly—the bus is booked and paid for!"

Joan's story was punctuated by Siobhan.

When she hung up forty-three minutes later, she immediately rang Ronnie. Again, I was glad that I could only hear one side of this chat.

"Joan is okay!"

"I know."

"I said that."

"Weird. Apparently, the police see similarities between those murders."

"Ballymena—just before my hen weekend."

"I know. There was even a murder in her hotel two weeks ago in Liverpool!"

Our eyes met. Siobhan looked at me strangely. I pushed open the back door and lit a cigarette.

I had my back to Siobhan but could still hear her every word.

"Yes, Dad, some guy with a hat was seen by one of her neighbours leaving the apartment block. Very scary for her."

I looked round. Siobhan waved to get my attention and cupped her hand towards her mouth to indicate that she wanted a drink. She then held her index finger and thumb out in front of her face very close together to let me know she wanted a small one. I poured a half-glass of chardonnay and handed it to her. She was listening to Ronnie. She moved the phone and kissed me.

"I'll let her know! And of course, I'll send her your number. She's awful good. She even offered to run us to Dublin in the morning."

I nearly choked.

"But sure, the taxi and bus are already booked and paid for."

"THANK FUCK!"

"Okay, Dad, I'll text or phone you every day. Love you. Tell Mum I'll talk to her soon."

"Love you too. See you next week."

She smacked her lips and hung up. She then looked at me.

"Did you know Joan had been in Liverpool the same weekend as your stag?"

I shrugged. "No."

She looked pensive. My heart stopped.

"Funny, did it never come up in conversation at work?" She was probing.

I was trying my best to be evasive. "We rarely talk in work, and when we do, it tends to be about a client."

I wasn't convinced she was buying this, but she didn't allow herself to think any further about it.

She kissed me. My heart started beating again.

My phone beeped. 'John from work'—a large heart icon. I sighed heavily as I headed to bed.

If I hadn't before, I was so looking forward to getting on that plane.

Chapter 33
The Big Suitcase

W e slept. I was glad we had 'christened' the bed earlier—my nerves were shot. The alarm roared at me at four a.m. My head pounded.

Our bags had been packed before the wedding. In November, southern Italy averages nearly twenty degrees or thereabouts—shorts all the way for me. I had a very small carry-on suitcase. Siobhan had to put her bag in the hold: hair straighteners, hairdryer, makeup bag, and fuck knows what else. We were only going for a week, and I told her no one would be looking at her.

She sighed wearily. "Not even you?"

I didn't respond.

The taxi driver texted that he was outside. I grabbed two beers for the bus to Dublin. Siobhan tutted.

"Cure!" was my terse, monosyllabic response.

We headed for the car.

I was glad to get into the back seat of the taxi. One week away, and I would try to sort this mess out when I returned. I could hear Peter Cox of Go West fame screaming in my ear: "I am the king of wishful thinking." I now had an earworm for the day.

The journey to Dublin was uneventful. Siobhan read and snoozed, and when she snoozed, I sipped beer. I simply couldn't be bothered to listen to her.

We got off at Terminal One and went to the Aer Lingus desk for Siobhan to leave her case. It always amazes me how many people are going to Sicily—or anywhere else, for that matter—in November.

Bag deposited, we made our way through security and went to have breakfast. We went into the Gate Clock Bar. Siobhan sat down, and I went to order food. I also ordered a double whiskey, which I necked at the bar.

We ate and talked about the wedding. Siobhan said, "On hindsight, it had been a great day." She apologised for her meltdown in the hotel room. I waved away her protests. She leaned across the table, kissed me, then lingered long enough for me to say, "Love you, gorgeous."

She smiled. "Me too, handsome!"

I could do a week of this, surely?

I bought a pair of sunglasses and a litre of Jameson in duty-free.

"Can't be too careful," I said to Siobhan as I lifted the whiskey. "They may not have Jameson in our hotel!"

She looked at me like I was a child.

I didn't care.

Our flight was called to boarding, and we made our way to our gate. I always wondered why they are called gates.

I slept for three and a half hours on the plane. It was the first time I had properly relaxed in weeks.

Siobhan wakened me and wiped the drool from my chin seconds before we landed at Catania Airport. I stretched and rocked my head gently from side to side.

I was so relieved to be here, and I kissed Siobhan.

She had the whole week planned. Normally, this would annoy me, but now I was just glad to be out of Belfast for a week.

Chapter 34
Mister and Missus Hill

As we left departures, I noticed a guy holding an A4 card with 'Mister and Missus Hill' written on it in black. Siobhan looked at me and smiled.

"Mister and Missus Hill," she said, wrapping her arm more tightly around mine.

It always annoyed me that she got to take a big suitcase, but I had to look after it! The taxi had been pre-booked and paid for. The driver hurtled through the tiny streets. I tried my pigeon Italian on him, but he wasn't very chatty.

"Buon pomeriggio, come stai?" I said.

Always say hello and ask how someone is, my mother would say.

He curled his lips downwards and simply said, "Bene, bene. San Vito Lo Capo, Hotel Sikania?"

I replied, "Sì," and settled back to take in the view. It was just over four hours by car.

We arrived in San Vito Lo Capo just after half five and approached the hotel, where we were greeted by Carlo, the youngest of the Panfalone family. The hotel reception was spotless and very white. We got booked in and made our way to our room. I was glad I had insisted on the most expensive hotel—I needed this. It was luxurious, and I loved how white it was. The bed was massive, and the white linen bedclothes were offset with sky-blue cushions. The sky-blue theme continued in the wall paintings, and in the adjoining bathroom, there were about ten blue tiles dotted around the brilliant white walls. The wooden floor was polished and had a high sheen.

Siobhan had let them know it was our honeymoon. There was a bottle of prosecco chilling in an ice bucket, a large bunch of flowers beside the bed, and a box of continental chocolates. The room had a beautiful view of a bay in the distance. I was commenting on how nice the room was when my hand slipped, and the cork flew just past Siobhan. We laughed.

We drank and ate chocolate before showering and making love.

We were booked into a restaurant called 'Vico de Santi' for eight P.M. It was only six twenty-three, so we decided to take a stroll. On the way out, I asked Carlo, "Dove si trova Vico de Santi?"

Siobhan was impressed. Carlo wasn't. I was screwed when he gave me directions in Italian. He realised and reverted to English with a cheeky smile.

The village was gorgeous—beautiful streets with bright, colourful doors, red-tiled roofs, and whitewashed walls.

The food was delicious. Siobhan and I both loved seafood, so we were in heaven.

Siobhan asked if we could eat here all three nights. I didn't see why not. She put her cardigan on as we walked back to the hotel, wrapping both arms around my left arm. For some strange reason, she always liked to walk on my left.

We arrived in the room. Siobhan poured out the rest of the prosecco. I fished out the Jameson. We had a drink, made love, I showered, we slept. It was seventeen degrees, so I put the air con on low.

After breakfast, Siobhan phoned home. Peggy said Ronnie was in great form and had been saying how impressed he was by how attentive Joan had been in Siobhan's absence.

When she told me this, I froze. I had been able to forget all about the fun that awaited me when I returned home.

Siobhan, for the first time, expressed reservations about Joan.

"Not sure I like her calling in on my mum and dad while I'm away. Strange behaviour."

I agreed wholeheartedly and calmly said, "Maybe we should start to distance ourselves when we get home?"

Siobhan said nothing.

I still had my phone on flight mode. I didn't want to look.

Our first day, Tuesday, was spent doing what I wanted. We visited Forza D'Agro and Savoca. As we passed the crystal blue water, I was playing scenes from The Godfather in my head. Siobhan didn't like those films.

"Too violent," she said.

I loved them.

I had a great day picking out spots I recognised from the silver screen, and Siobhan enjoyed it too.

She looked beautiful today.

Again, we got to our room. I drank whiskey. Siobhan joined me. We fucked. We showered and got ready for dinner.

I took my phone off flight mode and waited for the onslaught. Four beeps. I slid my thumb up the screen to reveal all four messages had been sent by my mum.

Nothing from 'John from work.'

Day two, Wednesday, was spent at the beach, reading and sunbathing in the unusually hot weather—it was twenty-three degrees. I had left my phone off and on the charger back at the hotel.

We talked about children. Siobhan wanted four. I didn't care.

Coincidentally, we were both reading Steve Cavanagh books on our respective Kindles—me, The Defence, her, The Plea.

We returned to the hotel on foot. As we did, she phoned home. Peggy answered and assured her that everything was fine, but Joan had stayed the night before because there were still police all over the apartment block. She was frightened. It was Ronnie's idea.

When Siobhan relayed this information to me, the 'fear' returned.

We got to our room, had a drink, had sex, showered, and got ready for dinner.

We ordered the same food and a bottle of Malvasia wine. I was hungry, and the red mullet was beautiful. The wine was dry and sharp. I liked it.

Day three, Thursday, we went to Palermo. It was about seventy miles away, so we set off straight after breakfast. I drove slowly through Castellammare del Golfo, onto Alcamo, through Cinisi, and finally Monreale before stopping in Palermo itself.

This was Siobhan's day.

The Capuchin Catacombs—she simply had to see them. I thought they were a bit macabre.

We moved on to Palermo Cathedral. It was impressive, although being in two churches in the same week was a bit much for me.

We went to Mondello Beach before having a late lunch in Caffè del Kassaro.

The drive back to the hotel took nearly two hours, so we set off at five.

Siobhan showered. I poured a whiskey, showered, and we headed for our last dinner in Sicily.

Day four, Friday—the day I dreaded. I hate airports. I hate travelling. But it had to be done.

After breakfast, we said our goodbyes to the receptionist. Even Siobhan chipped in.

"Arrivederci!"

We drove to Catania and got a flight to Naples. We were staying in Naples for one night, then getting the ferry to Procida the next day.

Still nothing from Joan.

Long drive. Long day.

We arrived at San Pietro a Patierno Airport and got a taxi from the rank outside. I laughed to myself—one tiny detail Siobhan had not planned.

We were staying in a budget hotel called Relais Della Porta. It was nicer than I thought it would be. As we approached the reception area, I took Siobhan's hand. She looked at me and smiled.

I was wrecked. Siobhan was too.

We made love—of sorts. She showered. I emptied the whiskey bottle. I showered. We slept.

Chapter 35
Lambretta

D ay five: no breakfast in the hotel, so we grabbed some croissants and coffee on our way to Molo Beverello to catch the ferry. The journey to Procida took the best part of an hour. By the time we were disembarking, I was dragging Siobhan's suitcase and my own. She had a scarf wrapped around her neck, and she looked like Lana Turner.

In that moment, I loved her.

Siobhan had hired two mopeds for our stay. After the taxi had dropped us off at Hotel La Corricella and we had dispatched our bags, we got the keys to the Lambrettas and headed for the beach known as Il Postino. Apparently, Siobhan's favourite foreign-language movie had been shot there. She had made me watch it—I fell asleep.

We parked up our bikes and entered the beach. I took her hand.

"I love it. This is the very beach where Mario meets and falls in love with Beatrice." She grabbed my arm and snuggled in closely.

I didn't mind.

We sat on the beach. She closed her eyes and imagined. I, meanwhile, made for the mobile coffee shop. I ordered two cappuccinos, then changed it when I noticed he had beer. One cappuccino and a can of Stella. We sat; she sipped, I drank.

She was savouring the highlight of her honeymoon. I looked at her with her eyes shut and wondered how this was ever going to work out.

After an interminable two hours, we left, as we had decided to go for a spin around the island. I loved the brightly coloured roofs and doors on each of the houses.

I was tired.

Siobhan had booked La Caracale restaurant for eight, so after we arrived back at our hotel just after six, Siobhan phoned home. Peggy answered again and said that Joan had gone back to her own apartment but that Ronnie had insisted she come to theirs for dinner.

What the fuck?

I checked my phone: two texts from Joe, one from Paul, and a missed call from my mum.

Still nothing from Joan.

We ate and drank wine. Siobhan was so excited to have seen that beach, and I actually listened to her for once. She could be engaging when she tried.

I ordered a bottle of wine to go, paid the bill, and we started to walk back to the hotel.

"I love you, Colin Hill!" Siobhan held my hand very tightly.

"I love you too, Siobhan!" We kissed and rocked our hands backwards and forwards.

We got into our room. Siobhan actually ripped my shorts off. We made passionate love, and she fell asleep in my arms. I was glad that I had left my cigarettes, lighter, and wine within reach.

I sparked up and sipped wine. She didn't wake.

Day six: boat trip to Capri. "Shame not to when we're this close," Siobhan had said. I couldn't give a fuck.

E quello che è!

As they say in these parts.

She had booked us onto a river taxi, and we headed for Capri. "I'm so looking forward to seeing the Blue Grotto. It looks awesome in pictures." She accentuated "awesome" in a mock New York accent. I certainly didn't love her in that moment.

The Blue Grotto was a sight to behold, but I wanted to eat. Siobhan had booked a table at Ziqu Terrace restaurant, and I needed a drink.

We ordered food. I had a G and T; Siobhan drank water. We had wine with our meal. Fuck, it was expensive. I didn't care.

We got the taxi boat at eight p.m. We got a taxi back to our hotel. We were both a bit tiddly. Siobhan even put her hands between my legs as the taxi neared the hotel.

I was shocked.

I finished the wine. We fucked. She showered. I joined her.

I texted Joan.

Day seven: our last day. I had asked to include a guided tour of the Terra Murata prison. Siobhan said she didn't mind. Frankly, I missed most of it, as I had received a text from 'John from work':

"Hope you're enjoying your week of FREEDOM. Tell Siobhan I said hi!"

No fucking chance.

"I will see you very soon. I have a kettlebell class with Siobhan on Tuesday night. She has invited me to stay at yours after. Should be fun. Laters, sexy! I'm picking you up at the Europa bus station."

What the fuck? Siobhan hadn't said a word to me.

The rest of the holiday was a blur.

I couldn't wait to get home.

I didn't want to go home.

Chapter 36
Unfinished Business

We travelled. I was tired, and even Siobhan's breathing was starting to annoy me. I texted Joan:

"You and I have a lot of unfinished business! I look forward to finishing it!"

She texted back immediately.

"Your place or mine?" Three laughing emojis.

Joan did, indeed, collect us from the Europa bus station. She hugged Siobhan and winked at me over Siobhan's shoulder. She licked her lips. I dropped my head.

When we pulled up, Siobhan insisted that Joan come in.

"One wee glass of vino?"

I hated Siobhan in that moment.

Joan acquiesced. Of course she did. I shuddered.

Inside, Siobhan took her suitcase upstairs. I went to the kitchen. Joan followed. I poured a large whiskey for myself. She grabbed my neck and kissed me like I'd never been kissed before. I couldn't resist.

She heard Siobhan approach and, before letting go, whispered, "I've got big plans for us."

I drank the contents of my whiskey glass and poured another.

"Now, Chardonnay okay?" Siobhan looked directly at Joan as she asked the question.

"A very small one, please. I want to get out of your hair. You two lovebirds must have things to do!"

Siobhan was pouring the drinks. Joan winked at me and touched my hand. As Siobhan turned around, she saw Joan remove her hand and shouted,

"What the fuck are you doing?"

Joan apologised profusely.

"What do you mean? I was only greeting my boss!" She giggled. Siobhan did too.

"Sorry, I'm tired. Please forgive me." Siobhan hugged Joan and mouthed the word "sorry" in my direction. I shrugged.

Joan announced, "You know what? I'm just going to go. Sorry for the misunderstanding, and sure, I'll see you at class and for dinner tomorrow night."

She hugged an over-apologetic Siobhan and me and left.

We went to bed and slept.

Chapter 37
Friday Night

I carried on the affair because I had no choice. In fact, the affair became my normal. The marriage became my hell.

That kiss changed everything.

Siobhan became increasingly aware of me distancing myself. Donna would call me and give off about Siobhan spending so much time at hers. She was also flirting with me—and she was Siobhan's cousin. It was a mess. Joan had me over a barrel, and Ronnie and Peggy could see no wrong in her.

Siobhan suspected something but hesitated to voice her thoughts. Most Fridays, I would cause a row. Joan was getting more and more desperate, and if we had a row, Siobhan would go to Donna's. It just made things easier. I was struggling with what I should do. I wanted to spend time with Joan, but Friday night was when Siobhan wanted us to tidy the house, then sit and watch crap on TV and judge me for having a couple of drinks. Meanwhile, Joan went out with the guys from work.

I must have absentmindedly decided what I was going to do as I drove home. I didn't want to be the cause of the row, but if I was infuriating enough, Siobhan would start on me.

As I walked through the door, I could hear her clanking about in the kitchen. Obviously, the fucking house cleaning had already begun.

Fuck this.

I walked slowly into the kitchen and nonchalantly opened the fridge door. Siobhan looked round from the sink with that face, disapproving as always. She was wearing that green dress that fell effortlessly over her substantial curves. She looked great against the black patent cupboard doors of our newly installed kitchen. I just couldn't bring myself to hug her and embrace the moment.

"Hey? How's you?" I enquired as I began to loosen my tie. I hate wearing a suit, but protocol demands that I do.

"You're not starting on the beer already? We have so much to do before we can sit and relax."

The drone.

"Hey to you too." Sarcasm had become my go-to.

I knew I was probably going to be a bastard at some stage so I could make an excuse to disappear, but I didn't think it was going to be this easy.

"For fuck's sake, do you have to use Friday night as an excuse to get fucking plastered?" She hung the apron over her shoulders— the one with the Houses of Parliament emblazoned on the front. I have to say, I preferred the one that had the suspenders and lacy underwear. I suppose her choice of apron was her way of telling me that sex was off limits again unless I behaved myself and was a good boy. Not much chance of sex with her tonight.

"Who made you the boss of me?" Infantile and infuriating, even by my own high standards.

"We're supposed to be a partnership here. You know— teamwork, companionship, a fucking tidy house, even if only for the weekend. Is that too much to ask?" She paused. "Well, is it?"

She brushed the front of the apron, and I wished I could bring myself to just join in. But I simply didn't want to.

By this point, I could just hear mumbles. I had completely zoned out. She brushed the apron again and sprayed some bleach-type stuff over the kitchen worktops. Apart from anything else, I hated that smell.

My whisky glass was clean. I could see it sitting prettily, winking at me from behind the open cupboard door, its sheen reflecting beautifully against the deep black surface.

Time for overdrive.

"Look, I've had a fucking rough week. I don't need to come home to you behaving like my fucking mother. I can do what the fuck I like when I'm in my own house—without you dictating. Or at least, I thought I could."

I removed the tie, took my jacket off, and pulled my shirt from inside my belt. Liberating.

Her voice had risen a few decibels by this stage.

"Are you going to help with the housework or not?"

"What I'm going to do first of all is sit down, watch the news, relax, and yeah—whether you fucking like it or not—I'm going to enjoy a few beers. So there."

"No. Screw this. I'm not doing another Friday night like this." She pulled the apron over her head, looked at me with complete contempt, and slapped it onto the hob.

"Look, I am only asking you to consider my feelings. I do have feelings, you know."

"That's a laugh. You, YOU have feelings? The only fucking feelings you have happen in your trousers. When was the last time you took the time out to ask me—ME—how my day at work was? Like you actually care!"

It had started now.

"I don't appreciate that language."

"Oh fuck, fuckity, fuck, fuck, fuck. You are so fucking frustrating. Why do you always play the language card? It adds absolutely nothing to any debate or discussion."

She put her hands on her hips. She looked stunning. Her blonde locks fell over her statuesque shoulders as she loosened her bobble—a clear indication that she was in the mood to leave. I think she enjoyed these shenanigans as much as I did.

"Yeah, yeah, like we ever have any debates or discussions. This is a complete dictatorship. You are a complete control freak. I hate constantly worrying about what bloody mood you're going to be in!"

"Oh, bloody, bloody. Who's using bad language now? It offends my sensitivities when you speak to dear sweet me in that tone."

I was on a roll.

"There is absolutely no need to use sarcasm. It is the lowest form of wit and is just another example of your passive-aggressive nature."

She shook her hair loose and ran her fingers through the front of it. She looked fucking amazing. She was in great shape.

I think I could cheerfully kill someone at this stage, and she just happens to be here right in front of me. I wonder, with an inner smile, if I could kill her and get away with it or if some freak accident could just take her away so that I wouldn't have to live like this anymore.

I do love her. Really, I do love her, but she drives me mad like no one else in the world is capable of doing—a madness that is bordering on the clinically insane. This passive-aggressive, control freak of a woman should be the centre of my whole world. Try to imagine that someone could mean so much to you and at the same time infuriate the life out of you.

Why, oh why, do we make life so difficult?

I often wonder if I should have settled for some sort of mediocrity, some sort of quiet acceptance of life.

Wouldn't it be so much easier?

No rows, no sarcasm, no passive aggression, no bad language—but then, having been there for so long with Siobhan, the lack of excitement would make you want to gouge your eyes out with a size 7 ¾ knitting needle.

She ran her hands down her side and settled them on her hips again.

"You're not even listening to me. Why do you drift off into that wee world of your own? You just throw insults about me being sarcastic and my passive aggression, then go into a world of your own. You say you have feelings, and then you say nasty things about me. Suppose you're just thinking about my feelings? Some fucking chance. The day you care about someone else's feelings more than you care about your own precious feelings will be a cold day in hell."

She sighed and brushed past me as she began to make her way down the hall. Her black heels clicked against the wooden floor as she stormed away. I wanted to run my arm across the pile of dishes and smash them all over the floor, but inside I was laughing, just a bit.

"Can we stop this? It isn't going to get us anywhere. It's a Friday night, and we don't want to start the weekend like this. Truce?"

I knew it was probably too late for this kind of conciliatory intervention, but somehow I knew I could use this remark as justification for my behaviour when she returned on Monday. She flung round in a rage, and she looked absolutely brilliant when she was angry—the green of the dress, the heaving breast, the faint outline of her underwear, all set against the look of rage that engulfed every sinew of her face.

"Fuck you and your truce. I don't believe you've met me before. Allow me to introduce myself—I'm a control freak and a sarcastic dictator who has mood swings. In your wee world, you probably wish I was dead. Well, trust me, we can all dream."

I flung my jacket around my shoulder and hung my tie around my neck. It was a dark blue tie, and I remember thinking at that moment how well it looked beside the light blue shirt and navy pinstripe suit I normally wore on a Friday.

"What the hell are you talking about? Do you really want to keep this going? Because, see, by now I do. I can't be bothered with your constant groaning and your blatant disregard for how I feel. So just leave me alone. I can't even stand to be in the same room as you."

I was in full self-pity mode at this stage and was actually enjoying myself in a perverse way. She tugged on her hair in complete rage and just screamed, "Aaaaggghh!!"

As she stormed up the stairs, I took a swig of my beer and lit a fag. She hated me smoking inside.

My phone vibrated in my pocket, and I went into the downstairs bathroom to check it. It was a text from "John from work."

"Can't wait to see you tomorrow night! Xxxxx."

A naked photo was attached.

I rubbed my groin as I couldn't help feeling a bulge in my trousers. I just wanted to be there right away. I pulled on the toilet roll holder and blew my nose—those god-awful scented loo rolls that she insisted on buying.

I looked at myself in the mirror. I grimaced, pursed my lips, and smiled. It is a weird experience looking at oneself in a mirror. We can all delude ourselves into how good we look.

It was a full-length mirror. I turned sideways and admired my physique, even though I was quickly becoming aware of my burgeoning beer-induced pot belly. When I returned to the kitchen,

Siobhan was standing, staring, and continued with the party mood. Her nose was twitching. She only did this when she was so far gone that she couldn't return even if she felt that she wanted to. She had opened the top two buttons on her dress to reveal her ample cleavage and just a peek of her lacy black bra.

She did look stunning.

"Don't you fucking worry. I can't even bear to be in the same house as you. I really don't think I can spend another weekend of this shit. Give me five minutes, and I will be out of your hair."

She pushed her arse against me, and I was careful to turn sideways. I was, after all, a bit excited. I hung my jacket on the door handle.

Why can I not bring myself to beg her to stay?

Joan.

I know where she is going, and I know that this is just another nail in the coffin of our relationship. I just don't care, and I just care too much. What am I supposed to do?

Listen to this or go for kinky sex tomorrow night?

I sipped on my beer and slowly removed my belt. I stared at the picture of four wine bottles that adorned the back room wall—a picture Siobhan had demanded we bring back from our honeymoon in Sicily. There were random letters across each bottle, and it was set against an alcove with corks strewn in front. I hadn't wanted the hassle of bringing it home and said so at the time, but now that we had, I found myself absentmindedly staring at it from time to time. I was rather pleased at her insistence.

I could hear her stomping down the stairs. I knew she had packed. I knew she was leaving. I knew that she would come back on Monday evening. I knew she would make me apologise for ruining her weekend—even though she would be out painting the town, even though she would be refusing to answer my calls and leaving me to stew in my own gravy.

It is madness; passive aggression is such a pain in the ass. But it means I can be in Joan's tomorrow night.

Maybe it is me who is the passive aggressor?

I don't care!

I can hear the front door opening, and I shout rather sarcastically, "Love you, honey!" I can see her back rushing out the door, and part of me wants to grab her and make her stay. What the hell is wrong with me?

I text Joan: Do you realise what you've done to me? Can hardly walk straight here. Will be at yours as soon as I can tomorrow night. Can't imagine what you have planned.

My phone vibrates almost immediately, and I open the message – a picture from Joan in her underwear. She looks amazing.

I look out the front window to see if Siobhan has left yet. She often sits in her car for ages at this stage, I suppose wondering if she should stay or go. Her car, or as she calls it, "BABY," is gone.

Sometimes I think she likes that car more than anything else in the world.

It was always her dream to own a Triumph TR7, and I managed to acquire a green one just last year. They had been out of production for over thirty years, but I somehow located one. The previous owner had had it from new, and he actually interviewed all interested parties. He apparently wanted to make sure it was going to a good home. He was terminally ill and wanted to ensure his "BABY" would be looked after by someone who would love and cherish it as he did.

Siobhan won the interview process. She proved to him, with her in-depth knowledge of everything about the car, that she was the only one he could trust. I paid for the car, and she promised to call and take him for a spin on a regular basis— and she did. She couldn't believe her luck. She washed that car inside and out every other day. She refused to take it through an automated car wash, afraid it would get damaged. I swear, I think she believed the fucking car was alive and had a pulse. She even talked to it.

I moved deliberately through the back lounge and pushed open the front room door. I loved the doors in this house. It was an old house, but we had the original doors dipped to remove the paint and rehung them. They were stained the same colour as the floors.

When I first moved in, before we were married, I borrowed an industrial sander and spent three weeks, night and day, sanding the floors back to the original wood. Why would anyone paint floors?

I slumped on the large corner leather sofa and screamed in that primal way—silently at first, then in a loud, uncontrollable, inconsolable roar.

I know I kind of made this happen, but that doesn't stop me from having doubts. The scream feels good, but it is a temporary high. I feel good for a minute, then I resign myself to the Friday night routine that has been my lot for the last four Fridays.

I had even been expecting this, so I prepared. I had gone shopping on the way home and bought a litre bottle of sixteen-year-old single malt whisky, some beer, and a selection of cheese and crackers. I suppose I wasn't only expecting this but also hoping and planning for it.

Joan.

I simply had to clear the way for the games tomorrow night.

I went to the kitchen, which was strewn with the dishes I had wanted to smash all over the floor earlier—it was a complete mess! I suppose Siobhan had a point, but it struck me as funny how she always stormed out when the kitchen was a mess, even though she was a self-confessed clean freak.

At least my good whisky glass was clean. There was something cathartic about drinking good whisky out of a good whisky tumbler—heavy-bottomed glass with delicate sides. Large blocks of cheese and a range of crackers were carefully laid out so they formed a kind of mountain range, one that I was going to slowly climb, hydrating—or rather dehydrating—copiously with sixteen-year-old single malt.

I filled the glass with ice, the only other substance I would allow to touch my whisky.

I was relaxing.

What music to listen to? I always find it difficult to select the right music to suit my mood in this situation. I want to scream. I want to laugh. I want to cry. I want to feel emasculated. I want to feel angry and happy—a dilemma.

So it will have to be a selection of tunes from a wide range of vinyl.

I make a list as I slowly digest my first glass of Glenfiddich.

You're the Best Thing – Paul Weller (Though really, it could read Worst.)

Honey, I Miss You – Bobby Goldsboro (Though really, it could read Shut the door on your way out!)

I allow myself a little snigger at the shut the door on your way out retort—it gives me a sense of freedom.

Hurt Myself – Christina Aguilera This hits the spot, and I hope—just hope—that this is how she is feeling. She should be. Although, do I really care?

SEMI-DETACHED

I look at my watch. It is exactly 8:28 on another Friday night alone, so I start the music. A full-blast rendition of Whitesnake's Fool for Your Loving No More (air guitar at the ready).

I watch myself gyrate in the long rectangular mirror that runs the full length of the living room wall—full flow.

I settle back in my wrinkly old tan leather recliner, take a large gulp of my whisky, pour another large glass, and sigh. Another large gulp. Another large glass. I put the CD on repeat.

I abandon the list and just stand at my large selection of vinyl in their red rack—a rack where the music is carefully laid out in alphabetical order.

This is my doing. I can be a wee bit anally retentive about my music. This is a small thing to some people, but it is huge for me.

You see, I hate when people play a record and either don't return it to its cover or, even more infuriatingly, return it to the wrong cover. She does this all the time, and while I found it funny at the start, it now just makes me mad. I am convinced she does it deliberately. I think she even moves albums about from cover to cover when she hasn't even been listening—just pure badness.

It's like this: when you want to listen to The Blue Nile singing "Happiness" (including the line "Now that I've found peace at last," which is really apt at this stage in my life), and you open the cover only to find one of her god awful Rolling Stones albums inside, it infuriates you to the point that it takes you right out of the mood.

Any number of songs could please my ear at this stage. I settle for Ocean Colour Scene's Moseley Shoals. Track one, large and testosterone laden, "The Riverboat Song." I pump up the volume and settle back to enjoy my whisky.

I slurped loudly. Seeing that I was on my own, I could do whatever the fuck I liked. I was starting to get a buzz from the whisky. It was that pleasant stage when everything feels a little fuzzy. I started to gouge down on the cheese and crackers. The blue cheese was delicious with the whisky. I drank hungrily because I just wanted the pain to go away, but for other reasons, I wanted it to be tomorrow.

I sat and composed a drunken text or two, actually one that was loving and one that was loathing.

"I love you. You're the best thing that ever happened to me. I want you to come home, and I want you to feel special and loved. Please, can we stop this before we completely ruin our weekend? Xxxxxxx"

I was just about to press send on my phone but couldn't bring myself to grovel, with all the implications for tomorrow night. I then composed my second text message as I took another large swill of my whisky, managing to spill a large dollop on my new tie, which I hadn't even managed to take off my shoulder.

"Shit." I brushed the tie as I was composing my second text.

"I can't stand you. You make my life hell. You completely control everything that we do, or should I say don't do? I hope you enjoy your weekend. I know I will because I won't have to stick your constant groaning. I'm just gonna get drunk and hate your guts."

I went to save it to my phone memory, wiped my tie again at the same time, but in my now slightly drunken haze, I hit the wrong button. My phone flashed a message:

"Your message has been sent to Gorgeous Siobhan."

I gasped. I had really just been sitting, fantasising. I didn't actually mean to let her see any of that. My phone made the Siobhan noise.

"Message received from Gorgeous Siobhan."

I dreaded opening it, and my dread was justified.

"Fuck you. And to think I was just driving into the driveway to try to make up with you. I can honestly say that I don't care if I ever see you again. You are so horrible to me!"

I staggered to my feet and stumbled to the front door just in time to see the back of her racing green car roar up the street. I ran to the gate, and she gave me a one finger salute as she sped off.

I turned and stumbled back towards the door. The next door neighbour just looked at me and tutted in complete contempt. His cardigan, ripped at the elbows, hung over his grotesque belly.

I often wondered how he had gotten so fat, given his absolute antipathy for anything alcoholic. He must have eaten an incredible amount of food. He'd be better off relaxing and having a drink, I thought to myself. I passed on the one finger salute. I didn't want it anyway.

He was kind of justified in his contempt. I could imagine that he and his young family were pissed off at the constant stream of loud, expletive-filled rants that emanated through their walls. But I didn't really give a fuck.

I tried to phone Siobhan. I told myself I wouldn't grovel. I'd just try to ring her once. As I expected, she didn't answer. However, my phone beeped.

"1 message received from Gorgeous Siobhan."

"You really don't expect me to talk to you? I couldn't stand to be near you tonight. I will phone you Tom."

I couldn't work out why she was calling me Tom. Who the hell is Tom?

I got another text from Joan. It was another picture message. I was frightened to open it but excited at the same time.

Wow. She had stripped completely naked and was reclining on her deep black leather sofa. Her heavily tanned body looked immense against this backdrop.

I drank some more whisky.

I put the whole album on repeat, as I had heard "The Riverboat Song" about 20 times by now. I just settled into my whisky with OCS still roaring in the background.

"Never saw it from the start."

I gulped down more whisky and just roared at my own stupidity, then smiled at the possibilities for tomorrow night.

I set the glass down, ate some more cheese and crackers, and realised how drunk I was. I studied the bottle and shrugged my shoulders. For all that was left, there was hardly any need for the glass anymore. I just poured the last of my nectar straight down my throat from the bottle.

I was so drunk, and it was only 10:57. And I had no whisky left.

I found myself imagining all sorts of possibilities. My mind was going all over the place, but I could also feel myself drifting off, with Simon Fowler roaring:

"Then I'm waiting, standing on the corner."

One last look at the photos of Joan. Mmmmmmmmmm.

I was comatose.

Chapter 38
Billy Sloan

I could hear OCS still in the background, but it was being interrupted by a constant low thud. I glanced at my new Tag Heuer. It was three minutes past five in the morning, and I thought I could hear Siobhan banging on the front door.

"Why the fuck did she not just use her key?" I muttered to myself as I dragged myself from my chair.

I was going to be a complete prick and pretend I didn't hear it – and I did for a while. My head was pounding, my mouth felt like it had a layer of foam all over it, I couldn't focus, and I could hardly even stand up. I staggered to the door and saw the outline of Siobhan and someone else turning to walk away. As I opened the door, I realised it wasn't Siobhan or any of her friends. What the hell were two policemen doing at my door?

"Good evening, sir. Are you Colin, husband to Siobhan Hill?"

"I am. What can I help you with? Has Siobhan been arrested? What has she done?"

My God, I was struggling to stand up. I felt like I had a concussion. I just wanted to be sick.

"Could we come in, sir? I'm afraid we have some bad news regarding your wife." He rubbed his chin and stared at his highly polished shoes.

"Don't you dare. That isn't even fucking funny, even by Siobhan's warped sense of humour. So you can go and tell her she didn't fool me."

My head was about to fall off.

"I'm sorry, sir, but my name is Constable Billy Sloan, and I have the unfortunate job of telling you that your wife has been

214

involved in a road traffic collision. I would prefer to come in if you don't mind." He looked serious. I was beginning to believe him.

My temples throbbed loudly. No. Surely not.

"Come in, please." I rubbed the stain on my tie. "You'll have to excuse the state of the place. I've just been sleeping on the sofa, and if I'm honest, I drank a whole litre of single malt."

As he passed me at the door, he removed his cap. He grimaced. It might have been the news he had to tell me, or it might have been the stale odour of whisky dying in me.

The three of us made our way to the kitchen, where I brushed some of the dishes to one side and poured myself a pint of water. I drank it in one mouthful. It didn't help.

"I'm afraid I have very bad news for you, sir. Your wife was involved in an accident, and unfortunately, she didn't survive. There was no other car involved. She died instantly." He was scratching his cheek and looking at his colleague. I reeled away. He must have been mistaken.

"You've got it wrong. She texted me earlier to say she'd ring me in the morning, and she would never do that if she wasn't going to follow through. So you see, you must be wrong."

I rested my elbows on the granite worktop and cradled my head in my hands.

"Sir, we believe she was sending a text message when she crashed. This could have been the cause of the accident."

This news wasn't helping.

My head was thumping so loudly now I wanted to fucking scream, but I couldn't even think to. I pushed the policeman and told him to get the fuck out of my house, that I was going to have him sacked for playing such a sick joke.

He tried to hug me, to comfort me, but I simply didn't want him or anyone else near me. I wanted him to go away. I just wanted to go to bed and nurse this hangover. When I woke up, this awful nightmare would be over. I told them to get out of my house, but they assured me they wouldn't leave until I had a member of my family with me.

The reality and the enormity of what I had just been told were beginning to sink in. Poor Siobhan. If only I hadn't been such a prick. Then the doubts engulfed me. I wanted them to go away so I could rewind the clock and make this not happen. We'd only been married two months.

"Get the fuck out of my house. You are not welcome here. You've got it all wrong. You don't even know what you're talking about. Just get out. I don't want or need anyone near me. Do you fucking understand? Siobhan will be home soon, so you better go and take your sick fucking joke with you."

He motioned to hug me again, but I just stared at him, and I think he got the message this time.

"Is there someone you can ring, sir? You really shouldn't be alone. This is a difficult time for everyone." He ran his hand through his hair and continued to look at his colleague as he spoke to me.

"No shit, Sherlock."

He rubbed his chin and sighed deeply.

"Sir, I am only trying to do my job. You shouldn't be alone. Is there someone we can ring?"

If I'm honest, he did seem to be genuinely concerned.

"Look, how many fucking times do I have to tell you I don't want anyone here?"

I was so confused and couldn't even think straight. I vigorously scratched my head with both hands, but it didn't ease the pain.

"You really need to let your wife's family know the tragic news."

Oh shit. How can I tell them? They will blame me. They never liked me anyway. Siobhan will have phoned Donna and told her we had a row. Donna will blame me. Fuck, the whole O'Neill clan will blame me. They will be glad they have got rid of me out of their family.

He tried to hug me again. This time, I let him. I just broke down and sobbed uncontrollably. My head was splitting, and I didn't believe what had happened, but I was blubbering the way Siobhan did when she watched a chick flick.

He hands me a handkerchief, and I blow my nose. Always graceful. I look at the residue I have produced and find myself wondering why the hell people do that.

"Could you tell her family? I don't think I could. They fucking hate me already."

I begin to imagine what I am going to wear to the funeral. Would I need an overcoat? Do I have a clean white shirt? Black ties need a crisp white shirt. Shit, what did I do with that black tie?

"We could tell her family, of course, but we find that in these situations it would be best coming from you. We could drop you off and go in with you if you like. You really shouldn't be driving. With the shock, and to be honest, you appear to be still drunk. Do you want to go and freshen yourself up? We can wait."

If I was going to do this, then carpe diem.

I ruffled my hair in an attempt to somehow extricate the pain in my head.

"Let's go. It would be better to get this over and done with. I'll just grab a coat."

I took a look around the kitchen and noticed Siobhan's favourite mug with a lipstick ring where she had been drinking her coffee before work yesterday morning.

I got into the back of the car and looked back at my house, our house, with its wooden floors and matching doors. As we pulled off, the policeman asked me for directions to Siobhan's parents' house. I mumbled something. 14 Elgin Street, I think. Then I slouched back in my seat and found myself thinking about the wake.

What do you need? God, the house is a mess. What will I dress Siobhan in?

It was then that it hit me. She was, in fact, dead, and I was on the way to her mum's gaff to break the news.

Fuck. Is there any way out of this?

We pulled up outside their house. It was a quaint old place that Ronnie kept in great order. It was in complete darkness. I looked at my watch. It was nine minutes past six. I suggested that we call back later, but they wouldn't let me prevaricate any longer.

I crawled from the car. My hangover had now taken complete control of me. My head went light, and I stumbled. Constable Sloan grabbed my arm.

We approached the door, and I just wanted to turn and run away, anywhere but here. We rang the doorbell, and after what seemed like an eternity, Ronnie turned on the hall light and opened the door as he fastened his dressing gown. The one Siobhan had bought him for Father's Day last year. He loved that thing.

He took one quizzical look at me with two policemen and just recoiled.

"NOOOOOOOO."

I went towards him, and he punched me square on the nose. I could feel the warm trickle of blood begin to cascade over my upper lip.

"Look at the shape of you!" he screamed. "You drunken bastard. Where is Siobhan? What have you done with her?"

He just stared at me as if I was a piece of dog shit that he had trod on.

"Siobhan died in a car accident, Ronnie. We had a row, and she stormed out. I'm so sorry."

I knew I was blunt, but I couldn't think of any way to dress this up.

"You should be. I told Peggy that our Siobhan marrying you would end up fucking killing her. Fuck, Peggy. Who's going to tell Peggy?"

Peggy appeared at the top of the stairs, bleary-eyed, fastening her robe and wanting to know what all the commotion was about. She took one look at me, bloody-nosed and crying, and said,

"Oh no. What have you done?"

She was always looking to blame me for everything.

"I did nothing. I just got the news myself. Siobhan was killed in a car accident last night, tonight. Fuck, I don't know anymore."

I looked at Billy Sloan, hoping that he would help me out with details. He didn't.

Ronnie was raging and screamed, "She wouldn't have been if she had never married you. You fucking waste of space."

"Now, sir, this isn't helping anyone," interrupted Billy Sloan.

He scratched his head under his cap and looked at me as if realising that I had been right about me not going with him to do this job.

"This is nothing to do with you, plod. You can go anytime you want and take that fucking waste of space with you."

Ronnie put his arm around Peggy and just grunted in my direction.

I was ashamed.

"Sir, I appreciate that this is a difficult time for you, but it is also a difficult time for all of those concerned."

Constable Sloan was doing his best, but to no avail.

"Get him out of my property."

Ronnie was angrier than I had ever seen him before, and trust me, I had seen him angry. He pulled his hair and just slumped into Peggy's arms.

He was distraught.

As I walked away with the policemen, I could hear Peggy saying, "He's drunk. Why is he drunk?"

I just shook my head and didn't look back.

I slouched in the back of the car and reproduced the handkerchief the policeman had given me. I asked him if he minded my blood on it. He just waved his hand and said, "Keep it."

I did.

I arrived back at my house, and Constable Sloan helped me to get out of the car. I stumbled again, breathless now and just wanting to be alone. I was strangely calm and found myself thinking about where I had left my black tie.

I put the key in the door and began to turn the latch, forgetting that I had company. I heard him say something like he was sorry for my loss and that he would call to see me tomorrow, though I couldn't, for the life of me, work out why he would be calling to see me tomorrow.

When I got inside, I rummaged about in the fridge. I just wanted a beer. I had bought a dozen bottles when I bought the whiskey. I twisted the top and drank the first bottle in one gulp. My head was pounding, but I needed a cure.

I opened a second and drank it slowly as my thoughts turned to the wake and the funeral. And Joan.

Fuck. I would have to get the house cleaned, and I definitely needed to get a clean white shirt. Suppose I could always buy one in town tomorrow?

I opened a third, and my head was beginning to clear. I took the third beer up to bed with me and fell asleep hugging it.

Chapter 39
Saturday Morning

I woke feeling freezing. I had spilled the beer all over my new shirt. Fuck. My head was pounding, and I just buried it in my hands.

I carried my head down the stairs, opened the fridge, and took out a beer. I looked at it and thought about whether or not I should drink it. I always had these thoughts when I was hungover.

"Look at you, drunken bastard. When are you going to take control of your life?"

I think I've had this conversation before.

This debate would go on in my head for a while, and then invariably, I would open the beer and slug it down. Today was no different. The debate in my head was still going on, and I could feel myself twisting the lid at the same time. Then the first mouthful would just feel right.

As I swallowed the first mouthful, I began to piece together the night before. I choked and spat beer all over the fridge door. Fuck.

I looked at my watch. It was half two. Jesus. I had slept for a lifetime. Maybe it was just a nightmare, and Siobhan had been calling me all morning while I was in my drunken slumber.

I frantically pulled the house apart, searching for my phone. I couldn't find it anywhere. Fuck, fuck, fuck. Where is it?

Eventually, I found it in the pocket of my now sleep-wrinkled trousers. I pressed the power button, but it was out of charge. I stuck it on the charger and took another mouthful of beer. I keyed in the security code, and when the thing came on, the phone began to beep furiously.

There were 24 missed calls from Donna. FUCK. It must have happened.

Then the text alert started to sound at the same time. The phone was going mad.

Text message from Twin Donna.

Text message from Twin Donna.

Text message from Twin Donna.

I saved her as Twin Donna because she looked so much like Siobhan.

Text message from "John from work" – interesting.

"How are you, sexy boy? Hope you had a good night on your own as you promised me you would. I had great craic with the lads last night, but I missed you. I'm so horny for you. Just played with myself. What time you coming over?"

I allowed myself to smile at the thought of Joan playing with herself. I was just about to jump in the car and drive to her house, but then the phone beeped again.

Message received from Twin Donna.

What to do?

I opened the first message from Donna. It chilled me.

"What the hell? How could you do this again? Siobhan is dead, and it's your fault. She told me yesterday that she just wanted a simple life and a Friday night climbing into bed with you. Then you threw her out. She was heartbroken, and me and her were going to do what we had for the last four or five Fridays—just sit in and talk about how much she loved you. Fuck you. PHONE ME when you get this. For fuck's sake, you only got married two months ago!"

I reeled for a second. Then I thought that I could drive over to Joan's before the shit hit the fan and just get a "hug."

Then the phone beeped again.

"Standing at your front door! You going to let me in or what?"

I stumbled towards the front door and opened it. There was no one there. I looked at the message again and saw that it had been sent at half nine.

I decided to take the bull by the horns and pressed the key that put me through to Donna. I held the phone away from my ear as it rang. After only a second, she answered.

"Where the hell have you been? I've been phoning and texting you all morning. Hell, I even called at your house FIVE times. You must have snibbed the lock. I couldn't get in. My uncle Ronnie is going to kill me."

"Sorry, I just wanted to be alone this morning."

(I could hardly tell Donna that I had fallen into a drunken sleep and woke having forgotten all about the night before.)

"I needed to get my thoughts clear. How are you?"

"How am I? How am I? How the fuck do you think I am? My cousin and best friend was killed last night, and it's all your fucking drunken, stupid, selfish fault. Hope you're proud of yourself."

I stared at the mirror on the lounge wall and reflected on how it needed straightening up.

"Donna, I don't need this shit right now. Siobhan started on me last night, and it was her who stormed out."

"I'm coming over. Hope you're not drinking. Put the kettle on."

Oh shit. Look at the state of this place. Need to get a wash, freshen up, brush my teeth, and clear some space in the kitchen. Fuck, do I even have two clean mugs?

I quickly threw all the loose, dirty crockery in the dishwasher, gave the worktops a rub, un-snibbed the door, and ran upstairs.

Jumped in the shower. Fuck, it was freezing. Just what I needed.

I vigorously scrubbed my teeth as the cold, refreshing water cascaded over my traumatised body—physically and emotionally traumatised.

I quickly towelled myself down, threw on a pair of jeans and a T-shirt, gulped some mouthwash, and swooshed it around my mouth for as long as I could without gagging.

As I walked down the stairs, the front door opened.

I shouted, "Siobhan?"

Donna's head appeared around the doorframe.

"It's Donna," she quipped. "Have you put the kettle on?"

Chapter 40
La Donna

onna and I just stood in the kitchen and stared at each other. The silence was deafening.

She was wearing a pair of tight, faded jeans and a purple T-shirt. I imagined she had just jumped up and thrown on the first thing at hand. She was every bit as beautiful as Siobhan, without the look of weariness that sometimes defined her cousin.

I poured the coffee, and we sipped slowly, still staring at each other.

Donna set her mug on the worktop and moved towards me with her hands outstretched. I felt awkward, set my mug down, and just hugged her. She broke down and cried uncontrollably. Then, suddenly, she started punching me with the underside of her clenched fists. I tried to hold her close—she was hurting me, for God's sake—but she pushed me away and silently mouthed, "How the fuck could you let this happen?"

Like it was my fault.

I just stared at her.

"No point in blaming anyone for this fucking mess."

I felt my nose tingle and remembered Ronnie thumping me in the middle of the night. I moved towards the mirror and grimaced at the sight of my swollen nose and the faint black rings beginning to form under my eyes. Bastard.

"Look at the shape of my face! Your uncle Ronnie's a psycho. He punched the face off me last night, as if I wasn't feeling bad enough."

"He was angry. I talked to him earlier—he wants me to bring you round to his so we can discuss this mess, make arrangements for the wake, etc." She rolled her neck, and her hair swished behind her back. "He was devastated. Surely, you can understand?" She was shaking her hair in front of her at this stage, just before dramatically throwing it back behind her neck again.

She was looking good.

"No fucking way am I going round there for him to lecture me. I'll make my own arrangements for my wife's funeral, thank you very much."

Fuck, I need a drink.

I tugged on the fridge door and stared at the beer in the bottom drawer. As I stuck my hand inside, the bottles rattled.

Donna sighed. "For Christ's sake, can we keep it together here? There are more people this affects than just you. Could we maybe leave the drinking until after we've made some arrangements?"

She walked to the sink and bent down to get a tablet for the dishwasher. I knew I shouldn't have been looking at her like that. I suppose I can console myself with the fact that she reminded me of my dead wife?

Just then, the door knocked.

I opened it to the sight of Billy Sloan standing there with a pathetic look on his face. He motioned to shake my hand, as if that was going to make a difference. I just stared at his outstretched hand. Awkward.

He took his hand away and asked if he could come in. I simply stood aside, and he brushed past me.

"Are you alone?" he asked.

"No, no. Siobhan's cousin Donna is in the kitchen."

Just as I finished, Donna sloped into the hallway.

"You must be Donna. I am very sorry for your tragic loss."

He motioned to shake her hand. Donna, obviously having better manners than me, accepted his greeting with warmth.

"What exactly happened?" she asked.

"All we know is that your cousin's car careered off the road and hit a tree. She died instantly. She didn't suffer."

He had this infuriating habit of rubbing his chin, as if he was deep in thought.

How the fuck does he know she didn't suffer? People talk some shit when it comes to this kind of situation.

"I have our preliminary accident report, which cites extensive head injuries as the cause of death. You'll need this information when you go to register the death."

"Thank you."

I could hear Donna talking, but it wasn't making any sense. They had a lengthy conversation about funeral arrangements—post-mortems, how to go about getting the body home to wake.

It was all a mumble to me. I just couldn't be bothered with this shit.

I was wondering when I could possibly get the time to escape to Joan for a "hug."

Message alert.

John from work: What you at, sexy boy?? What time will I see you? You will love what I have on. You'll love it even more when I take it off xxxx.

Fuck.

I wanted to get rid of these two strangers in my hallway and go ravage Joan.

Donna interrupted my daze. "Who was that?"

She never missed a trick.

Like it was any of her business.

"Just a friend from work. Going to text him, let him know what happened. If you'll excuse me."

I walked towards the living room and stumbled on the empty whiskey bottle, lying exactly where I had left it the night before when I knocked it over.

I fell into my old faithful chair.

I re-read the message from Joan and got excited. I began my reply.

I have some really bad news. Will text you later. Will definitely need a "HUG" today. This is big shit! X

I sent the message and got an instant reply.

Joan: MMMMMMMMMMM, I'm intrigued. Gisa clue?

I walked back into the hall. Donna had obviously had a word with Billy because he now suggested that all three of us go to Ronnie's house to start the ball rolling. He also mentioned that at least one of us was needed at the morgue to identify the body.

I never understood that.

They had her car, her license, her fucking identical cousin— why put anyone through the trauma of identifying an open-headed body?

Donna took over, saying we'd go together after visiting Ronnie and Peggy's. Didn't bother consulting me. What's new?

I checked my phone again.

I didn't want to go. I just wanted to get rid of everyone and head for my 'visit' with Joan. But I couldn't think of a way out.

I agreed, and we made our way to the car.

Donna drove. Billy followed closely behind.

I was shitting myself. Didn't know what to expect.

We sat in the car until Billy arrived at the passenger door, standing there fixing his hat and rubbing his chin. Again with the fucking chin-rubbing.

I walked behind them to the front door. As we neared the step, the door opened.

It was Peggy.

She brushed past Billy and Donna and moved toward me.

I instinctively put my hands up to protect my face.

Peggy just threw her arms around me and cried.

Through her sobs, I could hear her say, "You made my Siobhan so happy."

This was not the reception I was expecting.

Mind you, I still hadn't seen Ronnie.

Peggy let go and took my hand, leading me inside.

Ronnie shook my hand and gave me a hug.

Madness.

"Managed to get Patrick this morning," Ronnie said. "He's flying in from Gatwick in about an hour. I'll collect him."

Ronnie was in control.

Patrick. I liked Patrick. He was a bit of a rocket.

We stood in the O'Neills' front room, which always smelled musty to me. They called it the good room and only ever used it for special occasions.

This was a special occasion.

I hated this room.

Small. Stuffy. Peggy had it crammed with figurines.

It hadn't changed since the first time I met Siobhan's parents. Over-stuffed floral three-piece suite. That sickly mint-green plush carpet that left footprints when you walked on it.

The mantle on the red brick fireplace displayed silver-framed childhood photos of Patrick and Siobhan. Their evolution continued across the oak-veneered sideboard, concluding with the most recent addition—our wedding photo.

We agreed to meet at mine when Patrick arrived, so we could start making arrangements.

They kept talking around me.

I had stopped listening.

They hadn't noticed.

Donna and I said our goodbyes and made our way down the carpeted hallway. Red carpet with black stripes. I always thought it worked well with the magnolia walls.

Good contrast.

Chapter 41
Bleach

We made our way to the car, followed by Billy Sloan. We were to follow him to the mortuary. Donna took my hand. I looked back, and her aunt and uncle just stood there with one arm around each other, waving.

We approached the door, and the smell nearly knocked me over. I just hate the smell of hospitals—so clinical—and the bleach. Yuck.

We were ushered into a waiting room. Comfortable seats, mountain ranges glaring at us from the walls, dried flowers in the corner. I wondered who had set this cold room up. Had they researched ways of making relatives feel at ease? How could you?

We sat there in silence for what seemed like an eternity. I thought that rather than selecting the right décor to make people in this situation feel at ease, they should maybe speed up the process of identification. My God, they knew where we were, and they knew where the body was. What the hell was the hold-up? Donna and I sat in silence.

A dead silence.

The door was eased open, and Billy Sloan walked in, followed by a doctor or someone wearing scrubs. I instinctively stood up and brushed my left thigh with my right hand, ready for the handshake. I noticed a stain on my jeans, which was just in line with a similar stain on my T-shirt. Beer spill?

The doctor shook Donna's hand, and he just stared. I supposed he was noticing just how alike she and Siobhan were. He took my hand and said how sorry he was for our loss.

"You must be Siobhan's husband. If you could follow me, we will get this over and done with as quickly as possible. It's never easy, especially in such tragic circumstances."

232

God, people talk some shit at these times.

We all trudged through the door. As we did, my phone vibrated in my pocket.

John from work "So horny, big boy. Can't wait to ravage you. My fanny is eating the leg of me. What's the big news?"

If only she knew.

My mind wandered to the kinky sex that awaited me as we made our way through the door to the mortuary. I could hardly wait.

Donna was sobbing and gently took my hand again as they unzipped the body bag. I released my hand and stretched my arm around Donna's shoulders. Siobhan's mangled face peered from the slab. Donna shook her head and put it on my shoulder as she cried inconsolably. I nodded as the doctor began to zip the body bag up.

"That's her, OK," I blurted, as if I needed to say something.

My phone vibrated again. John from work. I knew it, but it seemed kind of inappropriate to be reading a message at this time and in this place.

We all exited the room, and I was given a form to sign confirming identification. I scribbled something illegible on the bottom of the form. Donna took my hand, and I quickly led her to the car park. I felt sick.

I pulled a pack of cigarettes from my pocket and fumbled to extricate one. I pulled on the end of it with intent. Donna looked at me and shrugged. I was supposed to be off them, but I needed some kind of comfort. I just shrugged. I could get away with anything at this stage.

Chapter 42
Joan

We were followed back to the house by Billy Sloan. As I turned the key in the latch, he coughed, rubbed his chin, and awkwardly strode up the driveway. I couldn't, for the life of me, think what else he could want. We shuffled into the hallway, and Billy produced some forms that needed signatures. I asked Donna to oblige and made my way to the kitchen.

Billy Sloan followed me and offered his hand. "If there's anything I can do or anything you need, please don't hesitate to contact me." He produced his card and indicated his mobile number at the bottom. I couldn't think how I would need him, but I accepted his card regardless.

By now, Donna had joined us in the kitchen. She handed Billy the forms and said she needed to go home to get showered and changed—she just felt dirty after the morgue. Billy gave a sympathetic smile.

"What time are Ronnie and Peggy arriving?"

I shrugged. "Don't know. I'm going for a walk when I get showered. Just want to be alone and try to get my head round this."

We hugged, and Donna left, assuring me she would see me later.

Thank God I eventually managed to get away. They were melting my head. Besides, I had a better option for some comfort. I showered quickly and pulled on a fresh pair of jeans and a clean navy shirt. I took my earphones out as I approached Joan's door, my heart pounding.

As I reached out to ring the doorbell, the door swung open. Joan had obviously been looking forward to me getting there. She turned, and I followed her through to the bedroom. Her skirt was so short that it revealed the bottom of her butt. Wow. Her suspender belt was so tight that I thought it was going to rip the top of her stockings. As she bent down to turn the bedside light on, I could see that she was going commando. My heart wasn't the only part of my body that was pounding now.

She looked at me and purred, "I hope you have been a good boy. Otherwise, I am going to have to discipline you."

"I've been very naughty, in fact. You wouldn't believe just what has happened." I was about to blurt out everything. She walked towards me, put her finger on my lips, and said,

"Ssh, come here."

As I walked towards her, I couldn't help but stare at her glorious breasts. I loved those surgically enhanced masterpieces. They were standing to attention at the top of the basque. I just wanted to bury my head in them.

She slowly unbuttoned my shirt, and as I went to talk, she placed her finger on my lips again and tutted.

"No talking. You're going for a ride. Just hold on to your seatbelt."

As my shirt slid from my shoulders, Joan ripped at my belt. I was so excited I nearly exploded.

"Stop, stop! Fucking stop! Siobhan is dead!"

Joan recoiled and slumped on the sofa.

"What the fuck? What do you mean? How can this be? What the fuck happened?"

"Car crash. Last night." It was my simple, measured response.

"Holy fuck. I've poured you a wee whisky—over beside the bed. Think you need that!"

"I shouldn't," I said as I gulped it down. "I have so much to do when I get home."

She looked at me quizzically and enquired, "You're not staying?"

"If you're not staying, then we have no time for small talk."

Small talk—I wish! Mind you, it was great to have this diversion at this time in my life.

"I have to go." I was aware that she was ready for sex, but this news had rocked her.

I made for the door.

"You'll come back later? I'm going to run over and see Ronnie and Peggy." I was surprised Ronnie hadn't already told her.

I left.

When I put the key in my own door, I could hear a commotion, and the whisky had hit me in the fresh air. Who the fuck is in my house?

Donna strolled from the kitchen. She looked uneasy as she stared at me, as if she'd worked out I had been drinking. She was wearing a green dress, almost a carbon copy of the one Siobhan had on yesterday. It was uncanny.

"Where have you been? Father Peter is here. He wants to comfort you and see what arrangements you want him to put in place for the funeral. Though I think John Jameson may have given you enough comfort at this stage. Go and freshen up. Try to fucking keep it together."

She turned to walk to the kitchen, and I couldn't help looking at her and wondering.

As I climbed the stairs, I could hear Donna mumbling something about me needing some time to myself.

I got into the shower in the en-suite and was just about starting to make sense of what I was doing when Donna nonchalantly walked in.

"What the fuck! Do you mind?" I was naked in the shower.

"Where the fuck have you been? You smell of whisky!" She rolled her eyes and tutted.

"I went for a walk and ended up at my mate's house. We had a couple of stiff drinks. You're worse than Siobhan."

It was freaky how she seemed to know. Siobhan never, ever questioned me like this.

She just looked at me. In a way, it was almost like Siobhan hadn't died. It was disconcerting having my recently dead wife's lookalike cousin standing in my bathroom, looking at me naked in the shower.

"Really, do you mind? I will be down in five minutes." I was pretending to be embarrassed.

"Just hurry up. Father Peter has been here for over an hour."

I could see the faint outline of her shape through my soap-filled eyes.

"Right, right. I didn't fucking ask him to call. I'll be down when I'm finished. A bit of privacy wouldn't go amiss." I was slobbering through the soap in my mouth.

As she walked out of the bathroom, she looked back, and our eyes locked.

Chapter 43
Yellow Towels

I stepped out of the shower onto the cold Italian marble floor. Siobhan was dead set on making sure every room in the house was just so. I took one of the carefully folded yellow towels—every towel we owned was yellow—from the hot press. After towelling down, I got dressed and stumbled downstairs to find not only Father Peter and Susan, but also Ronnie, Peggy, and Patrick. Outside of Siobhan, he was the only one of the clan who understood me.

Patrick immediately walked towards me and hugged me. I hate this shit. Father Peter offered his hand and his condolences. I gracefully accepted.

Ronnie coughed. "The body will be home tomorrow, so we need to start thinking about where we will wake Siobhan and how we are going to sort out the next couple of days up to the funeral."

"Hold on to fuck! What do you mean, 'where are we going to wake Siobhan'? We will wake her here in my own house, and if you don't mind, I will make the arrangements for my own wife's funeral and cremation."

Peggy was disgusted at me cursing in front of the 'family' priest.

"What do you mean, cremation?" interrupted Ronnie. "My daughter is not getting cremated. No way." He tugged on his ancient black tie and glanced towards Peggy for support.

He sobbed.

"Sorry, I think you'll find that I am, in fact, Siobhan's next of kin. Did you ever talk to her about what she wanted to happen if she died? Did you? Because I have. And if I'm not mistaken, she has explicitly outlined her wishes to Susan too!" I coughed and looked at Susan.

The atmosphere was tense. I knew Ronnie didn't want to wake Siobhan at my house, and I knew Peggy wanted to take control of all the arrangements. It's where Siobhan got it from. And although I knew I hadn't been the best husband, I wasn't going to let them bury my wife the way they wanted. It would be the way I wanted.

I stared at Donna, almost pleading with her to say something.

"It's true, Uncle Ronnie. Siobhan did want to be cremated, and she wants her ashes to be buried in your back garden under the apple tree. She has said that since she was about six years old. I know it's not what you might want to hear, but those were her wishes."

Father Peter shifted uneasily in my chair. "Don't you think we should consider everyone's feelings? I mean, Ron"—I had never heard anyone call him Ron—"and Peggy were, sorry, are Siobhan's parents. Surely their feelings should be considered too."

I was seething. "What the fuck has it got to do with you? No one even asked you to come to my house. I think your job is to sit and listen and do what you're asked to do—service, I think they call it."

"There's no need for that language or tone," suggested Peggy as she shifted uneasily in her longish black dress and looked at the priest in a conciliatory way.

I was getting fed up to my back teeth with all these people being in my space. I needed to see Joan again.

I also remember thinking how strange it was that people always seem to have an endless supply of black clothes for these situations.

"Look, Peggy, I am going to do this my way—or should I say, the way Siobhan asked me to do it! Surely that is simple enough for all of you to understand." I was on a roll. "Father, if you wouldn't mind leaving us to get the arrangements sorted, we will be in touch when we've made decisions."

Father Peter looked quizzically at Peggy. She shrugged—what else could she do? They were in my house. The priest dragged himself from the chair, his face red with rage. He slumped over Peggy and hugged her uneasily. Peggy pulled herself to her feet and motioned towards the front door.

The priest took the hint and trounced from the living room with Peggy in tow. I could hear Peggy making excuses for my behaviour. I was going to react but frankly couldn't be bothered anymore. I just wanted to get in touch with Joan.

Peggy returned to the kitchen and mumbled through her tears, "Can we all try to stay calm?"

She brushed the front of her black dress to try and smooth out some of the wrinkles she had acquired when sitting.

I retreated to the toilet and sent Joan a text.

Look, we will have to play it by ear until all this, but if I can get away, I will.

I got an immediate reply.

No, I can't believe this has happened, but don't worry, everything is going to be okay. I'm going to Ronnie's now, call over later if you get a chance.

I almost dropped the phone down the toilet.

There's nothing I would love more, but Siobhan's family are all here. They've fucking taken over my life. Can I text you if they go?

Laters.

Came the immediate reply.

Chapter 44
House Proud

When I returned to the kitchen, Peggy was rummaging in the cupboard under the sink, pulling out the cleaning supplies and throwing them onto the floor. I could hear her sobbing. I slowly placed my hand on her shoulder and fell to my knees. She grabbed me and held on as if she were about to fall off a cliff. We just embraced for a few minutes until Ronnie coughed and enquired whether we were going to get the cleaning started.

Peggy and I pulled ourselves to our feet and shuffled awkwardly. I grabbed the bathroom cleaner and said I would start upstairs. Donna took the vacuum cleaner and said she would begin vacuuming the bedrooms and stairs. Peggy was going to change the beds, and Ronnie and Patrick were charged with brushing and mopping the wooden floors that covered every inch of our ground floor.

We all set about our tasks. With all hands on deck, we got the house knocked into shape in no time. I couldn't believe how well it looked. Siobhan would spend hours on a Friday night, and the house would never look this good.

I was so glad when we had finished, as I thought they would leave and I could contact Joan.

"Right, now let's make arrangements."

Ronnie threw me. He had removed his black tie, and there was a noticeable drip of sweat emanating from just under his left nostril. He wiped it with his ever-present napkin, which he kept in his trouser pocket.

"What do we need to think about?" I asked.

"Well, let's see. Where are we going to put the coffin? I think the back of the living room. We'll need to move the table to the window, then people who call can congregate in the kitchen and front room. We need a crucifix and candles. We need to cover all the mirrors. We need a good photo of Siobhan to put beside the coffin. That policeman said she was so badly hurt that it would probably be best to keep the lid closed."

After what we had seen in the mortuary, the lid was staying closed.

Peggy was in full flow, even as she blubbered. Tears were dripping down her chin.

"The Mass," she continued. "We will need to sort out music and readings. Father Peter will celebrate the Mass. What will we put on poor Siobhan for the coffin?"

I couldn't help thinking that this was a moot point, given that the intention was to keep the lid closed.

"My God, what music will we use? We have to finish with The Lord Is My Shepherd. Nearer My God to Thee will be for the offertory procession. What about the Psalm? Will we have The Lord Is My Shepherd for the Psalm and finish with that Michael Joncas hymn On Eagle's Wings?"

"I love that On Eagle's Wings," interjected Patrick. He wasn't really getting the mood.

"Look, we can sort that all out with Father Peter. We will let him lead us with regard to the Mass," suggested Susan, who was looking completely lost. She was shaking and sobbing. I could tell she just wanted to be anywhere else—too many memories.

"How's your mum coping, Colin?" pried Ronnie. He was being so considerate.

Fuck. I haven't even told my mum. Can't do that tonight. She will be here and refuse to leave. No Joan.

242

"I haven't told her yet. I intend to call later. I don't want to tell her on the phone. She loved Siobhan like a daughter—more than she loves me, I think."

"God, we better go and let you get in touch with your family. Do you want Donna to go with you?" suggested Peggy.

"I don't want to. I think Colin has to do this himself. We should go and let him get on with things."

I was glad that Donna was being sensible. She started crying as she pulled a picture of Siobhan from her coat pocket. They trundled out in procession, all hugging me as they left.

Fuck. I do hate this shit.

Chapter 45
Joan Two

I returned to the kitchen and poured a beer. I was just about to take a slug when the doorbell rang.

"For fuck's sake, I wish they would just leave me alone."

I wasn't going to answer it. But then I thought better of it.

I walked slowly to the door and turned the latch. Joan was standing there, staring at me. I grabbed her arm and pulled her inside.

"What are you doing here? Fuck, Siobhan's family just left."

"I know. I've been sitting outside in the car waiting for them to go. I thought they'd never leave! I figured you could use a hug."

I put my arm around her, and she kissed me passionately, ramming her tongue in and out of my mouth. She unbuttoned her coat, letting it fall to the ground, revealing her completely naked body.

I buried my head in her breasts, and she turned her back to me, hands outstretched, leaning heavily against the wall. I quickly undid my trousers and slid into her, holding onto her waist as I moved with intent. I climaxed quickly, and she groaned.

We kissed.

I told her I had to go to my mum's and break the bad news. I suggested she come back later when I returned. She didn't want to leave me alone, but I assured her I had to do this by myself and was looking forward to seeing her later.

The truth was, I just wanted her to go. She had served her purpose at this stage.

I told her I'd text when I was on my way back so she could come round and spend the night. Reluctantly, she put on her coat and hugged me with a closed-mouth kiss. Then she was gone.

She told me later that she went to Ronnie and Peggy's to sympathize. They were so glad to see her that they didn't even ask how she'd found out.

She laughed when she recounted it. Ronnie had said, "Here, let me take your coat." She declined, saying she wasn't staying.

I ran upstairs, washed my face, brushed my teeth, and changed my shirt. As I revved the engine, I realized I was probably well over the limit for driving, but I couldn't let that small detail stop me now.

As I turned out of the driveway, I caught my neighbor's disapproving glance.

I was tempted to give him another salute.

If only he knew.

That judgmental glare will disappear when he finds out what's happened.

I allowed myself a small smile, imagining him shaking my hand and hugging me with condolences when he calls to the wake.

Fuck, people should be careful how they judge others.

Chapter 46
My Good Shoes

As I turned the corner onto the one-way street at the top of my road, a wave of blind panic hit me.

A random police roadblock.

The blue lights circled in slow, suspended animation, and I was pulled over.

As I slid down the window, I fumbled four pellets of Wrigley's Extra from their tinfoil casing—a vain attempt to mask my whisky-laden breath.

Futile.

"Good evening, sir. Can I see your driver's license?"

In the dusky light, with the glare of the torch in my face, I couldn't quite make out the officer's features. But I recognized the voice.

"Colin? How are you?"

It was Billy Sloan.

"I'm devastated. How would you be?"

I was hoping my response would garner sympathy.

"I understand. Hope you got it all sorted with Siobhan's family. Hope you're sober, big man." He rubbed his chin and cleared his throat.

"Well, I'd be lying if I said I hadn't had a stiffener, but just one."

I was hoping that would be enough to get me out of this.

"I'd say you've had more than one." His voice was measured. "I'm not sure I can ignore this."

Beads of sweat were forming on my brow—copious, like Ronnie's upper lip earlier.

"Tell you what," Billy sighed. "Given the circumstances, I'll let this slide if you park up at the end of the street and call a taxi."

"Thanks, Billy." I used his name in an attempt to gain his confidence. "I was only driving down to my mum's to break the bad news."

He didn't smile.

"Tell you what," he repeated. "Drive on, but do me a favor— take it easy and avoid Timbey Park. There's another roadblock there. Not sure they'd be as sympathetic as me."

"Cheers, Bill." Over-familiar, I know, but hey—he'd just let me off with murder.

I engaged first gear and rolled down the street.

I walked into my mum's house in a daze.

From the front room, a loud rendition of We Will Rock You seeped through the door.

"Where's Siobhan?"

That was always my mum's first question when I arrived alone.

"Did you hear a girl was killed in an awful accident last night? I hope it's no one we know."

She always jumped from one conversation to another before finishing the first.

Fuck. Make it easy for me, why don't you?

"She phoned me last night," Mum continued. "She seemed upset, said she was on her way to Donna's for the weekend. I hope you haven't upset that wee girl."

She shook her head.

"I was surprised, though. She said she'd call to take me shopping today, and she didn't. She wasn't answering her phone either. I hope she's alright."

She was, as always, wearing her apron. She lived in the kitchen, constantly cooking and baking—her way of showing she cared.

"That's why I'm here," I muttered. "Can I get a drink?" I motioned toward the kitchen.

"I think you've had enough! I hope you're not driving in that state."

She had an infuriating way of stating the obvious—and being right.

"Fuck this, I have something to tell you. I really could do without the lecture."

Dread clawed at my stomach.

"What's wrong?"

"A drink?"

"Sit down. What do you want? I think I have some of that whisky you like, left over from Christmas."

She scratched her head and walked toward the kitchen.

It was the smallest room in the house, yet somehow, she managed to make the most beautiful food in that tiny space. She'd recently redone it in anticipation of visitors before the wedding— cream cupboards, dark green tiles, the cooker facing the fridge.

There was only one open shelf, and that's where she kept the alcohol.

She reached for the bottle and poured a minuscule drop into a wine glass.

"Keep pouring."

She gave me that disapproving look only a mother can perfect.

She swayed back into the living room and handed me the glass. Just as I reached for it, the words tumbled from my mouth.

"Siobhan's dead."

The glass slipped from her hand, smashing against the tiled floor, spilling expensive whisky all over my favorite shoes.

Typical. Always given to drama and overreaction.

"You better be joking," she screamed, slapping my face.

I stood up, staring at her in disbelief.

"What happened? Where is she? Do her ma and da know?"

Forty-fucking-questions.

"Yes, everyone knows. That's why I came here—to tell you before you heard from someone else."

I rubbed my face, still stinging from the slap, and looked at her in disgust.

Silence.

"It was Siobhan who was killed in that car accident last night."

Mum was hysterical now.

My brother slouched in from the music room.

"What's wrong? Where's Siobhan? I heard this brilliant Counting Crows song—"

"I just know she'll love it. What's wrong with the drama queen?" Joe continued, barely glancing at Mum.

"Don't you fucking dare call me a drama queen," she squealed, running into the kitchen. She ripped a few sheets from the upright kitchen roll holder, blowing her nose and wiping her eyes.

"Siobhan was killed in a car accident last night."

Joe just stared. He visibly paled before slumping back into the green armchair. The one that sat in line with the blue chair, both opposite the red sofa. Shabby chic, Mum called it.

Composed now, he said, "What the fuck happened? That wasn't her that was killed on Annadale Avenue?"

He turned toward the kitchen just as Mum loudly excreted snot into her napkin.

"I told you we'd know who that was."

"Where is she?" Mum blubbered.

I just wanted to get out of there.

"What's happening? When's the funeral?" Joe asked.

"Oh fuck. Funeral. I can't take this in. Is she in your house?" Mum was beside herself.

"No, they're doing a post-mortem. The coffin will be released tomorrow morning."

"Do you want to have the wake here?" she asked, her voice rising in panic. "Might be better. You wouldn't want memories of beautiful Siobhan lying in your house in a coffin. Oh my God, Siobhan is dead."

Still flying.

"Nah, I already talked it over with the O'Neills. The wake will be at our house. It's what Siobhan would have wanted."

I wiped my whisky-stained shoe on the back of my jeans and asked if there was any chance of a drink.

Mum pulled me into a hug. "I'm so sorry."

For the first time, I broke down.

A Mother's Love's a Blessing.

I was crying uncontrollably.

"Do you want something to eat?" she asked, because food was her answer to everything.

"No, thanks. I just want to get home and be alone." I kept rubbing my shoe against my jeans, as if I could scrub everything away.

"No way," Joe interjected.

He seemed… strange.

"We'll come with you, help you tidy up, and stay with you."

"Joe's right," Mum agreed. "You can't be alone. Let me grab a few things and we'll come with you."

"For fuck's sake, I just want to be alone," I snapped.

"Well, you're not driving home in that state," she shot back. "Joe will drive and I'll come with you. We need to get your house tidied."

She shook her head, dazed. "My God, is this really happening?"

She was already removing her apron, and in one fluid motion, she had hung it up and slipped into her coat.

There was no point in arguing.

I gave in, reluctantly.

As we moved toward the car, Mum placed her hand on my shoulder and kissed my cheek.

A moment I would never forget.

I felt human.

As we pulled into the driveway, I noticed Joan's car parked strategically across the street.

I opened the front door and stepped aside, letting Mum and Joe enter first.

Donna walked up the stairs just as we came in.

"Hi," she said, glancing between Mum and Joe.

My God, she let herself in without even telling me.

This was an unwelcome development.

She turned to come back down, and Mum met her on the third step.

They hugged and cried.

"This is tougher for you than anyone else, love," Mum sniffled.

A Mother's Love's a Blessing.

Donna just stared at me over Mum's shoulder, shrugged slightly, and held on.

We moved uneasily into the kitchen.

My phone vibrated in my pocket.

I slipped into the toilet to check.

A text from Joan.

"I haven't left and I won't. I want to make you feel better. Will wait all night if I have to!"

I replied:

"OK. Will do my best to get rid of them. It won't be easy."

Chapter 47
House Prouder

Mum had already started with the vacuum when I came back downstairs. I put my arm on her shoulder and assured her that the O'Neills had already done all the cleaning. She stepped on the off button and began to put Henri away. She opened the fridge door and took out the loaf, butter, ham, and coleslaw from the fresh food drawer. Taking a knife from the cutlery drawer, she proceeded to make a mountain of sandwiches using the large bread knife she had taken from the mahogany knife block. It was all she knew—she had to help, and this was what she did best.

It was almost as if I wasn't there as all three of them started to reminisce about Siobhan.

"I remember going to see Neil Young at the Waterfront with her. She got all dressed up and was just so in the zone. Fuck, she sang along with every word of every song. She gave me such a hug when the encore finished—she loved her music," asserted Joe.

"Aye, she loved that concert," continued Donna. "She always loved talking about you and your love of music. She would laugh sometimes at how she thought she married the wrong brother."

My God, can they hear themselves?

"Ah, now, we all know she loved Colin more than she loved music. He made her sing," Mum joined in.

"Remember the time she tucked her skirt into the back of her knickers at Joe's wedding? Fuck, I laughed. She walked the whole way up to the front of the chapel with her arse hanging out, strutting and making sure everyone saw her. She looked so gorgeous. It was only when she sat down and felt the coldness of the pew against her bare cheeks that she realised what she'd done. Then, typically

Siobhan, she stood up and took a bow. The whole chapel just burst into rapturous applause. She had that effect on people."

I was getting fed up with this, and a naked Joan was waiting patiently in the car.

Laughing now, Joe kept it going. "We went to see this Queen tribute band one night in The Empire, and she was singing so loud the band stopped and invited her onto the stage. They let her sing 'Somebody to Love' à la George Michael. The place erupted. She wasn't a bad old singer. She was so high when she got off the stage that she made me take her dancing at Thompson's because she was too excited to sleep. Definitely an entertainer, that one."

I knew none of this. I hadn't realised Joe and Siobhan were so close. I should have—she was never out of my mum's house, and that's where he lives. I felt a wee tinge of jealousy. I knew I shouldn't, but I did. Don't ask me why—I just did.

"When was this?" I enquired.

"About four years ago. Remember when you went to Portugal for a week golfing with Sean? She probably told you, and you've forgotten."

She definitely hadn't told me.

I would have remembered this.

Joe threw in the bit about me being in Portugal because he knew I wasn't playing golf. He'd found out I'd been having a fling with a girl I met at the pub—she had told him all about it without realising he was my brother. By mentioning it, he knew it would stop me from asking too many questions. Bastard.

"What about the time she started salsa dancing? Remember? She would come into our house singing and dancing for us all. Fuck, she could brighten up any room," Mum said, smiling at her reminiscences.

"Right, right, I can't cope with this right now, please." I was beginning the process of getting them out of my house, piling on the sympathy. "It's too soon. I don't want to think of her in the past tense. Please."

Mum hugged me again, and I asked if they would all mind leaving so I could sit alone and watch the DVD of our wedding day. I thought this would pluck at their heartstrings. I couldn't think of any other way to get rid of them.

"Oh, I would love to see that again. Siobhan looked so radiant that day."

Radiant? That is a word people often use to describe brides, never any other time.

I looked sympathetically at Mum and said I needed to be alone, hoping they would understand. Initially, they were having none of it, but with my insistence, they soon got the message. Joe suggested they all go to the Errigle for a drink and wanted me to join them. I looked at him in amazement, still keeping up the charade, and said I couldn't face company. I didn't think it was appropriate for me to be out in a bar at this stage.

Mum playfully slapped Joe's arm and rebutted his suggestion. "It's not right. We should just go home—we can have a drink there. Donna, you come with us. Joe, you drive Colin's car, and you can get a taxi home." She turned to me. "Are you sure you want to be alone, son? I hate leaving you here to rattle about in this big house on your own. Are you sure you'll be okay?"

"I'll be fine, Mum. I just want to be alone with my memories. I will call you if I need anything, or if I need company, I'll get a taxi to yours. Thanks." I rubbed my shoe on my jeans once more.

As I waved goodbye at the front door, I could hear Joan's car engine revving—she must have had the heater on. I waited until I knew they were out of the street and was just about to phone Joan when the doorbell rang. I ran to the door and opened it quickly. My next-door neighbour, who was putting his bin out, just glanced, shook his head, and sighed.

Chapter 48
Wrong Room

Joan hugged me like she was never going to see me again. I wanted sex.

I started to unbutton her coat, but she began to say how sorry she was for being so insensitive earlier. I put my finger to her lips and said, "Ssh." I took her by the hand and led her to the bedroom. She looked uneasy.

"You okay?"

"This is your bedroom, you know... you and Siobhan's."

I looked at her quizzically. Who else did she think might sleep there?

"Yes. Is that a problem? It never was before!"

"Well, you know—dead man's shoes and all that." She scrunched her face and nodded away from the room.

"Sorry, wasn't thinking. We can go next door—the spare room."

"Are we sure this is a good idea? Appropriate?" For the first time ever, I noticed a vulnerability in her.

"We're here now. What else are we going to do—sit and talk about my mess? I've done nothing else all day." I tenderly put my hand on her shoulder.

"Our mess. I feel this too, you know." She slipped her hand around my waist.

"Okay, okay, let's just go into the spare room and lie in silence. I could do with a hug."

This was just my excuse to get her into bed at any cost. I knew we would be ravaging each other in minutes.

We walked to the spare room. Joan removed a litre bottle of Jameson from her pocket, took off her coat, and climbed under the blankets with nothing on but her shoes and a smile. I removed everything except my boxer shorts and climbed into bed beside her. We hugged.

We alternated drinking the whiskey from the bottle.

We just lay there in silence for what seemed like an eternity. Then she turned to face me, and our lips touched. We started to kiss passionately, tongues lashing. Joan moved her hand under the blanket and slid it slowly between my legs. I was so turned on.

She moved her head under the blanket, licking my chest as she made her way downward. I could feel her warm mouth envelop me. I lay back and groaned. She arched her back, got on her knees, and took me all the way down her throat. She licked her way back up to my mouth. We kissed again, and she slid over me, rocking up and down. I grabbed her beautiful tits and thrust into her as furiously as I ever had.

We climaxed simultaneously. She rolled off me, grabbed her coat, and pulled a pack of Marlboro Lights from her pocket. Flicking open her Zippo, she lit two cigarettes at once. Pulling heavily on one, she handed the other to me.

I dragged at the tip and exhaled with a sigh.

"You okay?" she asked.

As she pulled the cigarette from her lips, it stuck, and she inadvertently knocked the lit end off onto the quilt. I jumped and turned on the light. We quickly extinguished the smouldering ember. Laughing, we continued to smoke.

I left the light on—I knew she liked to see what she was doing.

We stubbed out our cigarettes, and Joan climbed onto the bed behind me. She began to massage my shoulders, circling her hands from my shoulder blades up to my neck and down to the base of my back. It felt good.

I lay still as she reached into her coat again, pulling out a bottle of baby oil. I heard the slap of her hands as she warmed it between them. Then she placed her lubricated hands onto my back, slowly circling again.

She became more industrious, moving her hands more aggressively, occasionally letting them slide down over my cheeks. Her fingers teased my arse, then her right hand slid between my legs. I arched my back slightly to allow access. She caressed my balls, rubbing me again.

I tried to roll over, but she squeezed her knees against my sides, holding me in place. I submitted. I felt her warm breath as she licked me, her tongue probing, fingers dancing. She stroked me firmly, rhythmically, until I was lost.

I woke some time later to find Joan massaging my chest. I pulled myself from the bed. She looked bemused.

I had a feeling we had to stop this.

I pulled my discarded shorts from under the duvet and stepped into them. As I slapped them around my waist, Joan sighed and pulled herself out of bed.

"We done here?"

"I just know that if we continue, we'll be caught, and this isn't the right time to get caught. You better go." I stumbled as I climbed into the left leg of my jeans.

Joan wasn't too pleased but begrudgingly accepted my request.

We walked to the front door. We kissed, and she turned to leave.

"I'll see you tomorrow," she said with a smile, blowing me a kiss.

Confused, I hesitated. "I don't think I'll get away."

"At the wake, dummy."

She laughed as she clicked down the driveway. I stood at the door, waiting for her car to pull away.

Chapter 49
La Donna Too

As I turned, I saw a taxi pull up and Donna alight. She walked up to me and hugged me. I just hoped she couldn't smell sex on me. She sighed and asked why I was standing at the door.

"Have you been smoking again? I hope not. We all have to keep it together here, Colin."

"What does it matter? I'll stop again when this mess is over." At least the smell of smoke had disguised the odour of sex.

"Can I come in?" She appeared to be a bit worse for wear.

I moved to the side and gestured toward the kitchen. She brushed past me, stumbling slightly.

"You okay? Mum make you drink all that wine?"

"Aye, I needed to get my head sorted. Do you have any Merlot?"

As I went to the wine cupboard, the house phone rang. I pointed at it, and Donna answered.

"Of course I'm here—neither of us wanted to be alone." She looked at me and rolled her eyes.

She was silent for a moment. "Please don't come round. Colin and I are just sitting, talking, and sorting things out for the funeral. Leave it till tomorrow, please. I'll stay here with Colin—I can sleep in the spare room."

Silence.

"When I got back to Siobhan's, Joe and Colin's mum were here, so we went down to hers and had a couple of glasses of wine. Colin is fine—he's upset, but I'm sure you understand that. We were just

261

going to head to bed. We're both wrecked. She was his wife, and she was my best friend and cousin."

God, she was such a natural liar.

Silence.

"Okay, I'll see you here about half eight. Night-night. Would you give Auntie Peggy a hug from me? Big hug to you. Love you all!"

She hung up. "Fuck, he can be a nightmare. Always criticising, no matter what."

I handed Donna the bottle of wine and a corkscrew. I hate those cheap wines with a screw top.

I needed to shower. I motioned toward the stairs and promised to return in five minutes. I bounded up, ran into the spare room, tidied the bed, lifted the discarded baby oil, opened the window, and placed the half-empty whiskey bottle on the dresser beside the door.

I climbed into the shower in my bedroom and let the water trickle over me. Placing my hands against the glass surround, I let the warm water massage my back. Great.

Having sorted myself out, I walked into the kitchen and noticed Donna had almost finished the wine.

"You thirsty?"

She looked at me and laughed. "What do you think? It's been a strange day, don't you think?"

"Indeed. Strange."

I went to the drinks cabinet and pulled out a bottle of single malt I'd had for years. It was for a special occasion—this seemed appropriate. I rinsed out my whisky tumbler and poured a large glass. The second bottle of Merlot clinked against my whisky bottle as I set them on the breakfast bar and pulled myself onto the high chair, facing Donna.

We sat and drank in silence. I realised I hadn't eaten all day, and it was 10:30. I didn't want to eat.

"Fancy a Chinese?" Donna asked, grimacing as she popped the cork from the wine. "If you were a proper gentleman, you would have opened that." She laughed, plonking the wine on the bar.

"Not really, but I suppose I should eat something, or this—" I pointed at the whisky glass "—will go straight to my head."

"It already has!" Donna giggled.

I rummaged through the drawer below the cutlery and found a menu for the local Chinese takeaway. I handed it to Donna and went to get my phone, which I'd left in the bedroom.

Joan had texted.

I wish I could have stayed all night and comforted you. Will see you tomorrow. Think I'm falling in love with you. Xxxx

My blood ran cold.

Fuck. The last thing I needed was someone falling in love with me. Not good.

I didn't respond.

I deleted the message and handed the phone to Donna. She found the number on the front of the menu, called, and ordered chicken curry with fried rice, satay beef with noodles, spring rolls, and a portion of prawn crackers.

She looked at the phone, pressed the stop button, and smiled.

"Fuck, you must be hungry."

"Always better to have too much than too little, I find, with Chinese food."

I laughed and slugged my whisky. Donna bubbled the wine through her nostrils and giggled. ·

"Rather be looking at it than looking for it," I added.

We drank as if we'd never seen alcohol before. We devoured the food—every last bit—and just sat drinking and laughing.

It was a haze.

I heard the alarm scream at eight o'clock and stretched my curled-up body. I rolled over in bed and felt my foot hit against another leg. I instinctively put my arm around Siobhan and buried my head into her back.

"Fuck, I'm dying."

I jumped out of bed in one bound as a fully clothed Donna turned to face me.

"What the fuck? What happened? How did we end up here?" I stammered, relieved to see I was still clothed too.

"Don't worry, we didn't do anything. We got pissed and just cuddled each other to sleep. Have you got any water up here?"

She was so fucking cool about this.

"This isn't good. Did you say Ronnie and Peggy were coming round this morning? What time?" My head throbbed.

"Half eight. What time is it?"

I looked at my watch. "Half five." I was confused. Siobhan always had the alarm set for exactly eight o'clock.

"I re-set it to give us time for a cuddle and some preparation before they get here."

Cuddle?

"Get some water and get back into bed. I'll re-set it for half seven. Stop fucking worrying. Have you got any paracetamol? My head's splitting."

I trundled downstairs, filled two pint glasses with cold water from the fridge, and rustled around in the medicine cupboard for headache tablets. I needed some myself.

As I re-entered the bedroom, Donna was just walking out of the en suite. I couldn't help but notice—she had such a good body.

"Did you get the tablets?"

I handed her the packet and one of the pint glasses of water. Nervously, I climbed back into bed and tugged the quilt up around my neck.

After re-setting the clock, Donna turned to me and wrapped her arm around my waist.

This just felt wrong.

She pulled herself into my shoulder, and we dozed off.

Chapter 50
My Head Hurt

Startled by the alarm, we woke. We looked at each other and silently agreed—no one needed to know about this.

After showering separately, we got dressed and went downstairs. I put on a fresh pot of coffee, grabbed my car keys, and headed for the door. I needed milk and the paper.

The car was gone.

I ran back inside, panicked. "My car's been stolen!"

Donna laughed—not the reaction I was expecting.

"Your car's at your mum's house. Remember? Joe took it last night."

I exhaled. Right.

"Take my car. What do you need?" She rummaged in her handbag. I didn't answer, just took the keys and left.

When I returned, the smell of frying filled the house. It was buzzing with people. The O'Neills had arrived. My mum was there too, along with Joe, busying herself in the kitchen.

My head throbbed.

Peggy hugged me without saying a word.

Ronnie cleared his throat. "What time is the coffin arriving?"

Fuck. The coffin.

"I don't know. Would you mind calling the undertaker?"

"Will do, son."

He called me son. Wow.

Mum just smiled that knowing smile, rubbing my upper arm as I made my way to the fridge for some water.

"I'm sure you two talked into the wee small hours," Peggy said. "I'll go make the beds. You were probably too tired this morning to even think about that."

Typical Peggy. Always helpful.

When she returned, she smiled at Donna. "I knew our Flo raised you well—you wouldn't even know that spare room had been slept in."

Donna smiled back. "She taught me well, indeed."

I felt the blood drain from my face. My head pounded harder.

Ronnie reappeared, clearing his throat. "They say it's on its way. Should be here in about twenty minutes."

"That's good," Mum interrupted. "We should all have breakfast in us by then."

I didn't want any fucking breakfast, but arguing was pointless. I nodded.

We all gathered at the dining table. Breakfast was served with care, like some kind of ritual. I poured tea for everyone, pushing my potato bread around my plate. I cut up the sausages and bacon but couldn't stomach eating them. Across from me, Patrick devoured his food. Donna smiled at me as she swallowed a piece of fried soda bread.

As Mum cleared the last plates, a heavy knock sounded at the door.

It was here.

Mum removed her apron—had she brought that with her?—and rushed to the door, already sobbing. She tugged at the latch.

"We have brought the remains."

I pitied these men in black. Three of them. What a miserable job. There had to be a high suicide rate in their ranks.

Mum thanked them, stepping aside as they rolled the coffin into the hallway.

"Where shall we place the remains?" one of them asked.

Mum motioned toward the living room.

They wheeled the coffin past the gathered family. Everyone was crying. Everyone except me and Donna.

I glanced at the brass plaque on the lid.

Siobhan Hill Died January 6th, 2019 Aged 33 Requiem in Pace.

The undertaker pursed his lips and nodded as he passed me.

I smiled.

They placed the coffin exactly where Peggy indicated. She pulled a lighter from her pocket and lit the church candles she had arranged on a lace-covered side table—one she must have brought with her. A framed photo sat beside the candles: Siobhan in her wedding dress, smiling.

I hadn't seen that picture before. Must have been taken in the O'Neill's garden before she left for the chapel.

I thought about being a bollocks and insisting on a photo of my choice, but I couldn't be bothered.

They were all crying now. Even Donna.

I wanted to go to Joan's house.

She shrugged and slipped into the wake room. She was in her element, hugging everyone. Ronnie, I thought, wasn't going to let go.

She said everyone at the office was devastated. She knew she had to come and pay her respects. She was surprised more people hadn't arrived yet.

The doorbell rang again.

It had started for real.

Paul arrived, accompanied by our cousin Michelle. Michelle just blended in—the kind of person you wouldn't notice, but whose absence you'd feel.

Chapter 51
The Tissues.

It was only ten past eleven when the doorbell rang. A fresh wave of sniffles filled the room as Mum and Peggy handed out tissues.

Father Peter and Joan stood at the door, both resplendent in black. Joan looked stunning—black suit, medium heels, a fur stole draped over her cleavage. As she stepped aside to let the priest enter first, she parted the stole just enough to give me a glance.

I was so turned on.

"I thought you'd have waited to come with the others from work," I whispered as she hugged me and kissed my cheek.

Across the room, Donna caught my eye. Her stare—it was exactly the way Siobhan used to look at me. For a second, it was like Siobhan was still here.

"Who's your woman with the black suit and the cleavage?" Michelle missed nothing.

"Just a secretary from work. Bit of an exhibitionist. She hasn't left for hours." Nonchalant. But Michelle wasn't fooled. She just smiled. She knew.

I managed to steal a moment alone with Joan. "What the fuck are you doing? Everyone's getting suspicious at your continued presence."

She smirked. "Relax. I'm doing what I have to do. Ronnie and Peggy would be shocked if I left."

I smiled.

"I could do with a hug."

She raised an eyebrow. "I'm a bit tied up here."

I shrugged.

She laughed. "I wish."

Incorrigible.

Laughter boomed from the kitchen. I wandered in to see what the craic was. My friends stood around, doubled over, pints in hand.

I smiled. The room fell silent.

"For fuck's sake, continue, please. Good to see you all."

I wondered if there was a collective noun for a group of awkward young men.

"How you keeping, Collie?" Stephen, the icebreaker.

"You know, had better weekends."

They all shifted uncomfortably as I pulled a case of beer from the fridge and handed them out. I found the bottle opener—inside the dishwasher, where I'd absentmindedly left it.

"You hear the one about the guy who writes to Dear Deirdre?" Stephen jumped in, and I was relieved.

"'Dear Deirdre, I was standing at my bedroom window looking at my next-door neighbor's topless daughter. I couldn't help myself—I just started knocking one out. I looked round, and my wife was standing there watching me, arms folded. My question is: does this make her a pervert?'"

We all howled. Ally nearly choked on his beer.

"Aye, what about this one—'I made a hotel out of small cheese biscuits... it's not exactly the Ritz.'"

Ally laughed at his own joke. The rest of us groaned, as we always did when he told one.

Frank joined in. Frank always joined in. We had an unspoken rule—whenever he told a joke, we all went silent. It was just our thing.

"Just got back from my mate's funeral… He died after being hit on the head with a tennis ball. It was a lovely service."

Silence.

He had a knack for being wholly inappropriate.

He continued.

"My daughter came running downstairs and said, 'Quick, Dad! Mum's limp and lifeless in bed!' I replied, 'Don't I know it.'"

Silence.

Jesus. Frank.

I figured it was my turn.

"Man texts his wife: 'I'm having one more pint, then I'll be home. If I'm not home in 20 minutes, read this text again.'"

Laughter erupted—just as my mum entered the kitchen. That look. She could kill the craic with a glance.

The boys all shifted, nodding politely, stepping aside to let her through.

She turned to me. "Can I have a quiet word?"

Without a word, they slouched out the patio doors into the garden.

Mum folded her arms. "I know this is a difficult time for you, son, but for God's sake, stop treating this like a party. You shouldn't be drinking, and they shouldn't be either." She gestured toward the garden.

I raised my eyebrows, polite but firm. "I appreciate your concern, Mum, but I need my friends around me. And they need to be here too."

I looked down at my beer, smiled, and took a sip.

Disgusted, she marched out of the kitchen.

I pulled another beer from the fridge, cracked it open, and sipped.

I waved the boys back in.

Stephen checked his watch. "It's time we were away—gonna head down to the Errigle. Pity you couldn't join us."

Joan winked at him. "I will."

I sighed. "Wish I could, but I think my ma would ensure it was a double funeral if I even suggested it. Call later, yeah? Or tomorrow. I need the laughs."

We did the awkward goodbye thing. I followed them to the door and watched as they disappeared up the street.

When I turned back, Donna was right behind me. She hugged me, kissed my cheek. She was getting inappropriately close.

A couple of hours later, the doorbell rang. Donna opened it to Mr. and Mrs. Smith.

Mr. Smith looked at her and simply said, "You're very like Siobhan."

He smiled.

Mrs. Smith moved past him, straight to me. She hugged me. "I'm so sorry for your loss." She glanced toward her husband, still chatting with Donna. "We both are."

We walked into the wake room, where Siobhan's closed wicker coffin rested. Some colleagues lingered around, murmuring condolences. I shook hands, nodded, thanked them.

I straightened the painting above the fireplace—an abstraction of brightly colored squares. I loved it. Siobhan hated it.

Joan still hadn't returned with the others from work.

Good.

Mrs. Smith approached me again. "I have a church function to attend." She gestured toward her husband. "Stanley's decided to stay on. I'm sure he'll find a lift with one of your workmates. He'd do anything to get out of a church function."

She smiled, squeezed my hand, and offered her condolences once more before leaving.

I excused myself as they were all drinking tea and devouring sandwiches. I made my way to the toilet in my bedroom and just sat down on top of the closed lid.

I sat for ten minutes.

I heard Peggy asking where I was and decided that I had better go back down and join the 'party'.

I closed the bedroom door and, as I turned, Joan was alighting from the main bathroom. She had changed into a little black number—fuck, it hugged her body so tightly that I didn't even have to imagine what she would look like naked. She smiled and pulled up her dress to reveal her nakedness below.

I looked towards my bedroom.

"Better not," she purred. "We will have plenty of time for that soon enough."

She pulled her dress down and slinked down the stairs. As she reached the hall, I heard Donna questioning her in an aggressive tone.

"Have you seen Colin?"

I opened and slammed my bedroom door and made my way downstairs.

"You okay? We were all wondering where you had got to," Peggy asked, concerned.

"Yeah, I just went and sat on my toilet. Wanted to be alone for five minutes."

Donna shook her head and gave me a knowing look.

I scrunched my face and shrugged my shoulders—body language that asked the question: "Is there a problem?"

"Can I have a word in the garden?"

I didn't want to, but I knew the suspicions she had would be confirmed if I didn't.

"What's going on with you and your woman?" she accused.

"Not sure what you're talking about," I said, hands upturned in an act of submission to her will.

"Her that's been here all day! Her that's running about hugging everyone! You sure there's nothing going on there?"

"Oh, her? Na, wise up. She's just a drama queen. Sure, you saw her at the wedding, for God's sake."

Donna had her reservations about how close Siobhan and Joan had become. I continued, "She loves being the centre of attention and takes every opportunity to show off her curves—deluded. I loved your cousin. Not liking this line of questioning, Donna."

I went on the attack.

"Do you think I have nothing more to worry about than your insecurities at this stage? Wise up! And, by the way, who woke up in my bed this morning? I'm just saying, like."

I put my hand on her shoulder. She wasn't convinced, but she seemed to begrudgingly accept this lame excuse. She shrugged and made her way back into the kitchen.

Joan was just leaving with Mister Smith. As I followed Donna down the hallway, she waved.

I nodded. Mister Smith was grinning like a Cheshire cat.

They laughed as they made their way to her car. I wondered.

Cousins, friends, well-wishers of all sorts came and went—awkward, shaking my hand, all offering the same line: "Sorry for your loss."

I hate this crap.

Do people really give a shit or, as I suspect, do they just enjoy the drama? Schadenfreude?

I was getting so fed up that I just wanted to scream at everyone to leave. Partly because I wanted to call to Joan's to see what she was doing, partly because I just wanted this all to be over, but mostly because I wanted to bury myself in a bottle of Jameson.

It was past half ten, and I couldn't take much more of this.

The door knocked. Donna answered, and I allowed myself a wry smile when I noticed my neighbour and his wife shuffling into the hallway. They made their way towards me; she hugged me, and he said they were so sorry for my loss and how much they loved Siobhan as a neighbour.

I sighed.

A backhanded way of letting me know that they didn't think much of me as a neighbour.

I couldn't care less.

They paid their respects and left rather quickly.

Mum and my brothers had left at about quarter to ten. Donna said that she was going to stay with me and Siobhan's parents and that we would spend the night with Siobhan.

The house emptied. I asked the remaining people to leave. Given the circumstances, my request was respected.

Ronnie, Peggy, and Patrick sat beside the coffin. Donna and I were on the opposite side. I had put two bottles of Jameson cask-aged on the table and five glasses. Ronnie poured himself one and asked if anyone else wanted to join him. We declined.

He sank a large glass and quickly poured another. He sank that too and then poured a third.

He stood with his back to us all. Peggy rolled her eyes—Ronnie was never good on the whiskey.

He continued to pour and neck the whiskey until, when I looked at the bottle, he was nearly three-quarters of the way down.

He stumbled and slurred, "This is all your fucking fault!" He still hadn't looked around.

Peggy sighed loudly.

"For goodness' sake, Ronnie, you know what you're like when you drink whiskey. Please stop before you say something that can't be taken back!"

"Fuck him! My daughter is in that basket, and it's his fucking fault! She was so damaged I didn't even get to say goodbye to her face, you fucking bastard!"

Peggy was shaking her head as she pushed her chair back.

"Patrick, you may give me a hand—he needs to go."

She looked at me and Donna and mouthed, "I'm so sorry!"

As she grabbed Ronnie's arm, she whispered loudly, "You know what you're like when you drink that stuff. We are leaving before you disgrace us any more!"

They left, with Patrick offering to return as soon as things were sorted. I assured them that we would be okay.

"Go home and look after your mum and dad. We will see you first thing!"

They left, with Peggy's apologies ringing in my ears.

Chapter 52
Awkward

I returned to the wake room.

Donna stared at me. "Get the wine open, will you? Fuck, I need a drink."

I popped the merlot, set a glass on the breakfast bar, plonked the wine down beside Donna, and turned to get my tumbler and bottle of Jameson.

We drank. Then we drank more. Then we started to laugh.

"God, that was awkward waking up beside you this morning. You think you're safe here?"

"Oh yeah, I just want to be close to my cousin, and at the minute, you're my best option. Lock the front door in case they come back, would you? Wouldn't want anyone to come in and catch us in bed." She giggled and winked.

"That's not going to happen." I wasn't even kidding myself at this stage.

We continued drinking for some time and woke again together. This time, semi-naked. This was becoming a habit. I seemed to remember us doing more than cuddling in the night. My God, what are we like? Maybe I was just imagining it.

The doorbell rang loudly. My head hurt so much. I woke Donna and told her to quickly go to the spare room.

She grabbed her mound of clothes and ran next door.

I pulled on my jeans and T-shirt and stumbled to the door.

"You look awful." Peggy fanned her face as she walked past me, followed by a head-shaking Ronnie and a blissfully self-indulgent Patrick.

Ronnie coughed. "Where is Donna?"

"To be honest, I'm not sure," I lied. "We had a couple of drinks last night. I left her sitting by the coffin and went to bed. Think I heard her leaving in the middle of the night." Fuck, this lying was so natural to me.

Peggy nodded at Ronnie, who reluctantly offered his hand and mumbled an apology for his behaviour the previous night.

I graciously accepted, choosing to ignore him staring and the unnecessarily tight grip.

We were still standing in the hall when we heard the bedroom door close upstairs. I shrugged. "Must have stayed. Frankly, I was too tired to even notice."

Donna looked fresh as she walked into the kitchen, wearing the clothes she had had on yesterday.

"God, I'm tired. Sat in the front room until half five, then I went to bed as I couldn't stay awake any longer." She smiled at me.

I must have looked guilty. No one noticed. They wouldn't for one second believe that Donna and I could be that 'sick'.

"Uncle Ronnie, can you give me a lift to mine? I want to get cleaned up and changed."

"Yes, yes, of course," he said absentmindedly as he approached Siobhan and rested his hand on the coffin.

We walked to the kitchen to give him a moment. Stifled sobs emanated from the wake room.

When Ronnie had gathered himself, they left, and Peggy made her way to the kitchen and started tidying up. Patrick put the kettle on and lit a cigarette. Peggy pointed at the back door, and Patrick knew this was her way of telling him not to smoke in the house.

He sighed and trudged to the back door, where he leaned against the frame and enjoyed his addiction. Mine too.

Mad.

Chapter 53
Another LBD

The doorbell rang. Peggy went to answer it. There was a posse of people, including my mum, Joe, and Paul.

This is going to be a long day.

Everyone was there.

Then the door started—people coming and going.

Mass cards.

Joan and Mister Smith arrived together.

She looked amazing in yet another little black number. She was more discreetly dressed than usual.

I needed to get a chat with her.

I did the rounds, shaking hands and having the same conversation with everyone.

"Sorry for your loss. I am sure you're devastated. How will you cope? Poor Siobhan! What happened? Did she die instantly? Will you live here? When is the funeral? Where is she getting buried?"

It was relentless.

Eventually, I cornered Joan in the kitchen.

"Something going on between you and Mister Smith?"

She looked surprised.

"No! How could I? It's just that my car is in for a service, and Mister Smith has just returned the favour—I just needed to be near you."

I bet he has been so good.

"You sure? He seems to want to give me the impression that there's more going on between you two than meets the eye."

"Of course I'm sure. He did want to come into my apartment last night, but I wouldn't let him. You can't blame him." She raised her eyebrows and smiled.

I had no clue. This explained the promotion and the transfer to the Belfast office.

Susan had just arrived in the kitchen.

Awkward silence.

Joan smiled and put her hand on Donna's shoulder. Donna faked a smile.

As Joan left the kitchen, Donna put her head in her hands and silently screamed.

Aggressively whispering, "What the fuck is going on with her?"

"I'm not doing this. I have told you I can't legislate for other people. Please listen to me now! Relax. Even if I could, I wouldn't go anywhere near her. My wife—your cousin—is lying in there in a box. Would you please catch yourself on? Try to keep it together."

I was hoping that Donna would accept this. Then I whispered, "For fuck's sake! You and I, last night—we did more than console each other!"

She smiled. She knew. She couldn't bring herself to be too angry with me.

"I'm staying here tonight." She was making sure I couldn't get anywhere near Joan.

My mates arrived again. It was 5:15 pm. They smelled of beer and were in great form.

Stephen was laughing as he told me about the ugly bird—his words—that Frank had gone out with the night before. All the boys were laughing.

Frank just shrugged. "You know me, big man—go ugly, go early."

He had this knack for saying disgusting things and getting away with it.

The jokes started. "You hear the one about the waiter?..."

I wanted to stay but knew someone would come in and disapprove.

I went back to the endless rounds of maddening conversations. Had to be done, I suppose.

The living room was covered with Mass cards. Some poor priest was going to have to say an awful lot of Masses.

I was starting to get pissed off with the guy from Siobhan's work who stayed for an unfeasibly long time and was, frankly, a wee bit too upset. Maybe they were having an affair. I was seething, but somehow it allowed me to justify everything that I did.

As the night wore on, the crowds dissipated. Then came the fucking funeral arrangements. I wanted to go to Joan's.

We all sat around the dining table with Father Peter. He had brought a list of suggested readings, prayers, and hymns. I said that the only thing I wanted to ensure was that the recessional song had to be The Blue Nile singing "Happiness."

Father Peter said it was impossible, as the diocese had decided that only music from a pre-approved list of hymns and choral music was allowed at funerals.

I was incensed. "Well, if you can't accommodate that request, we will find someone or somewhere who will."

"Calm down, Colin." My mum was only trying to help, but I could have cheerfully choked her.

"No song, no funeral. Simple. You lot can decide everything else."

"It was Siobhan's favourite song," enthused Joe. "She loved it. It has a very poignant and relevant lyric."

Him and his music.

"Now that I've found peace at last, tell me, Jesus, will it last?"

Peggy sobbed, looked at the priest, and nodded. It was agreed.

The hymns and readings were selected. Readers were assigned. Gift carriers, pallbearers, bidding prayers, singer, and organist were all agreed—same as at the wedding.

We all looked at each other. Donna was tired and asked if everyone would leave so that she and I could sit through the final vigil alone.

I watched as Ronnie was led down the path by Peggy and Patrick. He stumbled as he got into the car. He had spent the day finding comfort in whiskey, and his anger was replaced by an all-consuming grief.

Peggy had reluctantly left her daughter, as she wanted to get Ronnie home so they could comfort each other.

Some people wanted to stay all night. I asked them all to leave.

Donna had to go to her own house to get her black dress and coat for the funeral. She said she would only be half an hour.

I tried to reassure her that I would be okay alone, but she was having none of it.

As soon as her car pulled off, I grabbed my car keys and sped to Joan's.

She was expecting me—nothing on but stockings, shoes, and a smile.

We ravaged each other in the hall. We continued to thrust in and out of each other as we stumbled into the living room, still shagging.

Joan turned, knelt on the sofa with her back to me, arms outstretched on the back of the settee. I grabbed her breasts and rammed my body into her as hard as I could. She groaned loudly, and we orgasmed simultaneously.

I pulled my trousers up and made my way to the door. Not a word was spoken.

I raced to the house and jumped in the shower. I was just washing my hair when Donna walked into the en-suite. This was becoming a habit.

"There's a wee whiskey waiting for you downstairs." She smiled.

"I'll be down in a minute."

She opened wine and sat, drinking with some restraint.

Nothing was said. Frankly, no words were necessary.

Donna poured more wine. I poured more whiskey and pulled a bottle of beer from the fridge. We drank hungrily and in silence.

For the first time, the silence indicated our awareness of Siobhan in the next room.

Chapter 54
Sleepy Head

I woke alone in bed—thank God. I was just sighing with relief when Donna walked from the en-suite, unashamedly naked. I rolled over and groaned.

"You better get up and get yourself sorted. Ronnie and Peggy are on their way—the funeral is in three hours' time."

"What time is it?"

"Half seven. Come on, get a move on, sleepyhead."

Too familiar.

I waited until she left to put the coffee on, then showered and put my clean white shirt on. I put black socks on and black shorts. Mum had had my black suit cleaned, and it was hanging on the back of the wardrobe above my new shoes.

As I tied the black tie around my neck, I caught myself in the mirror. I looked well.

"You look great."

It seemed a wholly inappropriate remark from Donna. I smiled and poured myself a coffee. I wanted a cigarette, so I stood at the back door and inhaled deeply.

Donna was disgusted—she'd always loathed smoking.

I didn't care.

The doorbell rang. I pulled on the cigarette and fanned myself. If my mum knew I was smoking, she would kill me.

I asked Donna to get the door and rushed past her to the stairs so I could wash the stale smoke smell away and brush my teeth. I heard my mum's voice as I turned onto the landing.

"How is he, love?" she said as she hugged Donna. "How are you?"

Donna didn't respond.

Mum put the pan on. It was like a murder of crows had descended on my ground floor. Where do people get all the black clothes at such short notice?

I checked my phone and noted that I'd had two missed calls from Joan. Strange—she never phones me. She knows better. They had been placed last night, and no message had been attached.

I excused myself and made my way to my bedroom. I closed the door and tried to phone her. No answer. Again, no answer.

Something wasn't right.

How could I get away? My wife was getting buried from the house in two fucking hours.

I decided that I had to just walk downstairs and get into the car. I could think of something when I was driving.

Joan's front door was off the latch, and I tentatively pushed it slowly open.

I shouted, "Joan."

No answer.

I shouted again, only louder. Still no answer.

The living room was a mess.

As I slowly walked from the living room door, I saw Joan lying semi-naked and unconscious—maybe dead—on the floor. There had obviously been a struggle, and magazines were strewn about the ground.

I rushed to her and lifted her head in my arms. She was breathing but had a bloodied face.

I shook her. She wouldn't waken.

I let her head slide to the floor as I stood up. I started to edge backwards—I had to go. There were people who would be wondering where I was.

What the fuck?

I phoned for an ambulance as I made my way downstairs but didn't want to give my name. I told them they would need the police too. I slowly gave Joan's address as I made my way to the car. I was still talking as I pressed the button that beeped the car open.

I hung up as I turned the key in the ignition.

My head was all over the place.

I got back to the house with some of Joan's blood still drying on my sleeve.

I didn't care.

"Where the hell did you go?" Donna was starting to piss me off.

Fuck sake, it was like Siobhan hadn't died.

"I just wanted twenty minutes to myself. I went for a drive and a smoke. That's my wife in the box in there—I'm struggling to cope here. Do you mind?"

Mum put her hand on my shoulder.

Donna rolled her eyes and walked into the kitchen.

"You're going to have to eat something, son. It will be a long day."

"I can't even think about food, Mum," I said curtly.

"You know you have to eat something. You need to keep up your strength. Were you smoking, really? I can't smell it."

"I just wanted to be alone for a while."

"I understand, son. Please eat something. There's bacon and fresh bread sitting ready in the kitchen."

I gave in and ate, making sure she saw me.

Donna hugged me; she understood my need to be alone.

She just wished I would lean on her.

How could I?

There were people milling about in silence all over the place. It was like a morgue.

Ronnie coughed. "Who's the first lift?"

Fuck, how can he be so practical?

"Paul and Joe at the back, you and Patrick at the front? Is that okay?"

He coughed again. "That's grand, son. Siobhan would have wanted that."

Why do people feel the need to come out with this crap? How the hell would he know it's what Siobhan would have wanted? People talk some shit when they're just trying to fill space.

Ronnie was being nice to me again. I couldn't wait to get these fuckers out of my life.

Mum produced the Irish News. There were nearly a hundred death notices attached to Siobhan's name. The first was from me— I hadn't written it. Must have been Mum or Frank. I would have had some cheek to write the notice in the way it was printed.

"Hill, Siobhan (née O'Neill). Died tragically, as a result of a car accident. Dear wife and best friend. My heart was torn to pieces the minute I was told. I will miss your love and kisses and your warm and tender hold. You brightened up my every day, you just made me smile. I wish I could talk to you, if only for a while. My life has changed forever; nothing seems the same. I wake at night and call out your name. Sacred Heart of Jesus, have mercy on her soul. Sadly missed by your grieving husband, Colin. Gone but never forgotten."

I didn't want to read any more. "Leave the paper, Mum, will you? I'll read the notices later in the week."

"Okay, son. It's lovely that so many people thought so much of you and Siobhan, to take the time to put all those notices in the paper. It will give you strength when you read them when it's all over."

I couldn't care less if my colleagues, GAA clubs, or any other hangers-on wanted to express their grief. Why do people care?

The priest arrived with the undertakers. Someone must have organised all of this—I know I didn't. There was a hearse and two limousines for the chief mourners.

I glanced around. There seemed to be hundreds of people milling about the street. I was confused. Why did they all care? Some were holding bouquets, some were holding single roses, and some were just standing in complete silence.

Billy Sloan had cordoned off the street and was directing traffic. He nodded in my direction as he pulled his radio from its sheath. I watched as he responded to the crackly message he had received. He looked at me, completely bemused. I shrugged and made my way back to the relative safety of the wake house.

Father Peter began to say the final prayers. We all stood awkwardly, making the expected responses. I was amazed at how we all seemed to drift into automatic pilot when it came to these prayers.

He began, "Hail, Holy Queen, Mother of Mercy…"

We all joined in.

"Hail, our life, our sweetness, and our hope."

And so it continued.

A decade of the Rosary, the sorrowful mysteries.

The priest mumbled the first half of the Hail Mary; the assembled masses responded with the second half of the prayer—always beginning slightly before the cleric had completed his section. Always happened like this. Seemed rude to me.

As we absentmindedly offered our responses, my mind began to wander to Joan. I wanted to go there, to see if she was okay.

How could I?

"Let us take our daughter Siobhan to the celebration of her final Mass."

The priest kissed his purple stole and bowed his head in silence.

Chapter 55
God Alone...

I fucking hate funerals.

Just before the service started, Ronnie said it was strange that he hadn't seen Joan about.

"How to open such a sermon? How can any of us make sense of all of this? We must just trust in divine providence. God alone can help us cope with this—He did, after all, allow His only Son to die at an early age and in a tragic way."

What a pile of bollocks.

"God can help us make sense of this."

I have never heard such crap in my feeble little life.

First thing—he said God allowed His only Son to die. Therefore, He knew it was going to happen (in fact, He made it happen—not exactly comparing like with like, me thinks) and could prepare for the impending doom.

To be honest, how some misguided, dysfunctional, emotionally retarded cleric can try to help those suffering by referring everything back to some wandering preacher from 2,000 years ago just beggars belief. And these guys are supposed to be intelligent?

And make no mistake about it—this was a tragedy.

No shit, Sherlock.

"A beautiful life has been snatched from us, and we all feel the pain of the loss."

How the hell does he know it was a beautiful life? He didn't even fucking well know her.

Speaking of beautiful life—I held Susan's hand.

Pain—what the hell does he know about pain?

"A beautiful life, one with so much potential, one that was destined to touch many—yet tragically, it has been taken from us before the full potential could be realised."

Does he realise how daft he sounds? Mad as a hatter. How the hell does he know what she was destined to do or be? These people talk some crap.

Donna was sobbing. I did what was expected—put my arm around her shoulder and pulled her closer.

"Of course, her parents and her brother will never have another day when they don't think of her. This pain that they now feel will soon dissipate and become fondness in their thoughts. They will remember their beautiful sister, daughter, friend—a lovable person."

Fondness. That's an understatement. They are devastated, but I want this to be about me. He hasn't even mentioned me. Does he even know what he's talking about?

"Her friends, too, will be struggling to come to terms with this tragedy. How can we help young people to understand that which only God can make sense of? We must trust in His love for every one of His creations. God knows how you feel. He has endured such suffering—His only beloved Son struck down in His prime. It is in His infinite knowledge and understanding of the human psyche that we can find solace.

"To all of you young people, remember—God loves you. He knows how you feel. He feels your pain, and He wants you to know that you will gain a clear vision and understanding of what all of this means."

How the hell can he say this? How the fuck can he know this?

He talks some shit—does he actually believe this crap himself?

The sound of that rain relentlessly pelting on the tin roof is doing my head in.

Eventually, he got to me.

"And Colin, what can I say? The love of his life, and their life together had only just begun. Why, it was only two months ago that I stood and married them. Siobhan was so happy…"

He was droning on.

I zoned out.

Service over, we made our way to Roselawn for the cremation. The place was bunged.

The Blue Nile sang Happiness as the coffin was carried into the room.

Father Peter said some more words.

Patrick eulogised.

The second service ended with the wicker coffin beginning to slide backwards and Mark Hollis singing It's My Life.

Chapter 56
The Paradox

We all headed back to the Parador Hotel, as the priest had suggested at the end of the Mass. It was like a party of sorts.

I sat with my brothers and some close friends. The craic was good—always was when Sean was about. We cracked jokes, sipped beer, and probably laughed too much and too loud. Mum flashed me that look again. I just shrugged and carried on. This was my moment. Surely, anything I did today, of all days, was forgivable?

The customary soup, sandwiches, and finger food started to appear (and disappear) on the long table at the back of the room. Someone handed me a plate, but I wasn't interested. I made my excuses and went to the toilet—via the bar.

I couldn't help but notice the big sign crudely taped to the back room door:

NO ADMITTANCE PRIVATE FUNCTION

I laughed at the thought of it being called a function. Was waiting for the DJ to start.

The beer and whisky kept flowing. I was feeling that buzz again.

Donna came and sat beside me, put her arm around my shoulder, and just started to cry. I knew anyone watching would assume she just needed to be near her cousin's husband at a time like this, but that didn't make me feel any less uncomfortable.

She whispered, "Thank God that idiot from your work didn't show up today—I don't think I could have looked at her sneering face and inappropriate attire during the Mass. It was a lovely service."

Fuck. Joan.

I had completely forgotten about her. Suppose I'd been busy.

I didn't want to rush to phone her, so I waited a minute before saying to Donna that I was going for a smoke. I knew her loathing of the habit would give me a moment's peace to call Joan.

As I made my way to the smoking area—side door, that is—I was accosted by nearly everyone.

"So sorry for your loss. It was a lovely service." "Aye, lovely send-off."

God, I was getting fed up with all this shit.

I just wanted to phone Joan.

I managed to convince enough people that I wanted five minutes alone and headed for the door. I almost broke the cigarette as I hauled it from the packet. I spun the lighter wheel four times before managing a decent flame. I drew heavily on the unlit end, inhaled deeply—so deeply my head went light.

I fumbled my phone from my inside pocket, dropping it in the process. As I keyed in the security code, I noticed a missed call.

SLOAN BILLY (POLICE)

I had typed his name in bold capitals.

I paid it no heed and scrolled for Joan's number.

"John from work."

Pressed call. Held the phone to my ear.

Straight to voicemail.

"I'm sorry, the person you are calling is unavailable. Please leave your message after the tone."

I waited for the beep and blurted out, "God, Joan, I am so sorry about this morning—please call me when you get this. I couldn't help leaving you that way. Call me!"

I rang again. Still no answer.

"Please call me when you get this. You have no idea how sorry I am about this morning."

I slid the phone back into my pocket and took one last drag of my cigarette. Twisting my shoe on the butt, I turned to go back inside, fanning myself.

"Ah, Colin. Glad I caught you."

I turned.

Billy Sloan.

"I tried to phone you earlier."

"Might've escaped your attention, Bill—I was at a funeral."

"Can I have a quick word?"

Billy Sloan's appearances were becoming too regular—and tedious—for my liking.

"I'm kind of busy, Bill. You know, with all my family and friends? Could it wait until tomorrow?"

He looked at me quizzically, brow furrowed.

"I'm afraid, Colin, I think I'm going to have to ask you to come down to the station. We need you to help us with our inquiries."

I guffawed.

"Who's dead?"

He didn't laugh.

"You can come with us now, if you want. In the circumstances, you can get someone from inside to come with you. But I'll have to accompany you. In your drunken state, I'm not sure you wouldn't be a flight risk."

So fucking pejorative.

Donna emerged from the haze of my confused and distorted vision, already in her coat.

"I'll go. This shouldn't take long. And anyway, Siobhan was my cousin—I want to hear firsthand what they have to say."

It seemed okay by me.

Donna and I sat in the back of the panda car in silence. I was bursting for a piss.

"Fuck, Billy—me? A flight risk? You gonna tell me what this is all about?"

"If you just come with me, you can go inside and make your excuses. Then we can head to the station. You're not under arrest—yet—but we do need your help with our inquiries."

My head was spinning.

What could he possibly want with me?

Joan?

I shrugged and trudged back inside. The whole room fell silent, eyes fixed on the policeman shadowing me.

"I have to go to the station—something to do with the car crash."

Mum rushed over, launching into the confused detective.

"For God's sake, couldn't this wait until tomorrow? We're in mourning here!"

"I'm sorry, madam, but this cannot wait."

"Well, then, I'm coming with him. He shouldn't be alone today, of all days."

As soon as we arrived at the station, I was ushered to the toilet, accompanied by some pimple-faced cop.

He just stood at the door, arms folded.

At first, I had stage fright.

But that was soon overcome.

Chapter 57
B and B.

I was led to the holding cell, passing Donna in the foyer.

"My God, Colin, what is this all about?" A confused and bewildered Donna, like myself, had no idea what was about to unfold.

Billy Sloan was accompanied by a suited companion as he slowly walked into the room.

"Do I need a lawyer?" I sniggered—they didn't!

"That might be a good idea." The suited cop introduced himself as Chief Inspector Forbes. Initially, I thought he said Morse and allowed myself an inner smile.

"What the fuck is this about?" I was starting to get worried.

Billy Sloan proffered, "As I said, you're not under arrest yet," he paused, "but we do need to ask you some questions about your whereabouts this morning—and possibly last night."

I laughed. "If that's the case, why did you need to bring me down here? You could have asked any one of the hundred or so people that were in the Parador. What is this about?"

"I am going to record this conversation for our records." He pressed a button on the tape recorder on the desk in front of me. "Are you sure you do not want a lawyer present?"

I just shook my head.

"For the purposes of the tape, Mr Hill has indicated that he does not wish there to be a lawyer present."

"Can you tell us your whereabouts this morning between 8:45 am and 10:15 am?"

The suited copper was almost militaristic in his questioning style.

"That's easy." I pointed at the door Donna was sitting behind in the hallway outside. "I was with Donna the whole time."

This was serious.

"Ask Donna." I pointed at the door again. "I was getting ready for my wife's funeral, and then we left the house and followed the coffin to the church—you were even there directing traffic, Bill. Surely you remember."

I was feeling confident now.

"Can I ask the make, model, and registration plate of your car, sir?"

"Sure. It's a bright red Audi A5 S-Line, reg LIB 7723—I think, or is it 7732?"

I had nothing to hide—or so I thought.

"That car hasn't moved from the door for two days. What is this about?"

"Your car was seen at the Knock Apartments near the carriageway this morning, and a man fitting your description was seen making a phone call as he approached your car and drove off. Can you help us?"

My heart sank.

"I think I need a lawyer."

I settled back in my seat and asked if I could possibly get a drink. Billy Sloan suggested a black coffee. I glared at him and shrugged—I was really getting fed up with his judgements.

Forbes pushed a phone towards me and suggested I ring my lawyer.

I dialled the number on the antiquated piece of paper, and Mick answered on the first ring—he always did; he was so full of his own importance.

"Mick, hi, it's Colin."

"I know that. What did the cops want with you? Where are you?"

"Ormeau Police Station. Could you come down? I need advice. I need you here."

I knew praise and drama were the one sure way to set our Mick into overdrive.

"Jesus, pal, I'm on my way. Don't say a word until I get there! Taxi's ordered." He indicated in a loud whisper, the way you do when you're on the phone to someone else, "Terry, order me a taxi ASAP."

He always said "ASAP" rather than spelling out the four letters. I suppose for him, it increased the drama and highlighted the urgency.

"I'm warning you—don't say a word until I get there. Give me five minutes."

Mick was my old school buddy and a bloody genius—but as I sat looking at C.I. Forbes and Billy Sloan across the desk, I went cold. Mick was the one person in the world who liked to drink more than me.

After what seemed like an hour, the phone squealed, and I started in my seat.

"Okay, can you show him in, please?"

As Billy returned the receiver to its cradle, he glanced at me and said, "Your lawyer's here."

Mick strode purposefully into the room, pushing past the female cop who had been leading the way.

"This better be good because I will have both your guts for garters if it isn't. This man—my client—has rights, and you simply trampled all over them when you arrested him today of all days."

Mick was in full flow. I laughed at the "my client" bit.

He sat down beside me, and the sweet smell of single malt just seemed to fill the room.

He winked at me.

"I would like a consultation with my client so we can sort this sorry mess out. I can't believe that this couldn't have waited until tomorrow—whatever it is."

The policemen shoved their chairs back and stood in front of us. The room went dark—I hadn't realised just how big a man Billy Sloan was.

They slammed the door behind them as they left, and Mick, for some strange reason, began to laugh.

"Mick, for fuck's sake, keep it together. This could be serious."

He stopped laughing.

I told Mick everything—or as much as I was prepared to divulge at this stage. He was astounded. He looked at me with absolute disgust.

He got up and, without speaking, went outside. I could hear his animated voice as he conversed with Billy Sloan.

"There's no way you will let him go with me?"

Billy coughed. "We couldn't. These are very serious crimes—no way we can let him out. There's a woman lying close to death in the Royal Victoria Hospital. She was raped and strangled."

"I didn't do any of this!" I squealed at the top of my voice.

"If I'm honest, he might be safer here tonight. If what he's accused of broke over there in the Parador, I think you might have another murder on your hands. I can't look at him. Can you let him know that he's here for the night? I'll be here first thing."

A disgusted Mick left the police station.

"Will do."

Mick left. Donna went with him. Billy Sloan returned to the interview room, read me my rights, outlined the crime I was going to be charged with, and asked me to accompany him to a holding cell.

"You've got this all wrong! I didn't do any of that!"

"If I were you, I'd say nothing more until your brief gets back in the morning."

"What? You're keeping me here overnight? Fuck sake, my wife got buried today!"

He looked at me and sighed. "That's what makes it so much worse."

They had taken my phone and removed my cigarettes and lighter. I sobered up very quickly and was gasping for a smoke.

"No chance," was his terse reply.

I paced up and down, thought about Joan, even thought about Siobhan and Donna—I just wanted to get back to the party.

I tried to sleep. Food was left at the hatch. I didn't touch it. I asked for a cigarette. They laughed.

The longest night of my life ensued. I just wanted out of there. I was hungry and dehydrated. A rather nasty bastard of a cop brought me breakfast. There was coffee, water, and soggy toast. I

drank the liquids and, looking at the toast, thought, *You could never be that hungry.*

It was half eleven, and still, I knew nothing. I was cracking up.

Chapter 58
Pickled Onion

The nasty cop who made my toast soggy brought my lunch. It was a watery lasagne with two hard slices of garlic baguette. He brought another bottle of water, and I once again sucked it dry. I couldn't face the food—it looked and smelled horrible, and I would have sworn there was a very obvious piece of spittle in the middle of the pasta.

The door opened again. This time, Mick walked in with the cop—I was so relieved to see a friendly face.

"Did you bring me anything to eat?" I implored.

The cop mumbled under his breath while scoffing, "What kind of animal do you think I am?"

Fuck you, I thought.

I screamed at the door. I was so frustrated.

"I didn't do this! I didn't do it! What sort of fucking animal do you think I am?"

I waited. All I could hear was shuffling, paper, and footsteps. The cop laughed in the distance, and I resigned myself to my fate.

Mick looked at me with disconsolation in his eyes. "Have you any idea how much fucking trouble you're in, and all you can think about is food?"

"I'm fucking starving here!"

He set his briefcase down beside his highly polished oxblood-coloured brogues and motioned for me to sit on the bed. I hated the way he always wore pink shirts and ties with matching handkerchiefs—he was such a fucking walking stereotype.

I slumped.

The cop made some kind of gesture with his hands and walked out, leaving us alone.

"Got any cigarettes?" I was gasping for a smoke.

"No chance in here, mate."

I nearly cried.

"So, what is happening with Joan? Has she come round yet—so I can get out of this holiday camp? It's no fucking joke in here, man."

Mick's contorted face made me fearful of his answer.

Through gritted teeth, he said, "It's not looking good. Apparently, she had a very restful and relaxing night, but this morning they had to resuscitate her. She nearly died, for fuck's sake. They're saying the next seventy-two hours are critical. She's in a bad way."

I cradled my head in my hands and silently raged.

"Seventy fucking two hours? Can you not get me out of here before that? I really want to get home and washed and changed—I smell like that fucking cop who doubles as a waiter in here."

I was beginning to crack wise and crack up.

"You're going to have to stick with me. I'm doing my best, but do you—"

"For fuck's sake! The evidence against you is, as we say in court parlance, compelling. They have you at the scene of the crime. Your DNA is all over the gaff and, dare I say it, inside her. What the fuck were you thinking? It was your wife's wake! I can tell you that even if you do get out of here—and that's a big *if* at the minute—you shouldn't be expecting any kind of ticker-tape parade. Your mum is the only one still saying they must have gotten it wrong."

He was in full flow.

"If you'd been allowed out yesterday and returned to the funeral reception, I think Ronnie would have made sure your funeral was within the week. Do you have any idea what hurt and anguish you've caused? You're looking at a rape charge at the very least—right now, attempted murder, and if things get any worse, murder. You're staring down at least twenty-five years inside."

He looked at me quizzically.

His voice was starting to sound like noise to me now.

"What about that food? Any chance of getting me something to eat?"

Exasperated, he puffed out his cheeks, strode toward the door, and, almost in defeat, knocked slowly three times on the metal.

As the door eventually opened, he nodded in my direction and sighed. "He wants food. I'll go to the shop and return if that's okay?"

The cop reluctantly nodded. He was familiar with Mick.

Mick turned and walked away, his head rolling from side to side.

I sighed and just wished he would hurry up.

"Get me a Ploughman's sandwich, a Mars bar, a can of Coke, and a packet of pickled onion crisps!" I yelled at the door, hoping he wouldn't return with a salad and a nicotine patch.

After what felt like an eternity, the door slid open. To my amazement, everything I'd shouted for was in the bag he was carrying. He'd even sneaked in two miniature bottles of Jack Daniel's to mix with my Coke. Suddenly, everything felt good in the world.

I tore open the crisp bag, spilling half the contents on the floor. Scoffing them down, I licked my palm as bits slipped through my fingers. As I chewed the gorgeous, salty processed potatoes, I wrestled with the sandwich packaging.

I hate that fucking plastic—it's never straightforward. After five failed attempts to rip it open with my teeth, I finally managed to tear a corner free and peel back the cling film. I stuffed more crisps into my mouth and yanked a sandwich out of the packet. I ate gleefully.

It was only then that I noticed Mick looking at me with utter disgust. I shrugged. I couldn't understand what his problem was—I hadn't eaten in ages. I was entitled.

I ate too quickly. Immediately, my stomach felt bloated, and the Coke burned my throat, nearly exploding in my gut. I let out a loud, uncontrollable belch.

I looked at Mick and winked, then started to laugh.

Reluctantly, the corner of his mouth curled up, and he smiled too.

For a brief moment, all was good in the world.

I wiped my mouth with the sleeve of my jacket and grimaced as one of the buttons banged against my teeth.

"Ouch! Fuck, that hurt."

I cupped my mouth with my hand and sat down.

Heavenly.

Mick didn't waste any more time.

"Are you going to tell me what the hell is going on?" he asked, his tone sharp. "I mean, can you please explain to me what you were doing there on the morning of your wife's funeral? And why your DNA is all over the place? And—without meaning to be crude—it doesn't look good that it was, well, inside her, if you know what I mean."

I couldn't be bothered with all this crap.

I had eaten. I wanted peace, quiet, and time to enjoy my sneaky JD and Coke. Maybe even catch forty winks.

"Don't judge me," I said, stretching out. "I was having an affair with Joan. She's my secretary at work—sex on a stick. You've seen her about. You know what I mean."

"Fuck, I don't believe you, man," Mick scoffed. "Every single one of our friends would give their eye teeth to have Siobhan—just look at them! Let alone *marry* her. And there you were—*were*, sorry—married to her and playing the field? You're not even married three months!"

I cut him off.

"Are we here to talk about how my sick fuck friends coveted my wife, or are we here to discuss how to get me the fuck out of here?"

Mick shook his head, but I pressed on.

"As I said, I was having an affair with Joan. I called in the night before the funeral, and, well, one thing led to another. We had a quickie—I know, I know, I shouldn't have done it, but I was confused. I just found myself there."

Mick let out a faint tut.

Exasperated, I sighed loudly and continued.

"I phoned her several times the morning of the funeral and got no response. I was anxious to know if she was okay, so I just walked out of my house. When I got to her apartment, the door was slightly open. I called her name—no answer. I stepped inside, called her name again—still nothing.

"Fuck sake, Mick, she was lying there. What was I supposed to do? I lifted her head—she was breathing. *I swear* she was breathing."

Mick was listening intently now, so I kept going.

"I had to go, Mick. I had a funeral to get to. I phoned the peelers and the ambulance, but I didn't give my name. She was definitely breathing! I did all the right things. Why the fuck would I report it if I had done it?"

I stared at him. It made sense to me.

"I was shitting myself, Mick. That's why I didn't give my name. I just got in the car and left. I pushed the thought of her face out of my mind—it was starting to make me feel sick. I *swear* that's exactly what happened. Why would I lie?"

I paused.

"I swear!"

Mick pursed his lips and said, "Because you realise the amount of shit you're in? Look at me, Colin. *Is that really what happened? Truth now.*"

How patronising. I was raging. How did this not make sense to him? He'd known me all my life—why wouldn't he believe me?

"For fuck's sake, *why would I lie*? WHY??"

I was screaming now, a mixture of anger and frustration.

"I went home so we could have the funeral. I planned to visit Joan in the hospital later that day—wait, what fucking day is it anyway?"

I slurped from the tin cup, realising I had completely lost track of time.

"Thursday," Mick said flatly. "It's Thursday. For god's sake, you only came in yesterday. You *know*, the day your wife was buried."

Mick seemed agitated.

"Jesus, okay, my God, anyone would think I was Attila the Hun!" I sighed. "Look, what's the craic? Can you get me out of here or what?"

He bit his upper lip and sighed. "It's not looking good—but I'll see what I can get out of these bastards." He motioned toward the reception area where the police officers were standing.

I was getting weary.

Just then, the door flung open. It was him again. He waved Mick to the side and whispered something in his ear. This time, Mick looked slightly less irritated. He walked out of the room without a backward glance—but still slammed the door.

Mick turned to me.

"It's your lucky day—well, as lucky as you can get in a week like this." His voice was edged with caution. "Joan's come round. She's adamant you didn't rape her. Says it wasn't you who attacked her. When she was being strangled, a loud bang in the stairwell disturbed the attacker. They're double-checking things now, but it looks like you'll be good to go soon."

Relief flooded through me. I nearly hugged him.

I smiled.

"I wouldn't be smiling just yet," Mick warned. "We haven't even worked out where the fuck you're going." He scrunched up his nose. "There's a posse of people out there who would *gleefully* kill you."

Frustration churned in my gut. I buried my head in my hands. *What the fuck has it got to do with any of them?* This was my situation.

"If she said I didn't do it, then what problem does anyone have with me?"

Mick looked at me like I was the thickest bastard alive.

"In the name of all that's good and proper, have you *no* fucking idea of the hurt you've caused? Siobhan's mum and dad are *apoplectic*. Her brother has sworn revenge. The only one in her family who isn't physically raging is that cousin of hers—Donna. She seems to have calmed down. I was at their house. She was just sitting there, staring out the window, completely depressed. She's lost her cousin. But I swear, mate, I couldn't get over how angry she was when I told her what you were being accused of."

My stomach twisted.

"Who the fuck else did you tell? How the *fuck* did this get out?"

Mick gave me a deadpan stare.

"That's what I'm trying to tell you. *Donna.*"

Stupid bitch. I thought about how she'd feel if *I* told Peggy and Ronnie what *she'd* been up to.

Mick didn't even realise the irony in what he was saying. Was I the 'other half' he was referring to? How could he even know? I wasn't even sure of the reality of it myself.

"Not to mention *your* lot," Mick continued. "Except your mum. She doesn't believe you did it. But she *is* fucking raging about the affair."

I cut across him. "How the *fuck* does my mum know about the affair?"

Mick looked down at his lap.

"For fuck's sake, Mick, why didn't you just put a banner up over the *Parador*?"

I shook my head in disbelief. Inside, I was bouncing off the walls.

I needed a drink. I needed to talk to Joan.

"Can we go straight to the hospital?"

Mick spat out the water he'd been drinking, laughing. "Are you *fucking* having a laugh? For one thing, this is still an active investigation. You're *very much* a live suspect. It would look like you interfering with the chief witness." He furrowed his brow. "An *absolute* non-starter."

I just wanted out of there. The walls were closing in. My head was spinning.

Mick suggested that when I got out, we sneak off to a hotel for the night, just to keep a low profile. He said he'd act as the go-between with the families. He also *stressed* the importance of me *staying away* from Joan.

I agreed.

I just wanted out of there.

The door slammed. I grabbed my belongings, signed for them, and followed Mick out.

The cops still treated me like a *fucking criminal*, even though I'd done *nothing* wrong.

I tried to turn my phone on.

Dead.

"Fuck this. I'm going home," I muttered. "I've got to go at some stage. Why the fuck not now? It can't be *that* bad."

Mick let out a heavy sigh. "Are you *fucking* serious?"

I pulled heavily on a cigarette as we approached the car.

"Ronnie O'Neill. *Fuck that*. Peggy and Paddy are going to *fucking kill you*," Mick said flatly. He paused. "And when I say *kill you*, I don't mean a slap round the face."

I shrugged. "How bad can it be?"

I took another drag. My head was light.

"You *do* know that even your own mother is going to kill you, and your *brothers*," Mick warned. He paused again. "Fuck sake, I *told them all* I'd keep you offside tonight!"

I clapped my hands. "Good. Then they won't know I'm going home."

I smirked, raised my eyebrows, and dragged on the cigarette.

Mick sighed but had to admit I had a point.

I stubbed the fag out, and we got in the car.

I *loved* his shiny, blue Alfa Romeo. It was a *fucking flying machine.*

"You *sure* you want to do this?" Mick asked, gripping the steering wheel tightly, staring straight ahead.

I nodded.

The car *roared* out of the station, tearing up the road.

I put the window down, letting the air hit my face. I pulled out my recovered box of cigarettes and held them in front of Mick's face.

"You mind?"

"Not in the car, mate. I *just* had her valeted."

I rolled my eyes but let it go.

I couldn't wait to get home.

When we arrived, an eerie silence hung in the air. I waited for Mick to reverse into the driveway before getting out.

My neighbour stood at his front window, curtain clutched tightly in his hand. He just shook his head.

I stared at him and mouthed two words. The second was *off.*

I patted every pocket, searching for my keys.

When I found them, I stabbed at the keyhole and stumbled inside.

For a second, I half-expected Siobhan to greet me with a frown, to start a shouting match.

A cold shiver ran down my spine. That would never happen again.

Mick followed me in, making sure I was alone.

Satisfied, he checked his watch, pursed his lips, and pointed at the door with his thumb.

"Work, mate. You gonna be okay?"

I nodded hastily.

He turned to go but paused.

"Don't let *anyone* in, mate. I'm *warning* you. There are a *lot* of people who want you dead."

I shook my head as he added, "I'll phone you later."

And then, he was gone.

Chapter 59
It's Only Just Begun

I yanked the fridge door open, grabbed a beer, twisted the top, and sank it in one go.

Rummaging through the cupboards, I found that everything had been cleaned out. Someone had been here. I finally spotted my whiskey glass, poured a large one, cracked open another beer, and perched myself on the high chair at the breakfast bar.

Plugging my phone into the charger, I took a slow slug of whiskey and headed for the downstairs toilet.

As I washed my hands, I caught my reflection in the mirror. I stared. Splashed cold water on my face. Grabbed the towel, rubbing it roughly as I shook my head.

I muttered aloud, "This is your turn to mourn."

For a second, I felt smug. Self-satisfied.

I stretched and turned to walk out—just as the front door swung open.

Rage bubbled inside me. I wanted to be alone.

Donna walked in, oblivious to me standing in the hallway. She shook out her umbrella and placed it in the stand. Then she turned.

She saw me.

She squealed and jumped back.

"You fucking bastard!" she shrieked.

Then she launched at me, fists flying, slapping, punching, kicking.

"You bastard! You fucking bastard!" she kept repeating as she pummelled me.

Eventually, I managed to grab her arms, pulling her in so she couldn't keep hitting me.

"What the fuck are you doing here?" she sobbed.

I moved back slightly.

"I live here. I might ask you the same thing."

"I... I don't know what the fuck I'm doing," she cried. "I couldn't go home. I miss Siobhan. I miss you—you complete bastard. I wanted to be here... to feel you both. Mostly Siobhan."

I let her go.

We stood there, silent.

Then I walked to the kitchen.

She followed closely.

"How could you do this to me?" she asked. "With that bitch Joan?"

I turned, staring.

She was shaking now. "Ronnie is going to fucking kill you."

"Well, he can join the queue," I muttered. "And all thanks to you, by the way."

Her face paled.

I poured her a whiskey. She hesitated but took the glass.

"It's only half four, Colin," she whispered.

We drank.

She climbed onto the stool opposite me. Silence hung between us—thick, suffocating. The calm before the storm.

Then, she spoke.

"What the fuck were you thinking? Joan? Fucking Joan? And poor Siobhan—barely dead!" She shook her head, disgusted. "You are some fucked-up piece of shit."

She sipped.

She seemed to have forgotten her own betrayal.

I reminded her.

She cried.

I cried.

"What a fucking mess," she whispered.

I had to agree.

I refilled our glasses. Sucked on my beer bottle. Slumped, resigned.

We drank some more.

I tried to explain my shit situation with Joan—everything. Liverpool. Work. Bribery. Stalking. How she infiltrated Siobhan's family.

Donna wasn't convinced.

By the time we checked the clock, it was 8:43.

The whiskey bottle was empty.

She reached for her phone.

"Chinese?" she asked.

She ordered the same as two or three nights ago.

I wandered to the toilet. As I unzipped, I punched my security code into my phone. Slipped it into my pocket, waiting for it to kick in.

I caught myself in the mirror as I pissed. Jesus, I looked rough.

I felt rough.

Then my phone started.

Buzzing. Beeping. Whistling. Vibrating. Squealing at me.

Holy fuck.

Over fifteen hundred messages.

I couldn't deal with this now.

I had to deal with this now.

I didn't deal with it.

WhatsApp would show people I'd read their messages. I turned the phone off.

As the screen faded, I caught a glimpse of my missed calls.

Twenty-three.

From my mum.

I exhaled.

I couldn't deal with the fallout.

I wanted one night. Just one night alone with Donna.

The doorbell rang.

I froze.

Donna stumbled past me. I ducked behind the bathroom door.

"Chinese," she mumbled, unlatching the door. She handed the guy cash.

I breathed.

Walking out, I followed her into the living room.

She tripped into the space where the coffin had been. I fell on top of her.

We giggled.

I hauled her up, and we made our way to the kitchen.

As she grabbed plates, I was thinking, I need to put that dining table back. It works better at that end of the room.

I opened more wine.

We ate.

Drank.

In silence.

We were pissed.

Donna looked beautiful.

I woke at 5:39 a.m.

Naked.

Donna purred softly beside me.

My head felt like it was hanging off.

I staggered to the toilet, bracing myself over the bowl as I pissed.

All I wanted... was sleep.

I crawled back into bed.

Donna rolled over, wrapping her arm around my waist. I pulled her in, and we kissed.

I woke to the feeling of her massaging between my legs. She climbed on top, and we rocked. I enjoyed it, climaxing just after she did.

My head pounded as I stood under the shower, letting the water scald my skin.

My phone buzzed and flashed on the closed toilet lid. I had turned it on again.

Donna grabbed a towel and disappeared into the main bathroom.

Dressed, we made our way downstairs.

I made coffee.

Then I asked her to leave.

She hated it, hesitating in the kitchen.

I had to reassure her—whisper empty promises about a future together, about how being seen now would make things worse.

Reluctantly, she agreed.

I just wanted her gone.

I sipped my third cup of strong, black coffee and opened my messages.

They all followed the same pattern.

Disbelief.

Hatred.

Disgust.

Threats.

More hatred.

Even Donna's messages from before last night's bedroom gymnastics—so much venom before she ended up in my bed.

She was better than Siobhan. But not even close to Joan.

Every message was dripping with contempt.

Except two.

Mum. And Joan.

Mum's were desperate, repetitive.

"Colin, son, can you please contact me as soon as you can? I don't believe what they're all saying about you. Is it true? It can't be!"

"Please, I don't WANT to believe what they're saying about you!"

Then, Joan.

'John from work'—I needed to change that name.

"Hi, you okay? They say I'll be in here at least two weeks. Never mind me—how are you? You've lost your wife and been arrested."

Mick had called to see her.

"Let me know you're okay. I would love a visit. Can't wait to get a whole night with you! Don't worry, I told them it wasn't you. Everything will be fine, baby!"

My blood ran cold.

I wanted her out of my life.

The doorbell rang.

I froze.

Slowly, I made my way to the latch.

Mum and Joe barged past me without a glance.

Mum turned on me, eyes burning.

"What the fuck have you done? You've ruined so many lives— mine, our family's name. The O'Neills are devastated. You might as well have taken a gun and shot Siobhan yourself!"

She was shaking.

"Tell me," she whispered. "Please tell me it isn't true."

The pain on her face was unbearable.

I shrugged.

That was all it took.

Her expression crumbled. She was too hurt to scream. Instead, she uttered the words every child dreads hearing from their mother.

"Shame. And disappointment."

Joe scoffed, shaking his head, his hands gripping his temples.

I had nothing. No defense.

"I'm sorry," I muttered. "I didn't mean for any of this to happen."

Joe laughed. A bitter, cruel laugh.

"You didn't mean for this to happen? Mum, he's having a fucking laugh!"

He was enjoying this. Loving it.

"You're a fucking waste of space," he spat. "Ronnie and Peggy are on their way. You'll be lucky to get out of here alive."

He grinned. "I might even help Ronnie."

Panic surged through me.

"Who the fuck invited them?" I snapped. "I'm not ready for this!"

Mum shook her head.

"You should've thought about that before you did what you did," she said, her voice hollow.

Joe disappeared into the kitchen.

"Tea, Mum?" he called.

She sighed. Followed him.

"Yes, please, son."

She called him son. The way she used to say it to me.

The doorbell rang again.

Ronnie and Peggy.

The silence that followed was suffocating.

"Tea?" Mum asked.

Ronnie just stared at me.

He hadn't reached for me yet. That was something.

"You are not worth my time or my headspace," he finally said, voice low and dangerous. "What did my daughter ever see in you?"

Peggy rubbed his arm.

Then, he reached for the knife block.

My stomach dropped.

He lifted the large carving knife, holding it up, pointing it at me.

"Give me one good reason," he murmured, "why I shouldn't drive this through your fucking heart."

Joe laughed. "I don't think the fucker has a heart."

Mum just shook her head, over and over.

Peggy—calm, too calm—placed a hand on Ronnie's arm.

"Put the knife down, love."

Her voice was gentle. But her eyes were ice.

"He's not worth it."

She turned to me.

"You are dead to us," she said. "We want the money back. The eighteen grand we gave you for the deposit. You'll never be welcome by anyone in this family again. Do you even understand the damage you've caused?"

She exhaled, shaking her head.

"I hate you."

I had never heard her swear before.

"We should be demanding the whole wedding cost back too," she added. "Thirty grand, pissed away on a bastard like you."

Mum hung her head.

"We never want to hear from you again," Peggy continued. "Once you've given Joe the money, we're done."

She turned to Mum and Joe.

"This will drive a bus between our families," she said softly. "I'm sorry."

Then, she looked back at me.

"And you can tell that bitch—the one we took into our home, into our hearts—that if she ever comes near us again—"

Ronnie cut in.

"I'll strangle the bitch."

Mum turned to me.

The disgust in her eyes was like a knife to my gut.

She had loved the O'Neills.

Now, because of me, that was gone.

Ronnie, Peggy, and Joe turned for the door.

Joe was already reassuring them.

He would get them their money.

Mum stayed a moment longer.

She sighed.

"I'll never forgive you for this."

Her voice cracked.

"How could you?"

She turned to Joe.

"Take me home. I can't fucking look at him anymore."

They left.

I exhaled, pressing my palms into the counter.

I wanted a beer.

It was only 11:30.

The doorbell rang.

I opened it.

Mick stood there, shaking his head.

"No, thanks," he said flatly.

I frowned. "What?"

"This isn't a social call."

Chapter 60
Figaro

I texted Donna, "Coast is clear. Wasn't as bad as I thought it would be! Are you calling over tonight?"

My doorbell rang again. Ally and Mick were standing awkwardly, staring at the ground. They stood back as if waiting for me to invite them in.

I didn't want to.

I had to.

They walked past me. Ally didn't even look at me. I had never seen him like this before, even though he knew almost everything about me and Joan. "What the fuck's his problem?" Mick was less concerned. I recognised a car driving past as I closed the door. I think it was Mrs Smith's—a baby pink Nissan Figaro.

Ally still said nothing.

I told him about Mum and Joe and the O'Neills' earlier intrusion. "Beer?" I asked as I opened the fridge.

"I've spoken with the police." He shook his head again. "Trust me, you better not go near your woman Joan in the hospital. All they have is that she described the guy as short and heavy. Obviously, you're six-two and—" he prodded my tummy, "while the bay window is starting, you could hardly be described as heavy." He was sculpted like a modern-day Adonis.

I opened the beer and took a slug.

He continued, "I got a sense from that copper Forbes that they don't believe Joan."

Ally interrupted, "Are you sure you're telling us everything?"

"Fuck, of course I am. I have no reason to rape Joan, for fuck's sake, she can't get enough of me." I showed them some messages Joan had sent. This seemed to placate them, though Mick added, "Whoever did this tried to strangle her! She's lucky to be alive, and you, my friend, are very lucky she came round!" He nodded as he said this.

I wanted them to go.

Ally said he had to go back to work, and Mick followed him out the door.

I was just starting my second beer when my phone rang. Paul. I considered ignoring it. I didn't need another lecture. Thank God he wasn't anything like Mum or Joe.

"You okay, brother?" I put him on loudspeaker.

Forgetting I was on the phone, I nodded, then quickly followed with, "Yeah, as well as can be expected." I stopped myself.

"You have caused an awful lot of hurt, Colin. There are some people who will never forgive you for this."

Fuck, don't I know!

He went on, "Mum is devastated, says she will never be able to hold her head up again. She has done nothing but cry, says your selfishness has even robbed her of any chance of properly mourning Siobhan." He went silent, then, "I'm just saying, if I were you, I would keep a very low profile for at least a few weeks, or months even. Your Mr Smith will not be too pleased."

Oh my God, he would probably fire me—and Joan.

That bastard Joan has ruined my life. How could I be so fucking stupid?

She needs to go.

Paul got his bit off his chest and hung up.

I stared at the phone for ages before plucking up the courage to hit the button that put me through to 'work.'

"Good morning—oh, sorry, good afternoon—Smith and Partners."

I tried to be casual. "Hiya, Janet, it's Colin Hill here. Mr Smith about?"

She didn't even reply. Within seconds, I was talking with Mr Smith. I feared this conversation. I was right to.

Mr Smith began, "I am very sorry, but I have begun the process of terminating," he paused, "your contract."

I hung my head. I had gotten used to the lifestyle.

"I'm so sorry, Mr Smith, I didn't mean for any of this to happen!" I went to continue, but he cut across me. "You will receive the normal amount of severance pay. One of our cleaners will clear your desk. Let me be clear about this: the reputation of this company comes before anything. No way am I letting you, or anyone else for that matter, besmirch my good name—not on my watch." He wasn't finished. "You will never darken this door again, and expect the car back no later than tomorrow."

He hung up.

I stared at my phone again.

I quickly grabbed my car keys, ran to the door, jumped in, and sped to the off-licence. I grabbed some grocery essentials and prepared for the lockdown.

When I returned, I checked my phone. Joan had texted again.

"Sorry you're going through this without me. When I get out, all things will be different, you'll see! I have big plans for us! xxxxxxx"

Donna came over at eight. I had told her to wait until it was dark. We had sex in the hall. Sober sex. We drank from my replenished stock. I made fish pie. We went to bed. We had more sex.

She'd said that before.

I texted back, "I am trying to sort out this mess. Can you please leave me alone?"

Concentrate on getting better. Please don't text me again, as the police are watching my every move, and they are not sure they believe you! I'm begging you. I will not be able to see you until you're out of there, and it's just better if we don't communicate at the minute."

My lockdown continued for the next two weeks. Donna called under the cloak of darkness every night.

She was still calling with Ronnie and Peggy most days. She even called with my mother. The reports weren't good. At least I could see that my mother had started to read my messages again.

One more message: "Sad faces, I will see you soon."

I didn't respond.

She still wasn't responding.

How could I?

It was Sunday night. We had just finished a roast leg of lamb dinner when I received a call from Joan. I didn't answer.

She texted, "I'm getting out Tuesday or Wednesday. Can you pick me up? We can go back to yours or mine and have a cuddle."

"I have an interview in Dublin on Wednesday, and there is an information day on Tuesday. You will have to get a taxi to yours, sorry!" I was lying through my teeth.

I couldn't face her.

Donna took my hand as we reclined on the big corner sofa. I was about to turn on the TV when she stared at me and said, "I've missed my period!"

I had thought it a bit strange that she refused wine, but she had covered herself by saying she had to drive home later as she was going back to work tomorrow.

I was shaken.

Another me?

I was excited.

Donna said she was too.

She decided to stay at mine, always being careful to park two streets away.

This called for a celebration. I poured some whiskey. We went to bed, we made love, we slept.

When I awoke, Donna had already left. I was glad.

I turned my phone on and went to the toilet. When I returned, it buzzed. Joan.

"I'm struggling to manage this. Can we meet as soon as you get back from Dublin? We need to talk. I'm sure you would agree!"

I needed her to leave me alone.

Why hadn't she just died? Everything would be so much simpler.

"Did Mister Smith sack you too? I'm sure he did! I will get in touch over the weekend!" I pressed send.

My phone buzzed immediately. "Sack me? He says I will be getting your job for a trial period when I return. He even wanted to know if I wanted your car?"

Bastard. With me out of the way, he was making his move.

"He even took my keys and has gone to my apartment to get it ready for my return. He's had the decorators in. I can't wait to see it."

In my rage, I didn't respond.

When Donna returned, she was full of the joys of spring. She had bought something that was resting in a small gift bag with hearts on it. "Ah, Valentine's Day. Wonder what she got me?"

She patted her tummy. In my mulling over the whole Joan and Mister Smith situation, I had forgotten about her big announcement.

She hugged me. We kissed.

We ate dinner. For the first time in weeks, I didn't feel like drinking.

Joan continued to text every day, even though I had explicitly asked her not to.

It was mid-February, and the evenings had started to stretch. Donna had left early on Saturday morning. She was going shopping with her mum and Aunt Peggy. I was glad of the space.

Donna had said that her mother had asked her a strange question as she left after her visit on Friday night. "Something different about you. Have you something to tell me? A new man, perhaps?"

I nearly choked on my coffee, imagining Donna introducing me to her family.

Chapter 61
Night Caller

Donna came over at eight. I had told her to wait until it was dark. We had sex in the hall—sober sex. We drank from my replenished stock. I made fish pie. We went to bed. We had more sex.

My lockdown continued for the next two weeks. Donna called under the cloak of darkness every night. She was still calling with Ronnie and Peggy most days. She even called with my mother. The reports weren't good. At least I could see that my mother had started to read my messages again.

She still wasn't responding.

It was Sunday night. We had just finished a roast leg of lamb dinner when I received a call from Joan. I didn't answer.

She texted, "I'm getting out Tuesday or Wednesday. Can you pick me up? We can go back to yours or mine and have a cuddle."

"I have an interview in Dublin on Wednesday, and there's an information day on Tuesday. You'll have to get a taxi to yours, sorry!" I was lying through my teeth.

I couldn't face her.

Donna took my hand as we reclined on the big corner sofa. I was about to turn on the TV when she stared at me and said, "I've missed my period."

I had thought it strange when she refused wine, but she had covered herself by saying she had to drive home later as she was going back to work tomorrow.

I was shaken.

Another me?

I was excited.

Donna said she was too.

She decided to stay at mine, always careful to park two streets away.

This called for a celebration. I poured some whiskey. We went to bed. We made love. We slept.

When I awoke, Donna had already left. I was glad.

I turned my phone on and went to the toilet. When I returned, it buzzed. Joan.

"I'm struggling to manage this. Can we meet as soon as you get back from Dublin? We need to talk. I'm sure you'd agree!"

I needed her to leave me alone.

Why hadn't she just died? Everything would be so much simpler.

"Did Mister Smith sack you too? I'm sure he did! I will get in touch over the weekend!" I pressed send.

My phone buzzed immediately.

"Sack me? He says I'll be getting your job for a trial period when I return. He even wanted to know if I wanted your car."

Bastard. With me out of the way, he was making his move.

"He even took my keys and has gone to my apartment to get it ready for my return. He's had the decorators in. I can't wait to see it."

In my rage, I didn't respond.

When Donna returned, she was full of the joys of spring. She had bought something resting in a small gift bag with hearts on it. "Ah, Valentine's Day. Wonder what she got me?"

She patted her tummy. In my mulling over the whole Joan-Mister Smith situation, I had forgotten about her big announcement.

She hugged me. We kissed.

We ate dinner. For the first time in weeks, I didn't feel like drinking.

Joan continued to text every day, even though I had explicitly asked her not to. It was mid-February, and the evenings had started to stretch. Donna had left early on Saturday morning—she was going shopping with her mum and Aunt Peggy. I was glad of the space. Donna had mentioned that her mother had asked her a strange question as she left after her visit on Friday night: "Something different about you. Have you something to tell me? A new man, perhaps?"

I nearly choked on my coffee, imagining Donna introducing me to her family.

Chapter 62
Day Caller

With Donna gone, I was sipping coffee and smoking with abandon. I was thinking about how to get rid of Joan when I looked up, and she was standing in front of me.

"Why are you ignoring me?" She still had a faint red line around her neck. "We are in this together!"

She stood back. She looked amazing.

I stood. She approached. She wanted a hug. I wanted anything but. I made my feelings clear. She looked sad.

"We have lots to discuss," she continued as she sat on a patio chair. "How are we going to move forward?"

"WE?" I exclaimed. "There is no fucking we! I never want to see you again."

Her eyes widened. My heart sank. I feared her in that moment.

"You don't want to see me anymore? We will fucking see about that!" She pushed the outdoor table to one side and stood up.

"You have fucking ruined every part of my life! I have lost my wife, my job, my family, my friends," I pointed at the house, "I have lost my car. I will probably lose my home! And it's all your fucking fault!"

She smiled. "You won't get rid of me that easy." She was about to continue when Donna returned. She looked at me.

"What is she fucking doing here?" Donna flashed a look at Joan.

"Me? Me? What am I doing here? I might ask you the same fucking question."

Joan looked fantastic when she was angry. And she was angry.

336

Donna looked at me, patted her tummy, and said, "I'm here to see the father of my unborn child!"

Joan's nostrils flared. Her eyes widened even further than before. She looked right through me and ignored Donna.

"You will fucking pay for this!" She turned on her heel, and as I put my arm around Donna, we heard her car screech off.

"I'd been dreading this. I knew she wasn't going to go away easily." I shrugged.

Donna frowned. "We haven't heard the end of that one. Trust me on that."

We went inside and locked ourselves in.

We were just settling to watch Wanted on Netflix when my phone buzzed.

"I can't fucking believe you. I thought we had a chance. I thought the path was clear. I thought we had a future. As I said, you won't get rid of me that easily. That Donna better watch out. I will make sure everyone knows what a bastard she is. I had my suspicions during the wake for Siobhan. She was just too ever-present. I wonder what Ronnie and Peggy, your mum, and all the families will think when they find out."

My pulse raced, and I showed the message to Donna. We hadn't discussed telling anyone, and the enormity of what lay ahead of us was suddenly present in Joan's message.

Donna ran to the downstairs bathroom, crying.

My phone buzzed again.

"Mister Smith is on his way to mine. He wants to discuss my new position." I'll bet he does, I thought. "Maybe we will have a bit of fun too!"

If she was trying to make me jealous, it worked.

Donna returned. "This is a mess, Colin," she sobbed. "How are we going to sort this out? And don't even think termination. I wouldn't. I couldn't."

It had crossed my mind, but only fleetingly.

Donna sobbed all the way through Wanted. We went to bed, and as I brushed my teeth, I looked in the mirror and imagined Joan and Stanley Smith discussing more than one position.

Donna was sitting up in bed. She wanted to discuss our predicament.

I didn't.

She talked. I could hear but wasn't listening. I couldn't get the image of Joan and Smith out of my head.

Donna nudged me. "Are you even listening to me?"

I nodded but said I was tired and suggested we had all day Sunday to discuss it.

She gave in and went to the bathroom to brush her teeth and go to the toilet.

When she returned, I was pretending to sleep.

Chapter 63
Alibi

When I wakened, Donna wasn't there. The door was being thumped heavily as I peed. I washed my hands and turned the light on. As I looked out the window, I could see what looked like a uniformed Billy Sloan.

I thought the knock sounded familiar.

As I turned, Donna came into the room. "The police want you downstairs. They wouldn't say what it was about."

As I slipped on my robe and walked down the stairs, Forbes stepped forward.

"Colin Hill, I am arresting you for the rape and murders of Jane Sheridan in Ballymena on October 23rd, 2019. I am also arresting you for the rape and murder of Jennifer Sullivan on Saturday the 7th of November in Liverpool. We are also arresting you for the murder and rape of Sheila Jones on the twenty-first of November in Knock apartments, and finally—"

I started laughing. "What the fuck are you on about? You're insane! Murder? Rape? For fuck's sake, I've never done anything like this."

I looked at Donna, standing pregnant and starting to wonder. "I didn't, I swear."

"If I could just finish—"

I shook my head. "Fuck, there's more?"

He continued. "Finally, the murder of Joan Sanders in the same Knock apartments in the early hours of today." He paused. "Read him his rights and cuff him, please."

Susan blurted out, "He couldn't have done that! He was in bed with me all night."

I quickly agreed.

Forbes looked at her and, with a fake smile, said, "Madam, your evidence in the past has proven to be anything but reliable."

"But he has been here all night!" She was adamant.

He ignored her.

Billy moved forward, and as he was cuffing me, I was shoved to one side as six police officers in space suits passed me in the hallway.

"You have the right to remain silent…"

I started to zone out.

"We have a warrant to search the premises. Please move aside, madam."

Donna was crying heavily. What could I do?

I was frog-marched out to the waiting panda car. Sloan shoved the top of my head as he forcibly pushed me into the back seat.

"You're in some trouble now, boyo," he said, shaking his head.

Donna was shouting after me. "Don't worry! I'll phone Mick and Ally. I know you didn't do these things."

Forbes got in the passenger side, and Sloan was driving.

"This is a big misunderstanding!"

They weren't listening to me.

When we arrived, the policeman booking me in smiled in his disgust. "Knew we'd see you back here."

I didn't even bother trying to argue.

As I was ushered into the room for questioning, the handcuffs were removed, and I was told to take a seat. They left me alone. As they did, I protested my innocence. They weren't interested.

I rubbed my wrists. They were more painful than they had been in Liverpool. Then I held my head in my hands.

This couldn't be happening again.

I was there for three hours before the nasty bastard opened the door and tossed a plastic bag in my direction. Donna had obviously brought some of my clothes down.

I had said that I was saying nothing until Mick arrived, and I wished to fuck he would hurry up. I wanted—needed—water, and I didn't trust that man not to spit in it.

I wanted to see Donna.

I was going to protest but thought better of it.

It hit me in a wave.

Joan is dead.

Fuck me.

Happy days.

In my happiness, I had omitted to understand that while she was dead, I was in a police station being charged with multiple rapes and murders—including hers.

Forbes and Sloan returned. They got me a can of Diet Coke.

"Your brief has been delayed in court. It would be easier for everyone involved if you just admitted to what you did. The judge would go easier on you too."

Forbes looked at Billy. Billy nodded.

Forbes then ruffled his pages. "We have done further investigations, and CCTV footage shows you leaving Knock apartments at approximately three twenty-four on the morning of November twenty-first. Funnily enough, the day you got married."

I drank the Coke.

"Can you tell us your whereabouts last night between midnight and four A.M.?" Billy sat back and folded his arms as he said this.

"Where is Donna?" I assumed she had brought the clothes. "I need to talk to her, explain all this."

Forbes laughed. "You'll not be talking to anyone today, son. We have so much evidence against you that even Houdini couldn't get you out this time!"

I was confident that they didn't, and then he began. "For the tape," he pushed the button, and it whirred into action. After ten seconds, it beeped. "On October twenty-third, 2019, we have clear evidence from the Galgorm Manor that you were staying the night, and that just happens to be the night that—" he looked at his notes, "Jane Sheridan was murdered in her own bed."

"This is no time for humour, Mister Hill, I can assure you!" Forbes stood up. "The evidence we have is watertight. You did these awful things, you know you did, and what's more, we know you did."

I did panic a bit but simply said, "I'm saying nothing without Mick here!"

Just then, there was a knock at the door. Through the small gap, someone whispered something.

"Show him in," said Forbes, and seconds later, Mick walked in.

"Hope you're not questioning my client without me present, D.I. Forbes!" Mick was coolness personified.

"No questions, just presenting him with our damning evidence." Sloan smugly smiled.

Mick looked straight at Billy. "I don't remember talking to you. I was talking to the organ grinder."

I smiled.

Forbes repeated the evidence for Mick, and he began to look pale as he vigorously rubbed his face with his hands.

On second hearing, it did seem pretty bad.

Mick leaned in and whispered, "Just keep saying, no comment."

The tape was running.

The questions began.

"Can you account for your whereabouts on October twenty-third, twenty nineteen?"

"No comment."

"You were seen leaving the Hilton Hotel on Thomas Steers Way in Liverpool on November seventh at six twenty-seven A.M. Can you tell us why you were there?"

"No comment."

Mick nodded.

Forbes continued, "You're not helping your case by ignoring our questions!"

"No comment."

I was starting to enjoy this. Felt like I was in a movie.

The interrogation, if you could call it that, continued for ages. I must have said "no comment" thirty times. I had even started to say it before he asked a question.

They grew frustrated, and Forbes stood. He looked at his watch.

"For the benefit of the tape, interview terminated at four forty-four P.M."

He looked at me and grimaced. "We have applied for an extension on your warrant. Because it is rape and murder, we have asked that we can question you for up to ninety-six hours."

He told Sloan to take me to a holding cell. Mick said he wanted to talk to me, so he followed.

When the door slammed closed, Mick stared at me. "Talk about fucking déjà vu. What the fuck is going on? Care to explain?"

"I didn't do any of this, I swear."

I was about to continue when he butted in. "Doesn't fucking look that way, mate. I'm just saying, like."

He had a point.

"I've stuff to do at the office before I get home. Say fuck all to them," he pointed in the direction of reception. "I'll be back first thing. You take tonight to work out in your head how we're going to explain all of this."

He smiled, tapped the door, it opened, and he left.

Chapter 64
Pinotage

I opened the water bottle and drank. I wondered what Donna was doing—she could hardly confide in anyone.

Donna had phoned in sick to work and spent most of the day at the police station. She never got to see Colin and was, frankly, getting fed up with the dirty looks she was getting from the fat policeman at reception.

Eventually, realizing she wasn't going to see Colin, she decided to leave. As she drove, she made up her mind to stay at Colin's place—her toiletries were already there, it was closer, and she wanted to sleep in his bed.

She stopped at the off-sales and picked up a half-bottle of South African Pinotage. Baby or no baby, she needed a drink.

Next door, she grabbed a large sirloin steak and a bag of frozen chips. It was already dark when she pulled into the driveway.

She was exhausted.

As she opened the front door, she thought she heard something upstairs. Her heart skipped a beat. Setting the wine and food down in the kitchen, she went to check.

Nothing out of the ordinary.

Satisfied, she returned to the kitchen, turned the oven on, took the butter from the fridge, and dropped a dollop onto the skillet pan. She spread the chips on a baking tray, shoved them into the oven, and poured herself a glass of wine.

She was chopping garlic for garlic butter when she heard something outside.

A shadow passed the window.

Her pulse quickened.

A knock at the back door.

She hesitated, then peered through the half-closed blind. A faint outline—tall, broad. It looked like Ally.

Relief flooded her as she moved to the door and unlocked it.

Up close, under the dim light, she realized how tall and good-looking Ally was. Had she never noticed before?

She stepped aside to let him in.

"Won't stay long," he said. "Saw a light on, and since Mick told me Colin was arrested—something about four fucking murders and rapes—I had to check in. What the fuck?" Ally ran a hand through his thick, dark hair.

"He didn't do any of it," Donna started.

Ally cut across her. "Mick says the evidence is pretty compelling."

"Well, I was here last night. All night. And I know Colin never left the house, so he couldn't have murdered anyone last night. And the police are saying the cases are linked!"

Ally looked confused. His gaze flicked over her. "Still, it's going to be difficult for him to wriggle out of this one."

He shrugged. "Goodnight."

Donna double-checked that both doors were locked before sitting down at the table. She was halfway through cutting her steak when she felt it—

A presence.

Startled, she spun around, steak knife in hand.

Nothing.

"Jesus," she muttered, shaking her head with a nervous laugh.

When she finished eating, she cleaned up and made her way upstairs.

As she brushed her teeth, she caught her reflection in the mirror.

Even she could see how much she looked like Siobhan.

Absentmindedly, she ran her fingers through her hair, wishing it were more like Siobhan's.

The house phone rang in the distance.

She ignored it.

A shiver ran through her. The house was cold.

She hadn't packed any pyjamas—she never needed them before.

Rummaging through the top drawer of the dresser, she found a pair of fleece floral-patterned pyjamas. Siobhan's.

She hesitated, then slipped them on.

She climbed into bed and turned off the bedside lamp.

Darkness.

She lay there, thinking about Colin, the baby, their future—

Bang.

A loud noise outside.

Too tired to investigate, she pulled the quilt tightly around her and rolled over.

Sleep didn't come easily.

She was too aware of Colin's absence.

She couldn't wait for him to come home.

3:28 A.M.

The policeman on duty slid the hatch open to check the cell.

"Colin Hill' was scrawled in black marker on the white tile beside the door.

Inside, Colin lay fast asleep, snoring loudly.

Chapter 65
The Empresses New Clothes

In the morning, Donna crawled out of bed, grabbed a towel, and headed for the en-suite shower.

After drying off, she sat at Siobhan's dressing table, carefully applying Siobhan's foundation and drying her hair with Siobhan's hairdryer.

She reached for her jeans, then paused—she had no clean underwear, and she'd been wearing the same T-shirt for two days.

Opening the second drawer of the dresser, she pulled out one of Siobhan's black T-shirts. Then, in the third drawer, she found a selection of tights.

She was about to check the wardrobe when she remembered—Siobhan kept her underwear in the bottom drawer.

She knelt, opened it, and pulled out a black bra and a pair of knickers.

As she fastened the bra in front of her, a sudden tingle ran down the small of her back.

She spun around.

Nothing.

Heart racing, she slipped the cups over her breasts, adjusted them, and pulled on Siobhan's T-shirt.

Then she saw it—the black coat Colin had bought for Siobhan, hanging in the wardrobe.

She hesitated, then shrugged it on.

Turning to the mirror, she smiled.

She liked what she saw.

Donna had decided to stay at Colin's until he was released, but she needed a few essentials from her apartment.

She locked up and drove across town.

At her place, she grabbed jeans, shoes, underwear, makeup— though she wondered why she bothered. She and Siobhan were nearly the same size, maybe an inch or two difference here and there.

But now, what had been Siobhan's… was hers.

Stuffing everything into a small carry-on suitcase, she checked the kitchen clock—12:34 P.M.

She shut the door behind her.

On the way back to Colin and Siobhan's house, she stopped for groceries and another bottle of wine.

She called the police station, asking to speak to Constable Sloan.

"He's out on a call," the receptionist said.

"And Colin?"

"Nothing new."

That was all.

She sighed and hung up.

On a whim, she decided to stop by Peggy and Ronnie's house.

Patrick answered the door. His face was pale, his expression vacant. He stepped aside without a word.

Inside, Ronnie slouched in his chair, silent, nursing a drink.

Peggy stood and hugged Donna tightly, staring at her so intently that it made Donna uncomfortable.

"Cup of tea, love?" Ronnie finally asked.

Donna nodded, following Peggy into the kitchen. Patrick stayed behind, staring blankly into space.

As Donna sipped her tea, Peggy's gaze drifted to her coat.

"That's awful like one our poor Siobhan used to own," she mused.

Donna's cheeks flushed.

She tugged at the lapel and forced a smile. "This? Oh—this was... sorry, is Siobhan's. You know us two—we shared everything."

Peggy smiled softly. She had always loved how close Donna and Siobhan were. For a fleeting moment, it almost felt like Siobhan was standing in front of her.

They chatted about the funeral.

Then Donna hesitated before mentioning Colin's arrest, watching for their reaction.

Ronnie's face darkened.

"That bastard's name will never be uttered in my house again!" he roared, slamming his cup down.

Donna flinched.

"I want no one—no one—from this family having anything to do with him or his lot. Ever again." He drew a breath, shaking his head in disgust. "I hope they lock the bastard up and throw away the key."

Peggy just nodded.

Donna swallowed hard, setting down her cup. She quickly made her goodbyes.

As she moved to open the living room door to say farewell to Patrick, Peggy caught her elbow, squeezing it gently.

"Just leave him," she whispered. "He's been acting awfully strange this last wee while."

Donna nodded, hugged her aunt, and left.

Chapter 66
Jelly and Banana

I was still refusing to eat the food they brought to my cell, but I finally asked the policeman, *"What happens now?"*

"You'll be interviewed again when your brief arrives," he said. "Apparently, he's been held up and might not get here today. They got their extension, so they can hold you for up to ninety-six hours."

I checked my watch.

2:34 PM.

I had been arrested at 7:00 AM the day before. If my calculations were right, I'd been in here for thirty-one and a half hours.

And I still hadn't eaten.

The policeman left the tray and shut the door.

I glanced at the food.

A bottle of water. Something that looked like stew. A small tub of jelly. A banana.

I drained the water, peeled the banana, and ate the jelly with my fingers.

Then I dozed off.

When I woke, it was almost 6:30 PM. Still no sign of Mick.

More food arrived, but no one spoke.

My thoughts drifted to my father—the man who had taught me everything.

How to succeed. How to get the most out of life.

He was a brilliant businessman. I admired him.

He always told me, *"Friends only weaken you, son."* He had very few himself.

I could see him now, standing before me—immaculately dressed, hands hooked in his red braces, saying, *"The only thing that matters is success and everything that comes with it. A big house, a nice car, money in the bank, and a couple of foreign holidays each year."*

He used to laugh every time he said the last part.

Everyone respected him.

Or so he told me.

Night was falling, and I wished he was here.

He would have sorted this out.

I slouched against the wall, contemplating the injustice of it all.

I wasn't going to take this.

I stood up and shouted from the center of my cell:

"This is unfair!

I did nothing!

You bastards will pay!

I have rights!

You can't just walk all over me!

I'm Colin Hill!"

My voice echoed off the walls.

"I am an honest man! A good man! I *wouldn't—couldn't*—do these things! I'm innocent!

You have no evidence!

I want out of here!

I want a smoke!

I want a drink!

Where is Donna?

I can pace up and down all night!

I am not going to—"

The hatch slid open.

The pimply cop peered in, shook his head, and shut it again.

I clenched my fists.

"roll over! My human liberties are being trampled on! My dignity has been removed! This is an *injustice*!

You'll all be sorry when you realize I am an innocent man!

A good man!

An *innocent* man!

I didn't do it!

I *didn't!*"

I pounded on the door.

Sloan opened the hatch.

"Right, pipe down in there," he muttered. "Some of us are trying to work. Go to sleep. Your solicitor phoned—he'll be here first thing."

I wasn't sure if he was telling the truth, but I lay down.

Sleep came quickly.

Chapter 67
Twitching

Donna sat in the conservatory, staring at her small bag.

She barely noticed the noise at first.

Then—a violent *crash* at the front of the house.

She nearly jumped out of her skin.

Heart pounding, she rushed to the door.

A very drunk Patrick stood in the garden, a brick in one hand.

He was about to throw it.

"Stop it! For God's sake, stop it!" Donna yelled, waving both hands. "What the hell are you doing? Why are you here?"

Patrick blinked at her, confused for a second.

Then, recognition dawned.

He sneered.

"Me?" He laughed bitterly. "*Me*? Never mind *me*—what the *fuck* are *you* doing here?"

He reeled backward, laughing again as he fell against the oak tree.

Donna instinctively placed a protective hand over her stomach.

Patrick's laughter twisted into a slurred snarl.

"I *knew* it," he spat. "I *always* knew it. You're a complete, selfish b.tch. You were *always* jealous of our Siobhan. She was always better looking than you."

His lip curled.

"*Pregnant*, you bastard?" His voice was thick with drink. "You should be the one dead. And that fucker Hill? Wait till I see him. I don't know why I don't just fucking *strangle* you now."

The curtains next door twitched.

Donna tensed.

She didn't want everyone knowing their business.

Patrick tried and failed to stand.

Donna's fear spiked. She slammed the door, locked it, and stood frozen in the hallway, listening.

Through the frosted glass, she saw Patrick stagger out of the driveway.

She thought—*was he laughing?*

Shaking his head?

She wasn't sure.

Her hands trembled as she grabbed Ally's card from the fridge and dialed.

He answered on the first ring.

"Can you come round to mine and Colin's? Patrick's been here. He threw a brick through the front window."

She was sobbing.

"I'll grab my tools and a sheet of plywood," Ally said. "Be right there."

Donna exhaled shakily.

She liked Ally.

When he arrived, he hugged her before heading into the living room.

He rubbed his chin as he assessed the damage—the gaping hole in the window, the shattered blinds, the brick resting neatly on the dining table.

"Give me a hand moving this back," he said.

Donna helped.

Ally had spent a lot of time in this house, working to make it a home for Siobhan and Colin.

Now, here he was again.

As he opened his toolbox, he glanced at Donna.

"There's been too much death recently," he muttered, shaking his head. "It has to stop."

Donna retreated to the kitchen.

When Ally finished, he strode in, opened the fridge, grabbed a beer, and winked.

"Payment," he said, grinning.

He took a swig.

"That'll hold for tonight. I'll pick up a pane of glass at the yard tomorrow—I've got the measurements."

Donna nodded.

She handed him a key to the back door.

"I want you to come and go as you please until Colin gets home."

Ally took it, his fingers lingering against hers for a second.

Then he smiled.

Stared directly at her.

Finished his beer.

And left.

Chapter 68
Hello?

The house phone roared to life, its shrill ring cutting through the silence.

Donna flinched, her pulse spiking.

She grabbed the receiver. "Hello?"

Nothing.

Frowning, she pulled the phone away from her ear and tried again. "Hello? Who is this?"

A click.

The line went dead.

She hesitated before setting the receiver back down, then made her way into the living room.

Just as she was about to leave, the phone rang again.

This time, she answered more cautiously.

Silence.

But not empty silence.

She could hear breathing. Slow. Deliberate.

Her spine prickled.

She didn't speak. Instead, she slammed the phone down.

In the kitchen, she poured herself a glass of water, trying to steady her hands.

Then—ring!

Water splashed over the counter as she jerked, her grip on the glass faltering.

The phone kept ringing.

Donna clenched her fists and stormed up the hallway, grabbing the receiver. "Who is this?! Hello?! Hello?!"

More silence.

More breathing.

Her voice wavered. "What the fuck do you want? Who is this?"

Nothing.

The silence pressed in on her, heavier than before.

"Please," Donna choked out, her voice cracking. "Please leave me alone."

She sank to the floor, still gripping the phone.

Rocking back and forth, she whispered, "Siobhan."

Her mind raced.

Who would have the house number?

The O'Neills. Colin. His work.

But then she realized—anyone could look it up.

Her breath hitched.

She let the receiver slip from her fingers and crawled toward the stairs. Gripping the bannister, she hauled herself up, her legs weak beneath her.

At the bedroom door, she hesitated.

She stepped inside.

The bed was unmade.

Slowly, she reached out—her fingertips grazing the soft fleece of Siobhan's pyjamas.

With a strangled cry, she flung them to the floor.

She clambered onto the bed and yanked the quilt over her head, letting its weight cocoon her.

She sobbed until exhaustion took her under.

In the depths of the night, she stirred.

A familiar warmth pressed against her leg.

Colin.

She exhaled and reached for him—

Only to find the bed empty.

Her breath caught.

She scrambled out of bed, heart pounding.

Sliding down the wall, she clutched her stomach, her entire body trembling.

She felt so alone.

Then, a thought hit her like a slap.

Ally had the number.

And the calls had started just after he left.

Her mind reeled.

She shook her head. No. Ally was Colin's friend.

Wasn't he?

At 3:31 AM, the policeman on duty slid back the hatch of Colin's cell.

Colin was fast asleep. Snoring. Oblivious.

Morning came in dull shades of grey.

Donna dragged herself out of bed and stepped into the shower, the water scalding against her skin.

Afterward, she pulled on her own underwear, then reached for Siobhan's rust-colored turtleneck.

The fabric clung to her chest like a second skin.

She exhaled slowly.

She wasn't leaving the house today.

Chapter 69
The See-Through Window

The house phone rang, startling Donna. She exhaled in relief when she saw Ally's name on the caller ID. He was calling to arrange a time to fix the window. She found herself glad— looking forward to seeing him, even.

Ally pulled up just before noon, easygoing as ever. They chatted while Donna boiled the kettle. Settling at the table, they sipped their tea, Ally dunking a chocolate biscuit before speaking. "Any news on Colin?"

Donna shook her head. "Nothing."

Ally sighed. "I think he's a goner."

Donna's grip tightened around her mug. She was surprised— disturbed, even—by how readily Ally had accepted Colin's guilt. She said nothing.

While Donna busied herself in the kitchen, she caught movement in the garden. Patrick. He was making his way to the back door. She braced herself. But the storm never came.

He walked through the conservatory and slumped onto a high stool. For a moment, neither of them spoke. Then, Patrick shook his head and mumbled, "I'm sorry."

Donna blinked. He sighed, rubbing his face. "I was drunk. And none of this—" He waved a tired hand, "is my business."

Before she could respond, Ally stepped in from the living room. "Window's sorted."

Patrick nodded, pulling out his wallet. "How much do I owe you?"

Ally shrugged. "Glass was just under two hundred. Labour's free."

Patrick counted out two hundred and twenty pounds and handed it over. As Ally closed the patio door behind him, Patrick stood.

He glanced at Donna's stomach and muttered, "Don't worry. Your secret's safe with me." And with that, he was gone.

Feeling relieved, Donna called the police station. They told her that Colin's solicitor had arrived and he was being interviewed. She smiled to herself. Good. He'll be home soon.

Expecting Colin back, Donna drove to the supermarket for supplies. When she returned, she froze in the doorway. Ally was in the kitchen. He was sipping water from a glass. Her stomach twisted. Why is he here?

She kept her voice even. "Did you forget something?"

Ally nodded, patting his back pocket. "Left my chisel." He pulled it out, flashing it before tucking it away again. Then, as if offhandedly, he added, "Ran into Colin's old boss at the newsagents. Says he's glad he sacked him. Hope Colin's got solid proof he didn't do this."

Donna's spine stiffened. Ally spoke as if Colin were already guilty. She didn't like it.

"He has a very good alibi," she said firmly.

Ally nodded, unconvinced. Then, switching gears, he finished his water. "Gotta run—grabbing shopping for my ma. Knee's still giving her trouble."

He started for the door but paused. "You around for a while?"

Donna hesitated. "Yeah."

"Good " He smiled. "Got a few small sparking jobs to finish up. Might as well get them done before Colin gets out. I'll swing back in half an hour with my tools."

Donna nodded. Ally jingled his keys. "Still got mine." And then he was gone.

Chapter 70
She Smells Sanctuary?

Ally left. Donna cooked pasta with pesto and lemon chicken, poured herself some wine, and put on Pure Cult through the Bluetooth speaker, cranking up the volume.

"She Sells Sanctuary" eased in for about ten seconds before the drumbeat had her head rocking.

She finished eating, glanced at her watch, and decided to use the toilet before Ally returned. She made her way to the downstairs loo, flipping on the light as darkness had settled outside. Sliding her tights down, she sat, sighing.

Then she heard footsteps.

They were faint but definite, right above her, on the stairs.

Ally?

She quickly finished, washed her hands, and stepped out, calling, "Ally?" from the bottom of the stairs.

No answer.

Even though she was alone, she scrunched her face in confusion. She must have imagined it, she thought, heading back through the dining room to the kitchen. She flicked off the fluorescent light, reaching for the side lamp on top of the microwave

And froze.

A man's shoe.

Just inside the conservatory.

Her spine tingled as she saw the foot twitch. Then she saw his eyes.

He lunged.

Donna grabbed the carving knife from its block, swiping wildly. The blade caught something, flesh or fabric, she wasn't sure, but it gave her just enough of an opening.

She ran.

Slamming the kitchen door behind her, she bolted through the dining room, yanking that door shut too, pulling an upright lamp across it.

Behind her, doors banged open. He was following.

She sprinted across the large hallway, heart pounding, breath ragged. Behind her, a stumble.

The lamp. He had tripped.

Keep going.

She swerved into the spare room, figuring he would assume she had run to the main bedroom. She slammed the door shut, pressing herself against it, gripping the knife. On the dresser, an almost-empty whiskey bottle. She grabbed it too.

Then a voice.

High-pitched, eerie, crawling under her skin.

"I know you're in here."

She gripped the knife tighter.

"It's your turn, Donna. They all had to go. It's your turn now."

The door nudged open.

Now.

With all the strength she had, she swung the whiskey bottle. It shattered against his head. He staggered, falling back toward the bannister. Wood creaked. Splintered.

She saw her chance.

SEMI-DETACHED

Dropping the broken bottle, she rushed forward, ramming the knife deep into his stomach.

The bannister gave way.

He tumbled down all eighteen stairs.

Silence.

She slumped against the wall, sobbing, staring down at the crumpled, bleeding figure. He lay perfectly still.

Shaking, she ran into the en suite, searching for her phone. It wasn't there.

She grabbed the house phone from beside the bed and punched in 999.

"Police. Quickly, please. I've just been attacked. He's still here. I think he's dead."

Castlereagh Station. The dispatcher told her to stay put.

Then she heard a rustle.

Her breath caught.

Stanley Smith stood in the doorway, bloodied and swaying, holding the knife.

A macabre grin stretched across his face.

"The police are coming," Donna whispered, backing away. "You won't get away with this."

His grin widened.

"They won't get to you in time."

He took a step forward. She scrambled onto the bed, her mind racing. He raised the knife, ready to strike.

Then she heard the sharp crunch of glass behind him.

Stanley turned.

Ally.

Wielding a heavy spanner.

The swing was swift and brutal. The metal connected with the side of Stanley's head. He crumpled.

Donna collapsed onto the bed, hysterical. Ally moved toward her, arms steady, holding her as the front door burst open.

Police thundered up the stairs.

Billy Sloan.

Donna wrenched herself from Ally's grip, shaking, pointing.

"There's your fucking murderer. I told you Colin didn't do this."

Billy exhaled, rubbing a hand over his face.

The ambulance arrived. Paramedics lifted Stanley onto a stretcher.

He was still breathing.

Chapter 71
Stanley Wife

Later the next day, Colin was released from the police station. A recovering Stanley Smith was interviewed under caution, and he confessed.

That evening, Billy Sloan explained everything to Mick. Apparently, Smith had married into family money but never had control over anything. He resented that he had been unable to have children—and that it was his fault. He went on to say that Sheridan had stolen a lot of money from the company office in Ballymoney, Sullivan had stolen his clients in England, and Jones was just an attempt to frame Colin. It had nearly worked. Smith had wanted to ruin Colin's life for stealing Joan, and when he realized he couldn't have her, no one else would either.

"There are some fucked-up bastards out there," Mick muttered, shaking his head.

Colin signed for his belongings.

"No hard feelings," Constable Sloan said, offering his hand.

Unlike before, Colin accepted. "I told you it wasn't me."

Billy Sloan could only nod.

Two weeks passed, and I got a phone call from Mrs. Smith.

"I can only apologize," she said. "You must think I'm awful that I didn't know. I can't believe I was married—am still married—to that horrible wee monster."

I assured her it wasn't her fault. None of us had known. None of us had even suspected.

Then she asked if I would take over the running of the firm.

I gracefully accepted.

Finally, everything felt normal again.

I poured a whiskey and lounged on my leather sofa in front of my big TV. The football had just started.

Donna got home slightly later than usual.

She stepped in front of the TV. I sighed, reluctantly tearing my eyes from the screen.

I started to tell her my good news about Mrs. Smith when she blurted out—

"I'm bleeding."

I barely registered her words.

The commentator screamed that Mo Salah had just scored.

I was glad.

About The Author

L B McKenna has a master's degree in education and is a 61-year-old semi-retired teacher of Religion. He is from Belfast, Ireland and has two grown up sons, Eoin and Emmet. This is his first novel, but he has 3 more novels at various stages of completion. He has always found existentialism to be a fascinating philosophical viewpoint and was intrigued by Camus' views on the absurd.

"The only way to deal with an unfree world is to become absolutely free."

Camu

Printed in Dunstable, United Kingdom